Pride & Pyramids

MR. DARCY *in* EGYPT

AMANDA GRANGE
& JACQUELINE WEBB

sourcebooks
landmark

Published by Sourcebooks Landmark, an imprint of Sourcebooks, Inc.
P.O. Box 4410, Naperville, Illinois 60567-4410
(630) 961-3900
FAX: (630) 961-2168
www.sourcebooks.com

Library of Congress Cataloging-in-Publication Data

Grange, Amanda.
  Pride and pyramids : Mr. Darcy in Egypt / by Amanda Grange and Jacqueline Webb.
    p. cm.
  1. Darcy, Fitzwilliam (Fictitious character)—Fiction. 2. Bennet, Elizabeth (Fictitious character)—Fiction. 3. English—Egypt—Fiction. I. Webb, Jacqueline. II. Title.
  PR6107.R35P75 2012
  823'.92—dc23
                        2012014790

Printed and bound in the United States of America
UGI 10 9 8 7 6 5 4 3 2 1

ELIZABETH BENNET RAN DOWN the stairs of the Darcys' London home with a lightness that belied her thirty-five years. The Darcy family had just returned from Kent, where they had been visiting their de Bourgh relatives, and they were spending a week in London on their way back to Pemberley.

As she arrived in the hall, she met Darcy, who was still recognisably the man she had married fifteen years previously. In fact, if anything, he was more handsome. Age had improved him. His face had lost its former look of habitual arrogance and he wore an expression that made her heart lift. His dark eyes lit up as he saw her and he held out his hand, inviting her to join him as he stood looking up at an empty space on the wall.

"I think that spot will suit the portrait very well," he said, putting his arm around her.

Elizabeth followed his gaze and tried to imagine a picture of herself, her husband, and her children hanging there. As she did so, she felt how strange it was to have her likeness painted and then exhibited in such a way. Although it was nothing new for

Darcy, who had been the subject of a variety of portraits through-out his life, she could never quite accustom herself to having her picture painted. She always wanted to get up and stroll around the room instead of sitting still for the artist, and once the paint-ing was finished, she found it disconcerting to come across a life-sized image of herself when she turned an unwary corner in the gallery or on the stairs of Pemberley.

"I have just received a letter from Elisabeth Le Brun, and she has agreed to paint the portrait," he said. "I am glad. There is an air of informality about her work which will suit you very well."

Elizabeth, too, was pleased. Her namesake was famous for producing images of people with loose hair, flowing clothes, and natural poses, instead of presenting them in a stiff and formal manner. Perhaps this portrait would not be as trying as the others.

"Will she come to England?" asked Elizabeth.

"Alas, no, but she has agreed to work from sketches. Her assistant will make them for her."

"The young man we met last week? I cannot recall his name but I liked him."

"His name was Mr Paul Inkworthy, and yes, it is him."

"It is probably just as well she will not be coming herself," said Elizabeth, as the sound of her children's noisy play assailed her ears. "I think our children would frighten her away! At least now it is her assistant who will have the trouble of making them stand still, if such a thing is possible."

"Beth will be no trouble," said Darcy fondly, as they entered the drawing room.

Their eldest daughter was sitting on the window seat, quietly reading a book. Although named after her mother, and although she had her mother's dark hair and eyes, in all other ways thirteen-year-old Beth took after Elizabeth's sister, Jane. She was mild tempered and sweet natured, always seeing the good in others. With her calm and optimistic disposition, she went through life as serenely as a swan sailing on the water.

William, too, would be no trouble. At twelve years old, he was already much like his father: proud and honourable, although inclined to be haughty.

Eleven-year-old John, named after Elizabeth's father, took after Darcy's cousin, Colonel Fitzwilliam. The main grievance of John's life was that his father did not yet consider him old enough to follow in the colonel's footsteps by joining the army.

Laurence, two years younger, took after his aunt Lydia. Wild, enthusiastic, and energetic, he was always into mischief, and his eight-year-old sister, Jane, followed him into every scrape and piece of trouble.

"How unlike her namesake she is," said Elizabeth, looking at her daughter with fond exasperation.

Jane had just run in from the garden, bringing a trail of soil with her. It stretched all the way from the flower borders, in through the French windows, and then onto the rug behind her.

"And how like her mother," said Darcy, as his eyes drifted down to her petticoats, which were six inches deep in mud.

Elizabeth laughed.

"I have not provided you with very genteel children, I fear," she said.

"No?" asked Darcy, picking up Margaret, the youngest at six years old. "There are very few children as genteel as Meg."

Elizabeth looked at her neat little girl with love and affection. "With that I have to agree."

At that moment, John and Laurence erupted into an argument, while William tried to play justice of the peace and ended up with a punch on the nose for his trouble.

"The sooner the boys are back at school the better," said Darcy, adding pointedly, "All of them."

Elizabeth stiffened. She had accustomed herself to losing the older boys to their school each term, but she was not yet ready to let Laurence join them.

She had managed to keep him at home thus far because he had had a bout of ill health, but now that he was well again, the subject of school kept rearing its head. The idea was normal for Darcy. He himself had been sent away to boarding school, as had Georgiana. But for Elizabeth it was a strange thing, for she and her sisters had all been educated at home.

"Not yet," she said firmly. "Laurence is still too young. His tutor is giving him an excellent education and there is nothing to be gained by sending him away."

"His tutors are finding it difficult to hold his attention, and besides, I was at school by his age," said Darcy.

And see what it did to you, Elizabeth had to stop herself saying.

"Dearest Elizabeth, boys need discipline," Darcy continued teasingly but firmly.

"Dearest Fitzwilliam, they can find all the discipline they need at home," said Elizabeth, just as teasingly and no less firmly.

"Can, perhaps. But do? No. You are not very good at discipline," he said.

"My sisters and I—" Elizabeth began.

"But that is just it. You were born into a family of girls. We do not have just daughters; we have sons as well. I have given in to you over the girls' education, but now I expect you to give way over the boys' schooling. You cannot keep Laurence tied to your apron strings forever."

"Nor do I wish to," she said. "I know he must go to school eventually. But not yet."

Her cause was not helped by the fact that Laurence and Jane were now rolling around on the floor. Even to Elizabeth, who had grown up in a noisy, lively household, this was taking liberty too far. She set about restoring order, but it was more Darcy's authoritative tone that settled the dispute than Elizabeth's loving reasoning.

Once some semblance of calm had returned to the room, Darcy began to speak again, only to be interrupted by a knock at the door.

"Are we expecting anyone?" asked Darcy.

"Not to my knowledge," said Elizabeth.

A minute later, Edward Fitzwilliam was announced.

"Cousin Edward!" chorused the children.

Edward was in fact their father's cousin, a younger brother to Colonel Fitzwilliam. He had the same height and build but an altogether merrier disposition, as could be seen from the sparkle in his eyes.

"Edward!" said Elizabeth, greeting him warmly. "We did not know you were in town."

"I have only just arrived," he said, returning her greeting.

"What brings you here?" asked Darcy, depositing Margaret on the rug in order to shake his hand.

"Egypt," said Edward. "What else?"

"Egypt?" asked Elizabeth in surprise, adding, "You will stay to dinner?"

"I will do better than that, if you will have me. I was rather hoping I could stay for a week. Our town house is shut up at present. I could stay in a hotel but—"

"You will do no such thing," said Elizabeth, already ringing the bell and giving instructions for his room to be made up.

The children were still swarming round him, for he was a great favourite of theirs, and soon sweetmeats had made their way from his pocket into their hands.

Once the initial excitement had died down, Edward was able to take his place on the sofa. William sat on one side of him, Beth demurely took her place on the other side, and John sat at his feet. Laurence and Jane hovered nearby, while Margaret wandered over to a bag which Edward had left by the door.

Elizabeth and Darcy sat down on the sofa opposite and asked after his family. Between his answers, Edward told Beth how pretty she was looking, remarked upon William's height, and asked John if he were a colonel yet.

Laurence and Jane, having received their share of the attention, began to grow bored and drifted away to the door, where Margaret was examining the enticing bag. The children were unable to examine it more closely, however, as one of the footmen picked it up and carried it away.

"So Egypt still enthrals you?" Elizabeth enquired, as the servants entered with a tray of tea.

"Yes, it does," Edward replied. He turned to Darcy. "Ever

since hearing about our fathers' trip to Luxor as young men I have longed to go to Egypt and see the desert for myself. The tales they recounted on their return made my head spin with excitement. Do you remember, Darcy?"

"Indeed I do," said Darcy, though with less enthusiasm than his young cousin.

"Even now, when I think of the letters my father sent home, I can almost hear the noise of the markets and smell the exotic foods. I was not even born at the time, but I have always wanted to follow in his footsteps, to feel the heat of the sun on my face and gaze on the majestic, mysterious face of the pyramids, to set out down the Nile to the Valley of Kings and find an undiscovered tomb."

"You make it sound fascinating," Elizabeth remarked, somewhat enthralled herself.

"Edward has a lively imagination," Darcy said. "But he neglects to add that both my father and his nearly died on their trip. They, too, had hoped to find treasure, but they failed to find anything at all, despite owning a map they swore had been bequeathed to them by an adventurer they found dying in the desert. They came home with their health broken and their spirits in decline. Like most adventurers' tales, it is more romantic in the telling than in the experience."

"I should love to go there," declared John, his eyes shining with excitement. "I shall go there one day at the head of an army and we will find a tomb that no one has ever discovered before and bring back lots of jewels for you, Mama."

"Thank you, darling," said Elizabeth fondly.

"You must give me the chance to find it first, John," Edward said, patting the boy's head. "It will never do if you steal my thunder. Now, who wants some more sweetmeats?"

As Edward laughingly produced enough sweetmeats for the entire household and began giving them to Beth, William, and John, Elizabeth looked around for the youngest members of the family.

"Where are the other children?"

"Probably ran out into the garden when they heard I was about to bore you all with my stories of Egypt," said Edward. "And now, Darcy, you must show me the new phaeton you were thinking of purchasing on my last trip here…"

Laurence put his finger to his lips, admonishing his sister Jane to silence. The two children were not in fact in the garden, but on the landing.

Well used to obeying his commands in the pursuit of mischief, Jane nodded.

Both children waited with a patience that would have astonished their loving but resigned parents. They remained perfectly still in their hiding place, an alcove, while the servants deposited Edward's luggage in the room he habitually occupied when staying with the Darcys.

It was not his portmanteau, however, that interested them. They were hoping to see more of the battered leather bag, which contained all the most important documents and artefacts that he had collected in Egypt, and from which they were both banned on account of past transgressions.

They did not have long to wait. Soon Edward's valet

appeared, holding the valise. He entered the room and after a few moments reappeared empty-handed, continuing on down toward the back stairs and the servants' quarters.

When all was clear, Laurence took his sister's hand and led her quietly along to their cousin's private room, where they peeped inside. Reassured that there was no one else present, they went in.

"There it is, Jane," Laurence said, pointing to the familiar brown bag on a handsome walnut pedestal desk by the window. "You stand guard in case anyone comes."

Jane pouted. "No. I want to see as well." Although younger than her brother, Jane was his equal in obstinacy. She followed him to the desk and they both looked at the bag for a moment before opening it.

They peered inside, staring in wonder at the objects within. They had intended only to look, but a ray of sunshine suddenly escaped from the covering of cloud and shone through the window. It fell upon a figurine partially encased in a soft chamois cloth. It was decorated in tiny specks of coloured glass and lit up in front of them, dazzling them with its beauty, sparkling like a treasure from the cave of Ali Baba, their favourite nursery story of the moment.

Laurence picked it up, for once taking the utmost caution, and they both examined the figurine. It was a wooden statue of a slim, lovely young woman with a heart-shaped face and eyes that were elongated in the classic Egyptian fashion with kohl. The top was a carved headdress that appeared to be in the shape of a snake.

"It's beautiful," whispered Jane in awe.

She reached out to touch a necklace of sea green around the throat of the woman. The stones were cool to the touch and her little fingers explored the rest of the statuette eagerly.

"Let me see," Laurence demanded, grabbing the head.

"No!" Jane hissed, her usually sweet face flushed an unbecoming red. They might have continued to fight had not a voice at the door interrupted them.

"Papa forbade you to touch Cousin Edward's bag."

Both children turned in surprise. They had been so engrossed in the figurine that they had failed to hear any noise from the hall.

Margaret stood in the doorway, watching her brother and sister struggle for ownership of the statuette.

"We're not doing anything," Laurence said defensively and also mendaciously.

"Yes you are. You're fighting over Cousin Edward's doll."

The word "doll" had a startling effect on Laurence. He stopped trying to wrest the little figure from his sister, nearly causing her to drop it.

"I'm not interested in any stupid doll," he said, suddenly aware of his dignity as a nine-year-old boy. "In fact there's nothing very interesting in here at all. I'm going to go down to the pond and see if the frogs are out yet."

He ran out of the door and Jane followed automatically. Then she hesitated a second and looked back at the figurine in puzzlement, before shrugging her shoulders and following her brother. With a noisy clattering down the stairs, they were gone.

Margaret stayed where she was. For a moment she examined the little figurine from a distance; then slowly, almost dreamily, she entered the room and reached up to take the object in her hands. She smiled at the doll and then, humming a little song, picked up the chamois cloth and began to polish its jewels.

It was some half an hour later when Darcy held out a brandy glass to Edward. The children had all disappeared and Elizabeth had gone to speak to the housekeeper, leaving the gentlemen in possession of the drawing room.

"Your good health, Cousin. And now that you've admired my phaeton, expressed delight over Elizabeth's garden, and enchanted my children, perhaps you should tell me more about your reason for being in London," Darcy said.

"I am afraid you will disapprove," said Edward with a rueful shake of the head.

"Does it have anything to do with Sir Matthew Rosen?" asked Darcy, as he took a seat and stretched his long legs out in front of him. He took a sip of brandy. "Sir Matthew has written some very interesting articles for *The Times* recently, and I hear he is trying to find more patrons for his Egyptian dig. In fact, I believe he is even willing to allow some enthusiasts to join his party—for a consideration, of course."

Edward took a drink of brandy.

"I knew you would not approve," he said.

"Perhaps *not understand* is closer to the mark. If you want to go then I cannot stop you, but think carefully before you commit yourself. Egypt is a long way from home if you change your mind."

He was fond of Edward. More than fifteen years Edward's senior, he felt like more of an uncle toward the young man than a cousin and he remembered Edward's many boyhood enthusiasms with affection. They had come and gone like the will-o-the-wisp, full of movement and colour, but with the same ephemeral lifespan.

With the one exception of Egypt. Ever since he was five, when he had first heard his father talking about his trip to Egypt with Darcy's father, Edward had been enthralled by the very mention of the place, and this was despite the fact that both men had returned from their ill-fated adventure being poorer and also worryingly ill with strange diseases.

Elizabeth was right, thought Darcy; *enthral is a good word. It is as though they are bewitched by the place. Edward has never even been, and yet his eyes light up at the thought of it.*

"Luncheon will be ready shortly," Elizabeth announced, walking into the room.

"I was just asking Edward what his plans are while he is in London," Darcy said as he got up and poured her a glass of ratafia.

"Tell us all about it," Elizabeth said, spreading the skirt of her white lawn empire dress on the chaise longue. She took the drink and savoured it. "I take it you will be visiting the Egyptian exhibition at the British Museum? I do hope so. I have wanted to go there for some time. We could all go together; it would be good for the children. Darcy is always worrying about the children's education," she said teasingly.

Darcy took the teasing in good part, having become accustomed to it in the years of his marriage.

"By all means," he replied. "It would be interesting. The children have never seen the Egyptian exhibits and I think the older children in particular will be interested to see the Rosetta

Stone. Did you not acquire some prints of the Stone, Edward? I seem to remember you thinking you might be able to decipher the hieroglyphs."

Edward laughed.

"You are quite right," he said. "I was so excited by news of the discovery that I set to work right away, alas to no avail. It seemed as if it would be so easy, the Stone having the same message written in three different languages, one of them being the hieroglyphic language. But even understanding the other two languages was no help. Messages written in letters are one thing; messages recorded in pictures are quite another."

"There is no shame in having failed," said Darcy. "Better..." He stopped suddenly.

"Better minds than mine have tried and failed?" asked Edward.

"I was not going to say that," said Darcy.

Elizabeth and Edward both gave him a disbelieving look and he laughed. "Very well, I was. I would like to see it again," he mused. "I have not been to the Egyptian rooms for several years. When do you intend to go?"

"Tomorrow. I would be delighted if you would all accompany me. I have made an appointment to see Sir Matthew Rosen, but it should not take long. I would enjoy showing you around."

"I guessed as much," said Darcy.

"Sir Matthew Rosen?" asked Elizabeth.

"An authority on Egyptian tombs and artefacts," said Edward. "He has recently returned from an archaeological site near Cairo and I am anxious to talk to him."

"Then it is settled; we will visit the museum tomorrow. I am already looking forward to it," she said, her eyes sparkling.

She stood up as the gong for luncheon sounded in the hall, and the two gentlemen sprang to their feet. As they moved toward the dining room, Edward excused himself for a moment in order to retrieve a letter from his room that his father had given him for Darcy. Not wishing to delay the others, he bounded up the stairs two at a time and raced along to his room. But he stopped as he neared the door and heard a voice whispering softly. He walked slowly to the room and looked in.

Margaret was standing by the window, holding something in her hand, and talking to herself.

"Margaret? Are you quite well, my dear?" he asked. The child's soft brown curls were sticking to her face, which was flushed with heat. She turned at the sound of his voice.

"Oh, Cousin Edward, I was talking to your doll. She's very sparkly."

"Yes. Where did you find her?"

"I didn't find her. L—"

The little girl frowned and he guessed she was trying to avoid mentioning her brother's name. Edward was well aware of the fascination his leather bag held for certain members of the Darcy clan, and he smiled.

"Well, never mind. Do you like her? Her name is Aahotep."

"Is it? She's not very nice, is she? But I think she's rather sad."

"Why do you say that?" Edward asked, startled.

He had found the doll in the attic of his family home, along with several other artefacts his father had brought home from Egypt. It was of little monetary value, although the coloured glass made it look pretty.

"Because she was mean to someone and now she can't say

sorry although she wants to. And it's making her mean toward other people. But I feel sorry for her."

"Well, I expect she will feel better when she has had some lunch," Edward said gently.

Margaret gazed at him with clear grey eyes.

"She's a doll, Uncle Edward. She doesn't get hungry."

Edward smiled. "Well, I do and I am sure you do too. Come, let us leave Aahotep to ponder her evil deeds and go down to lunch, shall we?"

Margaret nodded and, taking his hand, was soon busily reciting the tale of her recent visit to Kent, where she had visited her great-aunt, Lady Catherine de Bourgh. Her unusually rosy colour faded rapidly and Edward dismissed it as a peculiarity of the very young. It was not until much later on that he realised he should have paid more attention to the littlest Darcy's pronouncements, but by then it was too late.

Chapter 2

ELIZABETH WOKE THE FOLLOWING morning with the feeling that something was wrong. At first she could not think what it was, but then she realised that no children were jumping on the bed or wriggling under the covers next to her.

She smiled as she remembered how horrified Darcy had been the first time the children had invaded their bedroom in the morning. He had been raised in a formal manner and he had seen his parents by appointment, usually for an hour after dinner, when he had recited whatever poem he had been learning or displayed his command of Latin. Then, having been smiled upon by his mother and inspired by his father, he had returned to the nursery, there to stay until the next appointed time. So when Beth had first toddled into the Darcys' bedroom, having escaped her sleeping nurse, he had been torn between delight at seeing her waddling toward him and an uncomfortable feeling that she should have stayed in the nursery.

Elizabeth had not had any such difficulties, and she had given Beth a hug. Darcy had been charmed, despite the feeling that it was wrong for someone as august as Miss Elizabeth Darcy to crow with delight as her mother, the equally august Mrs Elizabeth Darcy, tickled her and teased her. But then he had been overcome with love and affection and he had succumbed entirely.

The Darcys' room had become more and more crowded in the mornings as further children had arrived, until the older children had started to feel it was beneath their dignity to cavort in such a manner and had gradually absented themselves from the proceedings. Now Beth and William never came, John seldom, and even Laurence and Jane only whirled into the room about three mornings out of five. But Margaret always came. And yet here it was, past seven o'clock, and there was no sign of her.

Fearing that Margaret was ill, Elizabeth slipped out of bed and, throwing a wrapper round her shoulders, went along the splendid landing and into Margaret's room. She need not have worried. The early morning sunlight, creeping in through a crack in the curtains, illuminated a peaceful scene. Margaret was sound asleep, clutching her Egyptian doll, and judging by the murmurs that came from her cherubic lips, she was dreaming.

A slight creak alerted Elizabeth to the fact that someone else was walking along the landing and a moment later Darcy entered the room and put his arm round her.

"I thought I would find you here. It is not the same without Meg climbing on the bed, is it, my love? I am glad she has not outgrown the habit. She must be worn out after yesterday's excitement."

"Edward certainly knows how to exhilarate people," Elizabeth agreed.

"He does. He has always been carried away by his enthusiasms."

"Which is no bad thing," said Elizabeth. "I have been thinking for some time that I would like an adventure and Edward, with his talk of Egypt, is the next best thing."

"An adventure? Do I bore you, my love?" asked Darcy teasingly.

She put her hand up to his face. "Never. But we have spent a great many years having our family—wonderful years and I would not change them for anything—and yet now that the children are older, I find myself thinking of all the places I have never seen. When I was younger, a trip to the Lake District seemed like an adventure, but now the Lake District is familiar and I find myself longing for that sense of excitement again, the feeling that I am going somewhere different, to see something new. To be transported beyond the confines of my normal life, to experience something that cannot be foreseen."

"Then it is a good thing we are going to the British Museum. You can feast your eyes upon the Egyptian artefacts and imagine yourself exploring the pyramids!" he teased her.

Margaret stirred and then settled again.

"Let her sleep," said Elizabeth. "It will be a busy day for her."

"For all of us," said Darcy.

The busyness was already apparent when Elizabeth walked into the drawing room an hour later to find the boys already up and dressed, surrounded by books.

Edward, who was pointing out something of interest in one

of them, looked up with a laugh and said, "We breakfasted early, and ever since then we have been raiding the library for books on Egypt. Darcy has a fine collection."

Elizabeth was used to seeing William with a book, but it was rare to see either John or Laurence anywhere near one by choice, and she thought with satisfaction that Edward's visit had already been good for them.

Although she would never admit as much to Darcy, she did sometimes think that Laurence would benefit from school, but she hated the thought of losing him. He was her youngest son and she wanted to keep him with her. Now, seeing him so happy and engaged at home, she felt her somewhat guilty conscience being appeased.

"There are all sorts of interesting things in the museum," said William. "Did you know it was opened over fifty years ago and that it has lots of Egyptian artefacts in it?"

"The Rosetta Stone was found by a soldier," said John proudly.

"Only a French soldier," said Laurence scathingly.

"Some of the French fought bravely. Colonel Fitzwilliam said so," returned John. "I expect the Stone was found by one of the brave ones. The French invaded Egypt and they were working on the defences at Fort Julien when one of the soldiers saw the Stone sticking out of the ground," he explained to his mama. "It was near a place called Rosetta, which is why they called it the Rosetta Stone."

"But what is important," said William, "is that it has some writing on it, and the writing says the same thing but in three different kinds of writing. One of them is in Greek writing, and one of them is ordinary Egyptian writing, and one of them is hiero… hiero… hieroglyphs, which are a kind of pictures. I can read and write Greek, so if I could make a copy of the Stone, I might be able to work out what the hieroglyphs mean."

"No, you wouldn't," said Laurence. "No one can read the hieroglyphs yet, not even Cousin Edward."

"And if not even Edward can read them, what hope is there for anyone else?" asked Elizabeth.

Edward laughed and moved some books so that she could sit down.

"I appear to have taken over your drawing room," he said.

"Never mind, I do not have time to sit down anyway," she said. "It is time we were all getting ready for our outing. Fitzwilliam has given orders for the carriages to be brought round and they will be at the door in half an hour."

"Then we had better be ready for them," said Edward.

There was a flurry of activity, but by the time thirty minutes had passed, everyone was ready; even Margaret, who had at last roused herself and who was holding her doll tightly in her hand.

Edward delighted the children by suggesting that he should go in the carriage with them while Darcy should drive Elizabeth in his new phaeton. The suggestion delighted Darcy and Elizabeth almost as much as it delighted the children, for as much as they loved their offspring, they valued having time alone together.

The morning was bright and sunny, with the first feeling of spring in the air, and Elizabeth could not have been happier as she took her place beside her husband. The two-seater carriage, which had an open top, was pulled by a pair of matched bays, and they cut quite a dash as they moved out into the road.

Darcy drove with skill through the London traffic, past brewers' carts, hackney carriages, and ponderous coaches, while Elizabeth revelled in the feel of the soft air on her cheeks. By the time they arrived at Montague House, which housed the museum, she had a healthy glow to her skin and her eyes were bright, prompting Darcy to seize her hand and kiss it as he helped her out of the phaeton.

She had a sudden memory of the first time he had helped her out of a carriage, and she saw by his expression that he remembered it, too. She looked down at their joined hands and then looked at Darcy, whose eyes were full of his love for her. Thinking herself the luckiest woman in the world, she took his arm and looked up at the splendid museum.

Ahead of them, the children were spilling out of the Darcy coach. They had all been given strict instructions by Elizabeth to be on their best behaviour, but she need not have worried: the large and imposing building had its effect on them and they went quietly inside.

As they did so, she noticed the effect Beth had on everyone they passed. Without ever trying, Beth managed to charm people. They looked at her quiet, self-assured figure and felt the goodness she radiated. Coupled with her undoubted beauty, it entranced them, young and old. And yet Beth was unaware of it.

William looked around him with interest, while John's eyes searched for any display of weapons the museum might have. Laurence, for once overawed, held Jane's hand, and Margaret followed on behind as Edward led them to the Rosetta Stone.

"You seem to know your way," said Darcy.

"I have seen the Stone before," said Edward.

"How long has it been here?" asked William.

"Thirteen years," said Edward. "Colonel Turner brought it to England when the French surrendered to the English in Egypt. He presented it to the king, and the king said that it should be put in the museum."

"I should like to see the site of the battles," said John. "Colonel Fitzwilliam has told me all about Aboukir Bay and the triumph of our armies. I wish we could go to Egypt," he added wistfully.

They arrived at the Stone. Beth, who had shown little interest in the proceedings, was captivated by the hieroglyphs.

"Look at the beautiful pictures. That one looks like a bird," she said. "And that one looks like a shepherd's crook."

"It looks like a lot of squiggles to me," said Laurence. "If it's been here for thirteen years, why hasn't anyone found out what it says yet?"

"Because the language is very different from anything we are used to," said Edward.

William took out a notebook and started copying the hieroglyphs, but Edward said, "There is no need for that. I have a print of them in my bags. I will give it to you when we return to the house."

Elizabeth was as intrigued as the children. The Stone seemed very exotic and she could almost feel the heat of the desert as she looked at it. How wonderful it must be to travel, to see the pyramids and deserts, to float down the Nile and smell the unfamiliar scents that permeated that strange world!

"I will have to leave you here for a while," said Edward. "It is time for my meeting with Sir Matthew."

As Edward was about to leave them, Darcy took him to one side.

"Does Sir Matthew know you are the son of an earl?" he asked.

"Of course," said Edward. Adding, with a sudden smile, "How else do you think I managed to arrange an interview with him?"

"I suppose it would do no good to warn you that he is only interested in your family's wealth and status, not your enthusiasm?" asked Darcy. "Expeditions cost a great deal of money to pursue, and scholars are always short of funds."

"No good at all," said Edward. "Just as it would do no good for you to warn him that I am not just interested in his knowledge, but that I hope to persuade him to take me with him when he returns to Egypt."

He bowed and withdrew, leaving the Darcys to wander the room and exclaim over the strange treasures housed in the museum. There were Greek vases, marble statues, and even an Egyptian mummy, which delighted Laurence. John, meanwhile, was more interested in the collection of medals, and William perused the collection of books.

All was going well until Beth, looking around her, said, "Where is Margaret?"

Elizabeth looked round and realised that her youngest daughter had strayed.

"She went over there," Laurence said.

He pointed in the direction of an antechamber and then immediately lost interest in his smallest sister as Darcy pointed out a ferocious-looking sword. But Elizabeth and Beth went in search of Margaret.

The antechamber was darker than the main rooms, without

any windows, which rendered it mysterious and somewhat eerie. A few candles guttered on the bare walls and for a moment Elizabeth felt herself overcome with a sense of foreboding. The fact that there were no visitors in this particular room made it seem more sinister.

"There you are, Margaret," she heard Beth say.

She turned to see her youngest daughter staring at a set of painted friezes in the corner of the chamber. The little girl's eyes were set in enchanted wonder.

"What is it, my love?" Elizabeth asked, smiling, as she walked across to join both girls.

"Look, Mama. Margaret has found some pictures. Aren't they unusual?" Beth replied.

Elizabeth examined the pictures. They were set into a thick wooden board which had been propped up rather haphazardly against the wall. There were only six pictures, although it looked as though there was space for several more. Each picture was of the same figure, that of a woman with elongated eyes and generously curved body. But she was clearly not a sympathetic character. In every picture she was pictured surrounded by tiny corpses at her feet, who had obviously not died of natural causes.

"Oh, Beth, how gruesome…" Elizabeth began, but another voice interrupted her.

"Ah, early visitors to my *femme fatale*."

They all turned to see a man in his midfifties looking at them. He wore tightly fitting breeches, a long tailcoat cut away to show a rather faded waistcoat of cream brocade, and his cravat had been inexpertly tied. But his hair was his own, a faded brown with grey sideburns, and he smiled at them with merry eyes.

"Good day to you, sir," said Elizabeth, while Beth and Margaret curtsied formally. "My daughters and I seem to have strayed into an unfinished exhibit room."

"Unfinished and likely to remain so, madam," said the gentleman. "I donated these artefacts to the museum and intended to fill the room with antiquities, but my sponsors have lost their appetite for the venture. Can't say as I blame them, really. The minx in the picture isn't the best advertisement for inspiring the imagination of the British public. But I took a fancy to her story while I was in Egypt and picked up this little trinket in a bazaar in Cairo."

"You have been to Egypt?" Beth said with interest.

The gentleman smiled at her.

"I have, my dear, many times, for pleasure and in the pursuit of academic interests. It is a fascinating place."

Elizabeth said, "You are making us very envious, Mr....?"

"Rosen, madam," he said, tipping his top hat. "Sir Matthew Rosen."

"Sir Matthew, it is a pleasure to meet you," said Elizabeth, taking the introduction upon herself. "I am Mrs Fitzwilliam Darcy and these are my daughters Beth and Margaret."

"Enchanted. And what do you ladies think of my Egyptian lady? I admit to a certain doomed attraction for her, although I strongly suspect her story is no more than the figment of some wily souk keeper's imagination in order to sell a worthless bauble to a Western souvenir hunter."

He smiled as he said this, and Elizabeth laughed.

"She is certainly very wicked if these images are anything to go by."

"She wasn't very happy," said Margaret, speaking for the first time.

Sir Matthew looked at her curiously.

"What makes you say that, my dear?"

"Because it's true. People were mean to Aahotep, so she was mean back."

Now Sir Matthew looked at her in frank surprise. "However did you know that?"

"My daughter has a vivid imagination," said Elizabeth with a smile.

"And your lady looks like the doll Cousin Edward gave her, doesn't she? Look," said Beth, taking Margaret's hand and revealing the doll.

Elizabeth glanced at the wooden toy in Margaret's hand and noticed that it did bear a striking resemblance to the figure in the pictures.

"And who is Cousin Edward, young lady?" asked Sir Matthew, looking more interested in all of them now.

"My husband's cousin, Edward Fitzwilliam," explained Elizabeth, taking Margaret's hand.

"Would this be the Honourable Edward Fitzwilliam, with whom I believe I have an appointment imminently?" Sir Matthew asked, examining a pocket watch as he spoke.

Elizabeth smiled. "Indeed. He is looking forward to it very much. Edward has a great hunger for all things to do with Egypt, as my daughters will testify."

"Then I look forward to meeting him," said Sir Matthew.

Elizabeth sensed the unspoken comment that he had not been looking forward to meeting her young cousin before, which would explain why he was alone in a room devoid of nearly all decoration rather than trying to interest Edward in funding his trip.

"Yes, we must not detain you, Sir Matthew," she said, leading Margaret and Beth out of the room and into the light again.

Sir Matthew followed them, saying, "Good day to you, Mrs Darcy, ladies," and disappeared up a flight of stairs toward a set of rooms marked Private.

"Mama, we're over here," shouted a voice, and Elizabeth turned to see William waving to her.

Darcy and John were marvelling at a huge sculpture of an Egyptian pharaoh, but on seeing Elizabeth, Darcy moved across to her.

"The artefacts are fascinating," he said. "I've seldom seen all our children so captivated."

"It is good for them to see that matters educational do not have to be dull," Elizabeth agreed. "And yet I have to confess that this trip to the museum, far from satisfying my desire for an adventure, merely makes me want more. Darcy, you will never believe who we just met!"

"Tell me, my love."

"Sir Matthew Rosen himself. Margaret found a picture of the doll Edward gave her and while we were looking at it, Sir Matthew arrived."

"Surely he should have been at the meeting with Edward," Darcy said with a frown.

"He has just left to meet Edward. I rather felt he was reluctant to speak to him. We assumed that he was desperate for funds and prepared to do anything to obtain them, but it must be tedious to have to flatter those who think only of self-aggrandisement. I think Sir Matthew will be pleasantly surprised when he meets Edward, for Edward does not have a haughty bone in his body."

She placed her arm through his and was about to speak further when they were distracted by a museum attendant who was staring in alarm at Laurence and Jane. Both children were engrossed in a game which involved them touching the long, doglike snout of a statue of Anubis and then running away shrieking with laughter.

"Oh dear," she said.

She joined her husband in rescuing the room from the worst of their children's excesses, before organising an orderly departure from the museum.

As Edward had asked them not to wait, for he expected to be with Sir Matthew some time, they returned to Darcy House in the carriage, leaving the phaeton for his return.

"Congratulate me," Edward said as he burst into the ground floor sitting room much later on that afternoon.

"Congratulations, Cousin Edward," Laurence and Jane chorused together.

"Edward, at last." Elizabeth looked up from the pianoforte where she was engaged in giving Beth her lesson. "We missed you at luncheon. Did everything go well at the museum?"

"It went splendidly, dear Elizabeth," he said in exceptionally high spirits. "Where is Fitzwilliam? I have so much to tell you all."

"I saw Papa in the garden earlier. Shall I go and fetch him?"

Laurence asked, but he and Jane were off even before their mother had nodded her assent.

"Sir Matthew is the most interesting man I have ever met," Edward declared, sitting down on the Louis Quinze chair.

"Yes, we met him too," Elizabeth admitted, sitting down opposite him. "Beth, go and ask Molly to bring in some tea."

"He told me," Edward said, sitting forward, his eyes shining with enthusiasm. "He said he had been impressed by my family and that he was further impressed by my knowledge of Egypt's history and legends. We talked for hours, Elizabeth. I cannot tell you how marvellous it was."

"How marvellous what was, Edward?"

Darcy's voice from the French windows interrupted their conversation and Edward jumped up, unable to keep still for long in his passions.

"My talk with Sir Matthew Rosen. We discussed his forthcoming trip to Egypt at length, and in exchange for my sponsorship, he has agreed to allow me access to his dig. Can you believe it? I will sail for Cairo as soon as I can make my arrangements. I can hardly wait."

"You must be so excited," Elizabeth said, watching the young man pace the room. "I confess to envying you such a thrilling journey."

"I have waited all my life for this chance," Edward said. "Ever since my father told me of his adventures, I have dreamed of seeing Egypt for myself. To sail down that ancient river on a felucca among the crocodiles, to visit the pyramids under the moon, to experience for myself the Valley of the Kings. It is all I have ever wanted."

"Then we are both happy for you, Edward," Elizabeth said warmly. "And your father will be, too. You must write to him tonight."

Edward's expression of unalloyed delight faded somewhat.

"Yes," he said colourlessly. "I shall write directly after dinner."

"Edward, he does know about your plans, does he not?" Darcy asked.

Edward turned away from his cousin.

"He knows of my enthusiasms," he said. "He knows it has been my dearest wish since childhood to visit the land of the pharaohs. But if you are asking, Will he be pleased to hear that his youngest son will be leaving England in the next few weeks to take part in an archaeological trip to the Dark Continent? Then no, I fear that he will not be as delighted as you are at my good fortune. After all," he added bitterly, "I am the son of an earl. It is my duty to join either the army, the navy, or the church, not waste my time digging up bits of old pottery in the sands of a foreign country."

"I am sure that's not how your father views your interest at all," said Elizabeth, but Edward shook his head.

"If only that were true, but he has done everything he can to dissuade me from this course."

"Then perhaps you should listen to him," Darcy said. "Such an undertaking is full of dangers as well as excitements, and he knows more than most the price of such adventures."

Edward glanced up, anger and resentment in his eyes and Elizabeth was reminded that Edward was still very young, barely past twenty-three.

"It is no more dangerous than joining the army, and I could do that with his blessing," Edward said.

"I'm sure that once your father realises how important this trip is to you, he will understand. Sometimes, in concerning themselves with safety, fathers can forget the exhilaration of the new. Is that not so, Fitzwilliam?" she added as the maid appeared with the tea.

"Perhaps so," he replied as the children rushed in again, attracted by the plate of cakes which the cook never failed to add.

But as he watched Elizabeth dispense tea and pastries to the various parties, his expression became thoughtful as an idea began to form in his mind.

Elizabeth dismissed her maid and began to prepare for bed. She removed the combs from her long dark hair and picked up an elegant silver-backed brush as Darcy entered the room.

"Has Edward retired for the night as well?" she enquired.

She had left the two gentlemen to their port after dinner in hopes that Darcy might be able to impart some words of wisdom to their young guest. Despite managing to keep his mood from the children, Edward was still alternating between tremendous excitement at his forthcoming trip and bitter resentment at his father's disapproval of his chosen path.

"Yes, he has, although from the number of candles alight, I suspect he has little intention of sleeping straightaway."

"It is natural at his age to be so exuberant," she said, beginning to brush her hair.

Darcy crossed the room and stood behind her, taking the brush from her hands. She willingly relinquished it, for if there was one thing she enjoyed more than brushing her own hair, it was having Darcy brush it for her. But after a few minutes, she put her hand on his to stop him, for she could tell by his frown that something was worrying him.

"What is it?" she asked.

"Nothing," he said.

But she was not to be put off.

"There is something; I can tell. You are worried about Edward. You are not happy about this trip of his."

"It is none of my business. He is of age and free to do as he likes. Besides, travel broadens the mind and I think every young man should experience it at least once in his life. I admire his enthusiasm, but sometimes I feel that, for Edward, Egypt has not simply been an interest but an obsession."

"Are you worried that he will be disappointed?"

"I think it is more that I am worried he is too inexperienced to take care of himself abroad. He is very trusting, and there are plenty of people in the world who will be only too happy to take advantage of his generous nature, and his generous allowance. His father and mine were older when they undertook their trip to Egypt, and even they found themselves out of their depth. I am not sure you should be encouraging him."

"I cannot help encouraging him to follow his heart. You, above all, should know the importance of that. After all, would we be here now if we had followed the advice of older, wiser heads?"

"Perhaps not. Though I am not convinced the heads in our case were wiser."

Elizabeth laughed. "No, it was not very wise of Lady Catherine to visit me and attempt to bully me into saying that I would never marry you."

"Or to tell me that you had wilfully refused to assure her that there was no truth in the rumours, for that is what gave me reason to hope. I knew that, if you had really been set against me, you would have told her so."

"Then since things turned out so well for us, will you not agree with me that Edward should not be prevented from pursuing his passion? For who knows where it might lead?"

Darcy was thoughtful. "Perhaps…"

"Yes?"

"Perhaps we should go with him."

"Darcy, do you mean it?" asked Elizabeth, with a sparkle in her eye.

"I do," he said, smiling to see her so happy.

"But what about the boys' schooling?"

"We will be gone for less than a year and the trip will be educational. It will give them a chance to travel, and although it would perhaps be better for them to wait until they are older, such a trip might not be possible when they come of age. Europe has just emerged from a long period of warfare. Who knows when there might be another?"

"Oh, this is so exciting! Just think of it. Egypt! With its pyramids and palm trees and golden sand dunes. What an adventure it will be. We must start to make plans immediately—"

"However," Darcy interrupted as she got up, her eyes sparkling with pleasure, and ran to her escritoire. "Once we return, we will send Laurence to school."

Elizabeth stopped. "He is still so young."

"I was at school already by his age. He needs more society than his family circle can give him. He needs it for his own sake and for his future as well. He is ready to experience a life that allows him more companions of his own age and inclination."

"You mean he wishes to go to school?" Elizabeth frowned. "He has never mentioned it to me."

"Of course not. He does not want to upset you; he adores you, as all our children do. However, when you are not present he talks of little else but the day when he will attend a proper school."

As she stared at him, Elizabeth knew he was speaking the truth. She gave a sigh.

"You are right. I knew it must come eventually, and although I did not admit it, I knew only this morning that the time had come. When Laurence was running around the museum..." She gave a rueful smile.

"He is lively and energetic and full of enthusiasm, but he grows ever wilder as the days progress," Darcy agreed. "And what is more, he leads Jane astray. She will be far more ladylike without Laurence to lead her into mischief. So we are agreed?"

"Yes," she said.

"And we are agreed on the trip to Egypt?"

"Yes, a thousand times yes. It will be the holiday of a lifetime."

Chapter 3

ELIZABETH AND DARCY AGREED not to tell the children about the Egyptian trip at once, as the thought of six overexcited children was rather too much of a good thing, but they discussed it with Edward at the earliest opportunity. Elizabeth was not sure how he would take the news, whether he might think they were interfering, but she need not have been concerned, for he was enthusiastic about the idea.

"It seems only fitting that the two of us should go together," he said to Darcy. "After all, it is what our fathers did."

"If only we knew the name of the third member of their expedition, we could invite his son, too," mused Darcy.

"I did not know there were three men in the original party," said Elizabeth, who had not heard it mentioned before.

"Yes, there is a portrait of all three of them," said Edward. "I found it on a wet afternoon when I explored the attic. It was covered in dust and had obviously not been good enough for my father's refined tastes or he would have hung it in his study. The three men were painted in front of the pyramids."

"And do you not know who the third man is?" asked Elizabeth.

"I did not recognise him," said Edward carefully, adding, "I did not even recognise my own father. He had a beard, he was very thin, and his skin was as brown as a nut. It was only the ring on his finger which gave away his identity."

"And could your father not tell you?"

"He does not like to speak of Egypt. He fears it will encourage me. It is a pity we do not know of any artists who might be willing to come with us. I would like to have someone to record the expedition," said Edward. "We could have our portrait painted in front of the pyramids like our fathers."

Elizabeth opened her mouth, and Darcy said, "No, you cannot ask him."

"Why not?" she replied. "I am sure he would like to come with us."

"The poor man was of a nervous disposition. He jumped every time I spoke to him," said Darcy. "He would probably faint at the sight of a camel."

"You forget, my dear, that you are far more awe inspiring than any camel!" Elizabeth returned with laughter in her eyes.

"Do you mean you know someone?" asked Edward.

"Darcy has just commissioned a family portrait," said Elizabeth. "We were going to have it painted in London, or perhaps at Pemberley. But as we already have several family portraits with various Darcy houses in the background, I think the idea of being painted against a backdrop of camels, sand, and pyramids is an excellent one."

"I doubt if Paul Inkworthy will think it an excellent idea," said Darcy.

"We can at least ask him," said Elizabeth. "It would be an adventure for him, and I think he is in need of an adventure. He is very thin and pale, poor man; he has obviously spent too many hours sitting in a studio. Some sunshine is just what he needs. It would improve his nerves too, I am convinced of it."

"My dear wife, you are incorrigible," said Darcy.

"Alas, dear husband, I am. I will write to him and suggest the idea at once," said Elizabeth.

As she went over to her writing table, she had a brilliant vision of Darcy and herself standing in the middle of a glorious Egyptian painting, with their children seated in front of them. She imagined the girls in pristine white dresses and the boys looking immaculate in coats and breeches, surrounded by golden sand dunes. Then the impossibly perfect picture dissolved as her lively mind provided her with a more realistic picture: Laurence and Jane running about, Margaret sucking her thumb, and a camel eating the flowers on Beth's bonnet. Elizabeth laughed at herself then sat down at her desk, and taking up a quill pen, she started to write.

Darcy and Edward excused themselves. Edward went upstairs, while Darcy called for the carriage and set out for his club. He knew that Lord Potheroe would be there, and as Potheroe had travelled to Egypt the preceding year with his wife, Darcy wanted his advice.

As the carriage rattled through the streets, he felt his own excitement stirring. He had been deprived of a Grand Tour in his youth because of the Napoleonic Wars, which had ravaged Europe and made travel through France and Italy impossible. It had been a great disappointment to him at the time because as a boy he had listened avidly to his father's tales of Paris and Venice, and he had longed to see them for himself. And not only Paris and Venice. His father, in common with Edward's father and other young men of their generation, had extended his Grand Tour to include Greece, Turkey, and Egypt as well. Indeed, one of their friends, Lord Sandwich, had been so enthusiastic about these far-flung places that he had founded the Egyptian Society, opening it to any gentleman who had been in Egypt, and Darcy's father had joined.

It had been a disappointment to Darcy that he had never been able to do the same, but now his chance had arrived. The only thing troubling him was the fact that his father had suffered from various illnesses while in Egypt, and the whole adventure had weakened his constitution. There was no doubt that his Egyptian adventure had contributed to his early death, leaving Darcy an orphan at the age of twenty-two and Georgiana an orphan at the tender age of ten. Darcy did not want to expose himself, or his family, to the same evils, and he meant to take every precaution.

The carriage rolled to a halt. He descended to the pavement, drawing admiring looks from passersby, and went into the club.

As he had hoped, Potheroe was in his usual seat by the window.

"Darcy!" he said, rising, as he saw his old friend. "Join me."

"I would be happy to," said Darcy.

He sat down and ordered a drink, and the two men exchanged pleasantries.

"What are you doing in London?" asked Potheroe.

"We have been down to Kent to visit my aunt, Lady Catherine, and we decided to spend some time in London on our way back to Derbyshire."

"They are all well in Kent, I hope? Anne and her children are thriving?"

"Yes, I thank you."

"So when are you returning to Pemberley?" asked Potheroe, as the waiter brought Darcy his drink.

"Not for some time," said Darcy. "There has been a change of plan. And that leads me to the reason for my being here. I came especially to see you."

"My dear boy, I did not know I was such a draw!" said Potheroe, laughing.

Darcy smiled and then said, "It is not so much you, as your experiences. I am planning a trip to Egypt—"

"Egypt!" said Potheroe, startled. "Will Elizabeth not mind? It is a long way, you know, and you cannot go there and back in a day. Unless she intends to travel with you?"

"She does," said Darcy. "Elizabeth has always liked to travel, and when my cousin Edward turned up unexpectedly, he infected her with his desire to see Egypt."

"I see. It is not very sedate, you know."

Darcy laughed quietly, for there was nothing sedate about Elizabeth either.

"You will be leaving the children with the Bennets, I suppose?" Potheroe continued.

Darcy stretched out his legs in front of him and made himself more comfortable. "No, we will be taking them with us."

"Taking them with you?" asked Potheroe, surprised.

"Yes. It will be educational for them."

"Are they not a little young for that kind of thing?"

"If we wait, who is to say that the opportunity will be

available to them when they are older? You and I both know that wars can erupt at any time and make Europe impassable for decades. I do not want them to be confined to England forever."

"There is something in what you say. Even so, taking children to Egypt... You will need plenty of help. And, mind, not all of your maids and footmen will want to go with you, nor your tutors nor governesses either. It is a long trip, and life is very different when you get there. Not that I am saying it cannot be comfortable, because it can, particularly for a man of your wealth, but it won't be the same as being at home."

"That is exactly why we are going," said Darcy. "For an adventure. But I want to do everything I can to ensure the safety of Elizabeth and the children, which is why I came here to find you. You have been there recently and can give me your advice. I need to know how to travel, where are the best places to stay *en route*, and how to look after my family when we arrive."

"I will do so, and gladly. I will give you the address of the British Consul General out there and let him know you are coming. He will be glad to give you his aid. He will be able to arrange some suitable accommodation for you and have it waiting for you when you arrive. In fact, he will be able to help you with all your practical concerns. He was a great help to me when I was over there, even going so far as to arrange a suitable guard for us. It can be a dangerous place, but a few men following a party are enough to scare away any cutthroats and take care of things if help should become necessary. Not that I think it will: with our show of strength, we were never troubled by anything of that kind. And never fear, the guards are discreet. They will not be intrusive and you will soon forget they are there."

"Thank you."

"And of course you are free to draw on my experiences at any time."

"I hope that you and your wife will dine with us; we will be very glad of your company and I know that Elizabeth will be as eager as I am to hear of your experiences."

A date was set for the following week, and then they fell to discussing the travel arrangements for the Darcys' journey.

"I advise you to arrange matters so that you arrive in Egypt toward the end of August or the start of September; you do not want to arrive during the plague season in June, and it is best to avoid the Nile floods in August. I advise you to hire your own ship to take you to Alexandria from Southampton, it will be much more convenient than changing ships at various ports along the way, and for a man of your wealth it will not be difficult. There is a captain I can recommend..." Lord Potheroe began.

A few hours later, Darcy left the club with all the information he needed to make a start on the arrangements. It was not a small undertaking, transporting so many people so many miles, but it was stimulating and he found himself looking forward to the expedition with enthusiasm.

On leaving the club, he went to see his man of business and informed him of the coming trip, leaving him with a list of instructions based on Lord Potheroe's experiences.

By the time he returned to Darcy House, he found that Edward had taken the children riding in the park with their grooms and that Elizabeth was upstairs. He found her in her bedchamber, sorting through her clothes.

"What do you think I should wear in Egypt?" she asked, holding up two gowns.

"I have never been able to understand the mysteries of women's clothing, but I am sure that Lady Potheroe will be able to advise you. I have invited the Potheroes to dinner next week. They have been in Egypt recently, and they will be able to give us a great deal of help. I have already had the benefit of Lord Potheroe's advice as far as travel and accommodation go. I am sure Lady Potheroe will be just as helpful with the more domestic arrangements. Although you, my dear Elizabeth, will look beautiful whatever you wear," he said, putting his arms around her waist.

She laughed but was pleased nonetheless, and she slid her arms around his neck as he pulled her close, feeling a mixture of warmth and longing as he bent his head to hers.

"I am glad to see that you remember how to exaggerate my good points," she said.

And then she said no more, for his kisses left her neither the time nor the inclination to speak.

The next week was full of interest as they pored over maps, made arrangements, and wrote out long lists of things to do. Edward's father did not give his blessing to the trip but he did not forbid it, which was all that could be hoped for. Edward declared himself happy to travel with his relatives, particularly as Sir Matthew had sailed the day after their meeting. That being the case, he said he would rather wait and travel with friends, even if it meant a delay, than take passage alone.

Normal life was almost forgotten in all the excitement, but Elizabeth was reminded of it when the post brought two letters of interest. One was from Mr Inkworthy, who professed himself willing to travel with them to Egypt, and the other was from Mrs Bennet.

Elizabeth felt a twinge of guilt as she opened it, for she had said nothing of the proposed trip to her mother. She knew the information would provoke a strong reaction, either elation or despair, and an inevitable disturbance of Mrs Bennet's finely tuned nerves. And so she had refrained from saying anything thus far. There would be time enough for that once all the arrangements had been made.

Her twinge of guilt was soon replaced by a different emotion, however, for the contents of the letter gave her an idea.

"You have thought of something," said Darcy, who was writing a letter to Georgiana close by.

"Yes, I have. You know that Sophie Lucas, Charlotte's youngest sister, has recently been jilted and that she has been very unhappy," said Elizabeth.

"I remember you mentioning it, yes."

"Charlotte and Maria have both been worried about her. They invited her to stay with them, but although Sophie dutifully accepted the invitations and dutifully paid her visits, she showed no interest or pleasure in them. And now Mama writes that Mr Jones the apothecary is seriously worried about her and fears she may be going into a decline. Lady Lucas is in despair and does not know what to do."

Darcy stopped writing.

"I am very sorry for it," he said. "I liked Sophie. It cannot have been easy for her, being so much younger than the rest of the family, particularly as her sisters have both been married for ten years or more, and she is the only girl left."

"Even her brothers have now all gone out into the world," said Elizabeth, "which means that she is the only child left at home—although, at two and twenty, she is not a child anymore. I have been thinking that I will lack female companionship when we go to Egypt and that I would like another woman to talk to when so far from home. I cannot ask Jane to go with us, she is busy with her young brood, and I cannot ask Georgiana, as she is expecting again, but Mama's letter has led me to think I would like to invite Sophie. The change of scene would be good for her and give a new turn to her thoughts. She has always loved the children, and she would be a great help with them as well as providing me with some companionship."

"I think it a very good idea. If you can persuade her to come, then do so," said Darcy.

"The only drawback is that as soon as Sophie knows we are going to Egypt, Mama will know as well," said Elizabeth. "There is no such thing as a secret in Meryton."

"She will have to know at some time," said Darcy. "Or had you planned on posting her a letter from Southampton as we boarded the ship?"

Elizabeth's eyes sparkled mischievously.

"I must admit the idea had crossed my mind! But if I am to write to Sophie, I had better write to Mama at the same time. She will make a fuss, no doubt, but she is a long way away in Hertfordshire, and I will just have to bear her reproachful reply."

She could not complain about this minor worry, she thought, as she took up her quill, for the late afternoon was otherwise idyllic. All six of her children were behaving themselves beautifully. Beth was sitting by the window, embroidering a handkerchief; William was reading a book about the pharaohs; John was lying on the floor and reenacting the Battle of Alexandria with his toy soldiers; Laurence and Jane were playing chase, running in and out of the French windows without knocking anything over; and Margaret was talking to her doll.

Darcy, finishing his letters, went to join John.

"Playing with toy soldiers?" Lizzy teased him as he walked past her.

"Helping my son with problems of historical strategy," he returned.

"Do not get too carried away. Remember, the Potheroes are dining with us tonight. In another half hour, the children will have to go upstairs and we will have to dress."

"Half an hour is enough for us to win the battle, is it not, John?" said Darcy.

John nodded seriously.

"I only hope it is enough for Edward to return," said Elizabeth. "You told him we were expecting company for dinner, I hope?"

"Yes, I reminded him about it this morning."

Elizabeth was satisfied and returned to her letters.

As it happened, she need not have worried, for Edward walked into the sitting room soon afterward, just in time to bid the children good night. He was looking well pleased with himself and revealed that he had been with his tailor, discussing some new clothes he would need for the trip.

"You will be able to learn more about what to wear once the Potheroes arrive," said Elizabeth.

"The Potheroes!" said Edward, clapping his hand to his head.

"You had not forgotten?" Elizabeth said. "Even though Darcy reminded you?"

"No, of course not," he declared mendaciously.

"Then I think it is time you retired to dress, and we must do the same," said Elizabeth.

She tidied away her writing implements and then went upstairs, kissing the children good night before retiring to her room, where her maid had laid out a beautiful dinner dress. It had a high waist and narrow skirt, and it was decorated down the front with frills of lace. A newly fashionable lace ruff completed the outfit, but after a few minutes of wearing it, Elizabeth took it off, for although it looked very grand, it scratched.

Darcy entered the room a few minutes later, dressed in his evening clothes and looking as handsome as when she had first seen him at the Meryton assembly. His dark hair was combed over the fine contours of his head, and his figure—as hard and firm as when she had first met him—was encased in a black tailcoat, white ruffled shirt, and well-fitting pantaloons. That evening so long ago had sealed his fate, and hers, too. Despite the difficult start to their courtship, it had led to many years of happiness for both of them.

"You look beautiful," he said, kissing her on the neck.

She could not resist turning to kiss him and would have continued to do so all evening if she had not heard the Potheroes' carriage rolling up outside the house. Reluctantly, she pulled away from him and, equally reluctantly, Darcy let her go.

He gave her his arm and they left the room, descending the long and splendid staircase and arriving on the first floor landing in time to greet their guests.

They all went through to the drawing room, which, in common with other town houses, was located on the first floor. Edward was waiting for them, suitably attired.

He is very handsome, thought Elizabeth as she saw him in all his glory. *I wonder if he and Sophie...*

But then told herself that matchmaking was seldom successful and decided that she had quite enough to think about without such complications.

They were soon all talking happily together. The conversation was at first general, but as they went through into the dining room, dinner having been announced, it turned to the subject on everyone's mind.

"I am longing to know more about your trip," said Elizabeth to Lady Potheroe, as the soup was served. "Is the heat immense?"

"Well, my dear, it is unbearable at midday, although the evenings are delightful. You must be sure to take clothes of the lightest materials. Linen and muslin are best. And you must make sure to be well covered from the sun. We met a very agreeable couple while we were out there—do you remember the Wakeleys, Oliver dear?—they told us that one of their maids foolishly left off her shawl during a shopping trip to the market and was boiled as red as a lobster. The wretched girl was in pain for days and insisted on returning home as soon as ever she could move. But of course, if you take care, there is no need—"

Lady Potheroe chatted on at some length about the different

requirements for adults and children and Elizabeth listened diligently throughout.

Although she had never met the older lady before tonight, Elizabeth could not help but be charmed by her warm manner and matter-of-fact attitude to the perils of travelling in foreign lands. Lady Potheroe had already given Elizabeth more information on medicines to take and clothes to pack than any book could have done. Moreover, she had offered the name of her own seamstress for Elizabeth to consult.

By the time the dessert was brought in, Elizabeth felt much more confident about leading her children off on this marvellous, yet potentially hazardous adventure.

"Of course when you arrive at the Valley of the Kings, you will be amazed at how spectacular the pyramids are," Lord Potheroe said, as he took a spoonful of syllabub. "I couldn't take my eyes off them for the first three days, could I, m'dear?"

"It was the same for all of us, Oliver. The structures are so fantastic, one cannot help but feel dwarfed by them."

"It seems you were quite taken with Egypt, Lady Potheroe," said Darcy, smiling at his guest.

"It is impossible not to be," Lady Potheroe replied. "Indeed, just talking about it this evening with you young people makes me wish I was returning with you. But I cannot," she continued with a smile at Edward, who seemed to be about to invite her in his zeal to convert as many people as possible to his cause. "Our youngest daughter is finally getting married in three months time, and I barely have enough time to choose gowns with her as it is."

"Then our loss is England's gain," said Edward gallantly.

"However," Lord Potheroe continued, "do not let Amelia's enthusiasms blind you to the inconveniences of Egypt, and there are many. You should be aware of the dangers of drinking the water and the diseases that seem to be rife among the poor, even once the plague season has passed. And the animals can be deadly as well. Never be tempted to swim in the rivers, Darcy, no matter how hot it gets. The Nile crocodiles are the most fearsome creatures I have ever seen. We witnessed a male drowning a—"

"Oliver, this is hardly appropriate dinner conversation," Lady Potheroe interrupted gently.

Her husband looked awkward.

"You are right as usual, my dear," he said.

Elizabeth changed the direction of the conversation by saying, "Have you visited the British Museum recently? Edward had business with Sir Matthew, and we saw the beginnings of his exhibition room. He longs to fill it with treasures one day, but at the moment it is practically empty, apart from a few pots and a frieze of an Egyptian woman. She looked remarkably like the little doll Edward gave to Margaret—or, should I say, the doll which Margaret appropriated!"

Edward finished the last of his dessert and sat back on his chair. "Ah, you mean Aahotep."

"It is a peculiar little trinket," Darcy said.

"Egypt is full of such things, Darcy," Lord Potheroe said rather dismissively, but his wife held up a finger.

"Do tell us more, Mr Fitzwilliam. I adore Egyptian folktales."

Her husband smiled indulgently. "Amelia speaks the truth. Whenever we ventured into the souks and she spotted a vase or a tapestry or a rug with even a hint of a story—the gorier the better, I might add—I knew I would not be able to wrest her away until the whole ghastly tale had been told and my wallet would be lighter of a good few pounds."

The Darcys laughed as Edward pushed his plate aside.

"It is not a long story," he said, "although it is rather intriguing. I must confess a similar love of Egyptian stories as Lady Potheroe, and so I made it my business to discover what I could about Aahotep."

"Bravo, Mr Fitzwilliam," said Lady Potheroe. "We romantics must stick together. Please tell us the story."

"Yes, do, Edward," Elizabeth agreed eagerly. "Then I promise Lady Potheroe and I will leave you gentlemen to your port."

Edward bowed from his chair. "Very well then—although I warn you, I have no means of knowing how authentic this tale is…"

By now even Lord Potheroe and Darcy were intrigued and, encouraged by their enthusiasm, Edward began.

"Aahotep was reputed to have lived in the Old Kingdom Era—that is, during the period between 2686 and 2181 BC. She was, according to my source, a somewhat unpleasant creature, although perhaps we should not blame her too much for her wayward life. She was born the fifth daughter of a poor fisherman on the Nile and sold into slavery quite young when her parents decided they could not afford any more girls. She began her career quite humbly as a slave in the household of a grand vizier but soon rose to become a servant of some importance."

"Oh, let me guess," said Lady Potheroe smiling. "She was exceptionally beautiful."

"You have been teasing me, Lady Potheroe; you have heard this story before."

"Mr Fitzwilliam, the woman in question is always exceptionally beautiful; it is a staple of the best stories from every civilisation. Is that not so, Oliver?"

Lord Potheroe laughed. "You would know, my dear."

"Of course," agreed Elizabeth. "What is the good of a story if the woman is not beautiful and the hero not brave? Do go on, Edward."

"Well this beautiful woman was evil as well—"

"Not essentially evil, Edward," said Darcy, entering into the spirit of things, "just forced to become so as a result of circumstances beyond her control."

"Yes, indeed," said Lady Potheroe. "Was there a handsome young man with whom she fell in love and an evil older man who cast covetous eyes upon her?"

"Enough," cried Edward, laughing good-naturedly. "I can see my audience is far crueler than Aahotep could ever be."

"Dear Edward, we should not tease, and I do want to know the story before Mrs Darcy and I retire to discuss fabrics. Come, finish your tale."

The merriment of the company thus calmed, Edward continued.

"Very well; yes, Aahotep was very beautiful and, yes, she did eventually attract the eyes of a richer, older man who desired her enough to marry her and elevate her in society. She was clever as well as beautiful and helped her husband augment his riches, but he was less than just in dividing his newfound wealth with her, and when he died, she was able to govern her new business with greater freedom. It was whispered by some that her husband did not die of natural causes but was rather helped along the road by his less than loving wife, although he was not himself a popular man and most people were prepared to accept this as nothing more than jealousy. And then, she married again, a far richer husband, and enhanced his wealth as well, and after a few short years this husband too died. But life was precarious in those days. And then Aahotep married a third time, and this husband had a handsome young son named Ammon, of whom she quickly became enamoured."

Edward paused, and Darcy leaned toward Lord Potheroe.

"I fancy I can see where this is headed," he said with a smile.

"When her third husband died, Aahotep decided that the handsome young man would be husband number four," said Edward. "Except that he had plans of his own with a younger, equally beautiful girl. And when Aahotep was spurned by the young man and forced to watch his wedding celebrations, she went mad and poisoned their wine at the feast and laughed with insane glee as the whole wedding party died horrible deaths. Aahotep was the only survivor of the feast, but despite the pharaoh sending his most experienced men to apprehend her, she disappeared along the bank of the Nile and was never seen again. Of course, she was supposed to have been eaten by the crocodiles, although rumours persist to this day that one can see a mad woman fleeing the riverbanks when the moon is full. The two lovers were buried together secretly so that Aahotep cannot disturb them in death as she did in life. Only if she truly repents will she ever find them and be allowed to rest herself. And it is said," he ended, intoning dramatically, "that if their tomb is ever disturbed by anyone else, the guilty party, alive or dead, shall be struck down by a disease that no doctor can cure."

"Capital, dear fellow; well done," Lord Potheroe applauded. "Quite one of the best I have heard in a long time."

"And now we will leave you, gentlemen," Elizabeth said, as the servants entered to remove the dessert dishes.

The two ladies stood up and retired to the drawing room, where they discussed the clothes and other necessary items the Darcys would need in Egypt and on their journey.

Life was far less exciting for Elizabeth's parents than it was for Elizabeth as they passed their days in the village of Longbourn. There were no visits to museums and no plans for far-flung journeys. Instead, Mr and Mrs Bennet, having disposed of all their daughters in marriage, spent their days in peace and quiet at Longbourn House. This suited Mr Bennet, who had the calm his nature craved, but it suited Mrs Bennet less well. When she had had five daughters to think about, she had been constantly complaining but nevertheless happy. Now she was simply constantly complaining.

"I think I will walk into Meryton this morning," she said, as she presided over the breakfast table. She looked around at the empty seats and felt a sense of nostalgia for the days when every chair had been full. "I really ought to pay a visit to Mary."

Mary, after spending many years at home, had finally married her uncle's clerk and now lived in simple comfort in Meryton. Although she was the least favourite of her mother's daughters, she had the advantage of being the nearest, as the others had all settled many miles away.

"A good idea," said Mr Bennet, who never discouraged his wife from visiting friends or, indeed, from doing anything which would take her out of the house. "You must not let her feel neglected."

"And then I think I will write to Lydia and invite her to stay. We have not seen her for such a long time, and she is bound to be missing us. Ah! My dear Lydia. How happy she will be to see us again, and how happy we will be to see her and her handsome Wickham."

"We must not trespass upon their time," said Mr Bennet, taking a bite of ham.

"It will be no trespass, I am sure," said Mrs Bennet, as the mail was brought in on a silver salver.

She took the letters and glanced idly at the envelopes, then became more animated.

"A letter from Lizzy!" she said.

This made Mr Bennet look up, for Elizabeth was his favourite daughter.

Mrs Bennet started to read with a complacency reserved for the daughter who had married ten thousand a year and, incidentally, Mr Darcy. But as she read on, she exclaimed in amazement, "Why, Mr Bennet, whatever do you think?"

"I do not know, my dear," he said with a long-suffering air, "but I am sure you are about to tell me."

"Lizzy and Darcy are to visit Egypt. Well! What do you think of that?"

Mr Bennet was startled out of his usual imperturbability.

"Egypt?" he asked, and then he quickly settled back into his usual placidity. "Then I must ask them to bring me back some souvenir. Perhaps a map of the Nile or a crocodile tooth or—"

"Why, Mr Bennet, there is no need to ask them to bring back some souvenir. It would be far better for us to go to Egypt with them and buy some souvenirs ourselves. I am sure Lizzy and Darcy would be delighted to have us, and a few months in Egypt would set me up nicely."

Mr Bennet, however, was no more accommodating than he had been fifteen years before, when Mrs Bennet had desired to go to Brighton. He had refused to countenance a journey then, and he refused now. Having finished his ham and eggs, he remarked that it was impossible and then took refuge behind the latest broadsheet.

Undaunted, Mrs Bennet continued.

"Just think, Mr Bennet! The camels and pyramids, to say nothing of the company—"

"Then, indeed, let us say nothing of it," Mr Bennet remarked.

But Mrs Bennet was constitutionally unable to say nothing, and in the end her husband was forced to retire to the peace of his library.

Thus deprived of an audience, Mrs Bennet rang for Hill, who provided her with a more appreciative ear, and then carried out her earlier resolves: she must visit Mary at once, and then she must invite Lydia to stay.

"Remind me again why am I here with you, my love?" Wickham enquired charmingly as, several days later, he found himself on the steps of Longbourn House.

Lydia fiddled with the slightly grubby ribbon on her bonnet as they waited for the door of her parents' home to open.

"La! My dear Wickham, you know as well as I do," she replied, not even bothering to look at him. "We do not have enough money to live on, and we cannot pay the rent on the rooms we took in the hotel. Mama's letter came just in time to save us from another midnight exit. But now our problems are solved, at least for a week or two—longer, if you behave yourself. Be charming to Mama and polite to Papa, and they may let us stay a month."

"I will do my best."

He kissed her blithely on the neck, careless of the servant who might appear at any second to allow them admission to the house. Lydia could not help but smile, for Wickham was still very handsome, whether he wore his blue or his red coat, and she could never resist his embraces, however lightly given.

"La! Here is Hill," she declared, as the Bennets' long-serving, and long-suffering, servant opened the door. "Hill, is it not the greatest fun? What a lark to find myself at home again!"

Mrs Bennet hurried into the hall to greet her.

"Lydia! My Lydia! Why, how well you look. And Wickham, how handsome!"

Wickham bowed charmingly and kissed her hand.

"But come in! Come in!"

She ushered them into the drawing room, from which Mr Bennet had made a hasty retreat, and tea was immediately served.

There was plenty of news to relate, but Mrs Bennet could wait for very little of it and launched almost immediately into a story of how she was ill used, how no one considered her nerves, and how Elizabeth and Darcy were to go to Egypt!

"Egypt!" Lydia's somewhat weary eyes lit up. "La! Mama, how exciting. I would love to go."

She had a momentary vision of a palm-fringed watering hole, complete with picturesque camels and a host of young and gay people; and, to complete the view, she saw herself seated beneath a canopy, flirting with at least six sheikhs at once. For although she had been married for fourteen years, Lydia was barely thirty.

"My dear, do not mention such a thing, even in jest," said her mother. "It plays havoc with my nerves, for your papa has sworn I shall not go. I cannot see why not, for even Sophie Lucas has been invited."

"Sophie?" asked Lydia, startled and annoyed.

"Elizabeth proposes to take her."

"I do not see why she should take Sophie Lucas," said Lydia.

"Ah, my dear," said Mrs Bennet with a sigh, "neither do I, but Sophie has persuaded her to it, I have no doubt. The Lucases have always been artful. I remember when Charlotte Lucas stole Mr Collins away from beneath my nose, when everyone knew he was promised to Lizzy."

Lydia took no notice of this comment but replied, "Lizzy ought to have taken me," for she was feeling very much as Kitty had felt when Lydia had gone to Brighton and she had been left behind.

"I daresay she ought, but Lizzy has always been headstrong. She is going with Darcy's cousin, Edward Fitzwilliam—"

"Edward?" Lydia's face broke into a smile. "Oh, how I long to see him again. We met him at a ball given in the assembly rooms in Bath. He was forever flirting with me."

"I am not surprised," said Mrs Bennet. "You have always

looked well, Lydia. And now he has given Lizzy and Darcy the idea of going to Egypt. If only I could go to Egypt! But your father will not hear of it. I have told him it will do wonders for my nerves, but no one ever thinks of me. If only your father was more like Mr Darcy's father and Edward's father."

"Pray, what do their fathers have to do with this?" asked Lydia impatiently.

"They travelled to Egypt in their youth," said Mrs Bennet. "Lizzy told me all about it in her letter. Stay, I have it here." She read out the relevant section, adding, "I would like to travel to Egypt while I still have mine."

"Do they say where they intend to go in Egypt, Mrs Bennet?" Wickham asked with careless charm.

"Down the Nile somewhere, I believe," she said. "There is some talk of them joining an archaeological expedition with Sir Matthew Rosen, a most distinguished gentleman and scholar at the British Museum. Lizzy says he is very keen to take them and that Edward has already proved to be of invaluable help on account of the maps and other documents he has left over from his father's expedition."

The gong rang, signalling that it was time to dress for dinner. Lydia left the drawing room, followed by her husband, and as they climbed the stairs to their room—the very room in which Lydia had slept as a child—she stared at him with unabashed astonishment.

"La! My dear Wickham, I never realised you had so much patience in you," she said, opening her rather old-fashioned fan. "You seemed to encourage Mama to chatter, when of late you have not been able to contain your impatience in anything."

"I am always interested in what your mother has to say, my love," Wickham replied smoothly. "Visiting your parents has been a most profitable excursion this day, my dear." As they went into their room he took her hand, kissing it absently. "Most profitable indeed."

Chapter 4

Since they were not to travel until later in the year, so that they would arrive in Egypt when the fierce summer heat was over, the Darcys returned to Pemberley. They told the children of their plans and once the initial excitement had died down, life resumed its normal pace. William and John returned to school, and the other children were occupied by their tutors and governesses while Darcy and Elizabeth continued to host balls and parties. Their neighbours were, by turns, envious, astonished, and critical of their plans. But Elizabeth and Darcy, used to pursuing their dreams in the face of fierce opposition, took no notice of the talk they occasioned and continued to make arrangements for their trip.

Darcy wrote to all the British Consuls in the countries they would be visiting on the way and requested their help for the practical arrangements. In particular, he corresponded with the British Consul in Cairo, where they planned to stay for some time, and when all this was well in hand, he made further arrangements for the ship which was to carry them to Egypt. He was helped in this by his man of business, who dealt with many of the minor arrangements.

Then, too, he had to make arrangements for the life he would leave behind. Pemberley could not run itself, and although his steward was to remain in England, Darcy had to deal with many pressing matters as well as foresee any possible problems while he was gone.

One morning in the early summer, having ridden round the estate with his steward and noted any work to be undertaken in his absence, he returned to the house to find his wife and children sitting in the garden. They were bathed in sunshine as they worked and played, and his heart stood still as he halted for a moment, thinking he was the luckiest man in the world.

He had never imagined that his marriage to Elizabeth would bring him such a deep and abiding joy. He had almost resented the fact that he had fallen in love with her to begin with and had despised himself for rejoicing in her company and admiring her humour. When he had overcome his resentment and finally proposed, he had been angry that she had not fallen into his hands like a ripe plum, but had instead rejected him as the last man in the world she could ever be prevailed upon to marry.

It was only then, when he had insulted her and her family, that he had come to know how passionate, loyal, and constant Elizabeth could be when she knew herself to be right. But it was not until the succeeding months that he had learned she was also capable of change when she found herself to be wrong.

And, right or wrong, she was at all times strong and brave and true to herself, no matter what allurements (such as ten thousand a year and Pemberley), nor what threats (such as offending Lady Catherine and polluting the shades of Pemberley) were used to try and persuade her out of her own mind. And with this strength he had fallen more deeply in love. But he had never known that his love would continue to grow with every passing year, until he no longer knew how he had lived without it.

Parenthood, too, held many surprises. Both he and Elizabeth had been amazed at the strength of their love for their children, and they had found the whole venture more challenging, if more stimulating, than they had expected. Elizabeth, who had grown up in a family of girls, had been amazed at the propensity of small boys to wrestle at any available opportunity. Darcy had had no illusions about boys, having been to a school overflowing with them, but he had been surprised in other ways. Indeed, he had been astonished to find that his children, brought up in a happy, informal atmosphere—in contrast to his own, formal upbringing—had none of the awe of him that he had had for his own parents. Instead, they had unrestrained love, which he found extraordinarily fulfilling, and which he preferred enormously—even if it was sometimes a little exasperating.

With a formal upbringing, there would have been no noisy play in front of him, only "Yes, Papa," and "No, Papa." And although there were occasionally moments when he thought how wonderful that must be—usually when Laurence had led Jane into mischief—he was nevertheless wholeheartedly thankful that he had married Elizabeth and that he had experienced their fun-filled, exhausting, exasperating, yet joyful family life.

As he joined them on the lawn, William looked up from his book.

William is a true Darcy, he thought, for William was already conscious of his heritage and his future as the master of Pemberley. William had an air of gravity that the other children lacked. A *fine boy*, thought Darcy proudly, going over to his eldest son and asking him about his book, engaging him in an interesting conversation.

John was busy using books for a less exalted purpose. They lay about the grass, standing in for naval ships sailing on an emerald sea, as John reenacted the Battle of the Nile.

Laurence, for once, was still. The explanation for this remarkable phenomenon was to be found in the book he held on his lap, which contained a picture of an enormous crocodile menacing a suitably horrified man on a sandbank.

Beth was teaching Jane to sew, and Margaret was dressing her doll in their latest creation, a surprisingly successful imitation of an Egyptian gown.

Elizabeth was sitting in the middle of this happy scene. She looked toward the drive as the sound of carriage wheels filled the air, and Darcy remembered that Jane and Bingley were to visit them. He stayed only to kiss Elizabeth and tell her she was looking exceptionally beautiful, and then he went upstairs to change into fresh clothes.

By the time he joined Elizabeth again in the garden, Jane and Bingley were with her and all the children were playing together, chasing each other across the lawn.

The Bingleys were frequent visitors. Having left Netherfield Park a year after their wedding, they had settled in Nottinghamshire, some thirty miles from Pemberley. In the winter they often stayed with the Darcys, and in the summer it was not uncommon for them to drive over for a day. They customarily arrived before lunch and left after an early dinner, which allowed them to return home in the daylight.

Family news was exchanged, and Jane said, "I envy your trip. If the children were old enough, I would be persuading Charles to take us all, too. But with Eleanor less than two years old, it would never do. It is the talk of Meryton, you know. We have just been staying with Mama, and there is talk of nothing else. Sir William and Lady Lucas have decided to accompany Sophie to London in their carriage. They are planning to stay in London for a few days and then they hope to accompany you to Southampton, so that they may see Sophie safely onto the ship before returning to Lucas Lodge."

"I am glad they are so careful of her," said Darcy. "I think it an excellent idea."

"Yes. I think I must invite them to stay with us while they are in town," said Elizabeth.

Jane hesitated.

Elizabeth looked at her enquiringly. "There is something you are not telling me," she said.

"Only this," said Jane uncomfortably. "As soon as Mama realised that the Lucases would be taking Sophie to London and that the fourth seat in the carriage would be spare..."

"Oh dear," said Lizzy, but she could not help laughing at the sight of Darcy's face, which had fallen comically as he had a presentiment of what was coming.

"You mean to say that your mother is intending to come, too?" he asked.

"I am very much afraid so," said Jane.

"Cheer up, Darcy," said Bingley jovially. "It is only for a few days, you know, just while you are still in London."

"Is that really all, or will she accompany us to Southampton?" Darcy asked, dismayed.

"I am afraid so," said Jane. "To see you onto the ship and to wish you all *bon voyage*."

Lizzy could not help laughing, despite her own horror, for it was so like her mama.

"Do you really mind so very much?" she said, turning to Darcy.

He rallied himself. "No," he said courageously. "Or, at least, no more than you! But never mind, it will not be for long and the children will be glad to see her. We are taking them away from their grandparents for months, after all."

"I think, if we are to have the Lucases and Mama to stay for a few days before we set out for the port, we should also invite Paul Inkworthy to stay. Otherwise he will be the only member of the party not to know anyone. A few days at Darcy House will give him a chance to accustom himself to the children, as well as meet Sophie, before we leave the familiarity of England," said Elizabeth.

"A good idea. I will visit him when we return to London and invite him."

"When are you returning to London?" asked Jane.

"At the end of June," said Elizabeth. "That will allow us some time in town to have the final fittings for our clothes, as well as make other last-minute preparations before we set out."

"You will not forget to write? I am longing to hear all about it," said Jane.

"I will write very regularly, and you must write to me, too," said Elizabeth. "I want to know all about my nieces and nephews while I am away. I have an itinerary inside; I will give you a copy before you leave, and then you will know where we will be at any given time. If you send your letters to the British Consuls, they will hold the letters for us until we arrive, for we will be travelling at a leisurely pace and the post will go more quickly than we do."

"This artist of yours, is he any good?" asked Bingley.

"He comes highly recommended," said Darcy, "but I hope to see for myself when I invite him to stay with us before embarking on our voyage. I intend to call on him to issue the invitation."

"Would it not be better to write?" said Bingley. "You will give him more time to prepare if you do."

"Which is exactly why I intend to call. I would like a chance to see his studio so that I can examine some of his work without him having arranged it all for me in advance."

"His studio is, I fear, nothing more than an attic," said Elizabeth. "The address was not in a good part of town. You must not expect too much."

"Never mind. If the young man has talent, then I mean to give him the opportunity to rise in the world. If I like his work, I am thinking of commissioning a whole set of paintings from him, so that we will have a pictorial record of our trip."

"I like that idea," said Elizabeth, "but we will be away for months, and if he is to paint everywhere we go and everything we do, we will need a new gallery at Pemberley!"

"Well, and why not? Each generation of Darcys adds something to the house. We will add an Egyptian gallery. We might collect some antiquities, too. And once we return, I will be able to introduce him to many more patrons. There is nothing I would like more than to make his fortune, if he deserves it."

Elizabeth was gratified. It was one of the more wonderful things about their position, that it gave them an opportunity to encourage those with talent, and she found herself looking forward to all the paintings, with their exotic backgrounds, which were to come.

"You must bring some antiquities back for us, you know," said Bingley. "Upon my honour, I think a few Egyptian vases would look well in the hall. Do you not think so, Jane?"

"If you would like some, then I have no objection," said Jane. "But I would rather have some Egyptian cotton; it is supposed to be very fine."

As the two women began talking of fabrics and sheets, dresses and shirts, the gentlemen excused themselves and went down to the lake to fish.

"Upon my honour, this is a daring enterprise," said Bingley, as he reeled in his line, only to find a tangle of weed on the other end. He removed the weed and then cast it again.

"The trip to Egypt or entertaining Mrs Bennet in London?" asked Darcy.

Bingley laughed.

"I meant the former, but perhaps the latter will be more of a trial. We have just come back from Longbourn, where Mrs Bennet spoiled the children dreadfully. Charles and Eleanor have taken no harm from it, Charles being too old and Eleanor too young, but I was glad to bring Eliza and Harry home before they were thoroughly spoiled. And so you will be leaving us in July. How long do you mean to stay away?"

"For six months at least. The journey will take several months each way, and we intend to spend some time travelling down the Nile when we arrive. We will go so far from home only once, and we mean to make the most of it."

Bingley felt a tug on his line and landed a fish, and shortly afterward, Darcy's own line gave a jerk. It was with a sizeable catch, at last, that they returned to the house, where the fish were taken to the kitchens and served as one of the dishes at dinner.

Afterward, Jane and Bingley did not linger, wanting to be home before dark.

"Dear Lizzy," said Jane, embracing her sister. "I do not suppose we will see you again before you leave. Have a safe journey and remember to write."

Elizabeth promised to do so and the Bingleys departed. Then she went into the drawing room, where she wrote to the London housekeeper, apprising her of the fact that the Darcys would be entertaining five house guests when they returned to London, prior to their departure for Egypt.

June arrived, and with it the day of their departure for London drew nearer. The children had all but forgotten about the coming trip, having been engrossed in their summer activities at Pemberley, but their excitement began to mount as the boxes were packed, for the journey to London signalled that the journey to Egypt was not far behind.

Almost as soon as they reached London, Mr Darcy called on Paul Inkworthy. The artist's home was in a poor part of town, with narrow cobbled streets and overhanging gables. The houses were a relic of the sixteenth century, their black-and-white buildings giving evidence of the neighbourhood's Tudor heritage.

Darcy found the address, mounted the three precarious wooden steps, and knocked on the crazily askew front door.

There came a drunken shout from inside, followed by the sound of someone falling over, and then a window opened overhead, and a woman peered out.

"Aw, my life, it's a swell," she said, before shutting the window and running heavily downstairs to open the door.

"I am here to see Mr Inkworthy," said Darcy.

"Yes, sir, right this way, sir," said the woman, wiping her greasy hands on her even greasier apron.

Darcy followed her into the ill-lit interior and up several flights of rickety stairs, until she stopped on the uppermost landing, which was inches deep in dust.

"'Ere you are, sir," she said, bobbing him something that resembled a curtsey and holding out her hand.

Darcy put a coin into it and knocked on the attic door. A familiar voice called, "Come in," and Darcy opened the door, walking into the large attic room with a sharp sense of interest. It was bare of any furniture, save for a bed, a table, and a chair; but canvases, sketchbooks, paintbrushes, and all the paraphernalia of an artist's studio filled the large space. An easel stood over by the east-facing window, and on it stood a painting, while in the corner farthest from the easel, cleaning a paintbrush, was Paul Inkworthy.

The artist had his back to him, and Darcy had a chance to examine him for a moment, curious to know more about the young man who was to accompany them on their travels.

Mr Inkworthy looked much the same as he had on their previous meeting, and yet there was something different about him. He was still tall and thin—Darcy found himself wondering when the man had last had a good meal—and his dark, curly hair still fell in an unruly profusion over his collar, but he had an air of confidence about him that had been lacking before. It was evident in the line of his back and the angle of his head.

Darcy nodded thoughtfully. Before, Inkworthy had been in someone else's salon. Here, he was in his own studio, the master of all he surveyed—a small domain, it was true, but one full of riches.

Darcy walked over to the easel and was surprised to see a half-finished portrait of Elizabeth standing on it.

"Ah, yes," came a voice at his side.

He turned to see Mr Inkworthy, who had joined him noiselessly and was looking critically at his own work.

"You have painted my wife," said Darcy.

Some of the artist's former nervousness returned.

"Yes," he said, uncertainly, as if he realised he had committed a *faux pas* by painting another man's wife when not expressly asked to do so. But then the artist in him took over and he said, "I could not resist. It is the eyes, you see, they are so very fine. I noticed them as soon as I was introduced to her. It is not just the colour and shape, nor the fineness of the lashes, but the expression in them. It is extraordinary."

He stood looking at his portrait, lost in thought.

"You have caught it very well," said Darcy, impressed.

"No." The artist shook his head. "I have caught something of it, it is true, but my memory failed me at a critical juncture. I should have taken a sketch at the time but I neglected to do so, for which I have been cursing myself ever since. I could not remember the light in them, the exact glow, the sense of spirit… But I will capture it, I promise you. Now that I am to go to Egypt with you, I will have time to study those eyes at my leisure."

"Which brings me to the object of my visit," said Darcy. "Mrs Darcy and I"—he caught himself stressing Mrs, since the young man was so appreciative of Elizabeth, and since the artist possessed a certain charm. "Mrs Darcy and I would like you to join us at Darcy House tomorrow, so that you may spend a few days with us prior to setting out on our journey. It will give you an opportunity to become acquainted with us, with our children, and with our travelling companions: my cousin, the Honourable Edward Fitzwilliam; and a family friend, Miss Sophie Lucas."

Mr Inkworthy looked dazzled at such a prospect but managed to murmur his thanks. "I will need to bring my things with me," he added. "I hope there will be room for them all?"

"I am sure we can accommodate them," said Darcy with a smile, remembering the size of Darcy House—remembering, too, the spacious quarters he had arranged for them on the ship he had commissioned to take them to Egypt and the size of the house he had rented there.

The artist looked relieved, saying, "Then I will join you tomorrow, if that is convenient."

Now that the business was concluded, some of Inkworthy's former nervousness returned, as though he was suddenly conscious once again that his visitor was Mr Fitzwilliam Darcy of Pemberley, a man who could buy his studio and everything in it a hundred times, nay a thousand times over, and never notice what he spent. Remembering, too, that Darcy had a fine and imposing figure, which made his own spare frame seem even more scrawny, and a face which would have put a more handsome man than Paul Inkworthy to shame.

"Very well," said Darcy, adding the final, unwitting, touch to the younger man's sense of his inferior place in the world by saying, "I will send the carriage."

While Darcy was busy with Paul Inkworthy, Elizabeth was busy overseeing the preparation of the rooms for their guests. Having satisfied herself that everything was just as she wanted it, she finalised the list of essential and desirable things they should take with them and then went into the drawing room, where the children were playing.

"Have you any questions?" she asked them. "We will be leaving in a week, and everything must be ready by then."

Beth asked her mother's advice on which clothes she should take, a sure sign she was gradually leaving childhood behind and beginning to walk the path toward womanhood; William wondered if his allowance would be sufficient for him to bring some curios back to England; John wrote to Colonel Fitzwilliam, telling his idol that he would be visiting the scene of the Battle of Aboukir Bay; and Laurence chased a squealing Jane around the room, pretending to be a crocodile. Only Margaret was quiet, listening to her doll and then saying gravely that Aahotep was glad to be going home.

When she had answered the children's questions, Elizabeth relinquished them into the care of various tutors and governesses. She went out into the garden, where Darcy soon joined her.

"How peaceful it is!" said Elizabeth, as they walked along arm-in-arm. "There is nothing better than the London garden in July. It is small compared to the grounds at Pemberley, I know, but it is a haven of beauty and tranquillity, especially when the roses are in bloom."

She breathed in deeply to catch their scent.

Darcy stopped and picked one, then, stripping off the thorns, he put it in Elizabeth's hair.

"You are not regretting it?" he asked, looking deep into her eyes. "Our holiday will be anything but peaceful. You know what the Potheroes said; there is a great deal of noise and bustle in Cairo, and it lacks the luxuries we have here."

"I know, but I am not regretting it; quite the contrary, I am looking forward to it. But I still welcome moments like these, when we have time entirely to ourselves."

"Then let us make the most of them before our guests arrive," said Darcy, bending his head to kiss her.

Those few precious hours spent together refreshed their spirits, and when they went inside they were ready to welcome their guests, who would be shortly arriving.

Having sent the carriage for Mr Inkworthy, they gathered together the children and settled themselves in the formal drawing room. They were joined by Edward, who was eager to meet their guests.

Mr Paul Inkworthy was the first to arrive.

He entered the drawing room hesitantly, overawed by his surroundings, but he was welcomed cordially and invited to sit down.

He perched on the edge of a *chaise longue* and answered Elizabeth's questions as to the comfort of his journey, his health, and the weather nervously, while all the time looking at her with an artist's eye. He was introduced to the children and then to Edward, and he greeted them all with slightly less nervousness, again studying them with the peculiarly alert gaze of the artist.

As they continued to talk, his eyes wandered to the paintings adorning the walls, and Darcy said, "What do you think of my collection?"

"Good," said Mr Inkworthy, nodding thoughtfully, "although that one is, I think, inferior."

He spoke without any wish to offend, conscious only of the artistic merit of the piece.

"Indeed?" asked Darcy, interested.

Mr Inkworthy nodded, giving his reasons, and Beth surprised them all by joining in.

Mr Inkworthy looked at her in some surprise and then asked, "Do you paint?"

Beth nodded, pleased to be spoken to as an adult, and fetched one of her paintings, a watercolour of the garden.

"Interesting," said Mr Inkworthy as he took it, studying it at arm's length. "The colour is remarkable for one so young, and the..."

But unfortunately for Beth, who was glowing under the praise, the door opened at that moment, and Sophie Lucas walked into the room. Paul was struck dumb and rose slowly to his feet, captivated by her ethereal beauty. Edward, too, could only stand and stare as she made her way into the room, followed by her parents.

Elizabeth stepped forward to greet her, noting with satisfaction that Sophie's eyes had flickered slightly at the obvious effect she was having on the two young men. Such undisguised admiration was just what Sophie needed to restore her vitality, in Elizabeth's opinion, having been jilted by a young man who had led her on to satisfy his own vanity and then left her for an heiress.

Although the flicker in Sophie's eyes quickly died, it was a start, and Elizabeth looked forward to seeing what a few months in their company, in the exotic and colourful country to which they were heading, would do for her young friend.

The introductions had hardly been performed when Mrs Bennet made her entrance, calling out, "There you are, Lizzy. You have a new sofa, I see. And where are my grandchildren?" she cried, opening her arms to them and doing everything in her power to excite them.

Beth bobbed a curtsey, William shook his grandmother's hand, and John stood to attention, while Laurence and Jane flung themselves at their beloved grandmama, and Margaret embraced her knees.

"How you have all grown!" exclaimed Mrs Bennet. "I declare you are the tallest children for your age I have ever seen. Are they not, Lady Lucas?"

Lady Lucas remarked that her own grandchildren were taller, and Mrs Bennet replied that no, she had seen the Lucas grandchildren but recently, and they were, if anything, small for their age.

Elizabeth sought to divert her mother's attention by asking after her journey. But it was an unfortunate choice of subject, for Mrs Bennet remarked that the Lucas's carriage was very cramped and not at all comfortable.

Luckily, Laurence hit upon a better topic by saying there

were no carriages in Egypt, and they would all have to ride on camels. Mrs Bennet said he must take care that the camel did not bite him, to which Laurence replied that the camel must take care that *he* did not bite *it*. Mrs Bennet said he wouldn't, Laurence said he would, and the argument entertained the pair of them until the housekeeper mercifully arrived and showed Mrs Bennet and the Lucases to their rooms.

The children eagerly followed them, hoping for sweetmeats from their indulgent grandmama.

Elizabeth looked at Darcy as the door closed behind them and sank down onto the sofa, laughing. Edward laughed, too, and Mr Inkworthy, looking embarrassed, walked over to the window and effaced himself by admiring the view.

"Well," said Elizabeth to Darcy that evening as they dressed for dinner, finding themselves alone for the first time since luncheon. "What an exhausting afternoon!"

He smiled. "It was certainly entertaining."

"There was a time when you would have found it horrifying," Elizabeth said.

"I must have mellowed with age," he returned. "Besides, it had its satisfying moments. It was good to see Sophie becoming a little more animated."

"Yes, it was. Both Edward and Paul Inkworthy are very taken with her."

Darcy looked smug, and on Elizabeth wondering aloud why that was, he said, "Let us just say that I am glad Mr Inkworthy has another object for his attentions."

"Another?" she asked.

"When I went to see him in his studio, I found him with a half-finished portrait of you on his easel. He was at first uncomfortable to be discovered with it, but he soon lost himself in his enthusiasm for your fine eyes. He had caught them very well, but not well enough for his own satisfaction, and he promised me to do better once he had a chance to study you further."

"You do not mean you were jealous?" she said as he slid his arm around her waist.

"Jealous?" he asked innocently, kissing her on the neck.

"I do believe you were!" she said.

"Well, and what if I was? I am your husband. I have every right to be jealous if a gifted artist takes a fancy to my wife—even if he is not very handsome."

"No?" enquired Elizabeth provocatively. "He is not conventionally handsome, perhaps, but there is something very attractive about him. There is no denying he has a certain charm."

"It is a good thing we are not already on the ship, or I would be tempted to throw him overboard," Darcy said, nibbling her ear.

"Then perhaps I had better leave him to Sophie," said Elizabeth. "It will do her good to have two men competing for her attention. Besides, I already have the man I want," she said happily, turning in the circle of his arms and giving herself up to his embrace.

The next few days followed the pattern of the first. Mrs Bennet spoiled her grandchildren, who enjoyed all the attention—all except Beth, who, gratified by a real artist's praise, spent her days at her watercolours, glowing with pride when Paul noticed her efforts and made some kindly remark.

But Paul's real attention was given to Sophie, and he spent most of his time either sketching her or watching her in silent adoration.

Edward was not so silent. He endeavoured to interest Sophie in his enthusiasms and succeeded in bringing the occasional smile to her lips. But then she drew back, like a child drawing her hand back from the fire at the memory of a previous time when, seeking to warm herself, she had been burned.

Sir William and Lady Lucas spoke at length of their daughter Charlotte and Charlotte's husband, Mr Collins, who, with Mr Darcy's help, had acquired a valuable living. Elizabeth had to smile when Lady Lucas remarked that Mr Collins spent long hours with his parishioners and that Charlotte bore his frequent absences without complaint.

But the morning of their departure arrived without any real arguments, and Elizabeth heaved a sigh of relief as everything was packed and trunks were carried downstairs. She had the occasional sinking feeling that they would not be ready in time, but at last everything was done. The children were put in one of the Darcy coaches with their grandmama; the Lucases offered a seat to Edward, who accepted with alacrity; Paul Inkworthy accepted the offer of a seat on the box next to the coachman, leaving Darcy and Elizabeth to make the journey in Darcy's phaeton.

There had been some debate about whether they should travel for one long day or stay overnight at an inn and have two shorter journeys, but it had been decided in the end that they should break their journey so as to arrive at the ship feeling refreshed.

The decision proved a good one, for when they drove into Southampton the following day, they were not too tired to enjoy the wonderful sight which met their eyes.

"Well, what do you think of it, my dear?" asked Darcy as he helped Elizabeth down from the phaeton.

Elizabeth looked around her, taking in the busy harbour, which was full of hurrying men and women, horses, carts, and, above them, wheeling seagulls. She breathed in deeply, inhaling the salty, fresh air, as her eyes came to rest on their own vessel. She looked at it with awe. It was a large ship, freshly painted, which boasted two tall masts, each with five billowing white sails of increasing size and two smaller ones at the front. Sailors in rough working clothes, their hair dipped in tar, scurried along the decks. All about them was hustle and bustle.

"Magnificent," she said appreciatively.

Her children stared in wonder, for they had never seen anything like it.

John was gaping in something akin to adoration at the way the sailors scrambled up the masts with the agility and confidence of monkeys.

"So, John," came a familiar voice behind them, "do you think you might like a life in His Majesty's navy, rather than in the army?"

They turned to see Colonel Fitzwilliam, and John's face lit up. He took a step forward and looked as if he were about to hug his father's cousin, before pride got the better of him and he stood to attention.

"No, sir," he said. "It's the army for me."

"Good boy!" said Colonel Fitzwilliam approvingly.

John was not the only one who was pleased to see the colonel.

"Brother!" said Edward, greeting him warmly and clasp-ing him by the hand. "I wondered if you might come to see us off."

"I was in the neighbourhood and could not resist," said Colonel Fitzwilliam. "The Darcy expedition is the talk of the port. It is not often that someone can afford to commission a ship to take them all the way to Egypt. You were wise," he said, turning to Darcy. "It is no small thing to take a family so far. I think you will have good fortune, though; she is a fine ship. Her captain, too, is well spoken of." His gaze wandered from the ship back to John, who was eager for his attention. "It will be an opportunity for you to find your sea legs, John. As a soldier, you will often be transported to the scene of battle by the navy, and you must accustom yourself to life aboard."

"Yes, indeed, John," said Mrs Bennet, who had been silent for two minutes and could manage no more. "And I am sure it would do me good, too. Some sea air is just what I would like to set me up. A sea voyage is just what I need."

Elizabeth and Darcy exchanged glances, but otherwise ignored this hint, as they had ignored every other hint, large and small, dropped by Mrs Bennet since her arrival at Darcy House.

"I think I see the captain," said Darcy diplomatically. "Let us board."

They made their way up the gangplank. This mode of entry proved irresistible to Laurence, who ran up and down it several times until he nearly overbalanced. He was just about to fall into the ocean when he was caught by Paul Inkworthy, who was bringing up the rear.

The entire party was welcomed on board by a tall man of middle years, his fine military posture and smart uniform immediately proclaiming him the captain of the ship.

"Captain Merriweather, may I introduce my wife, Mrs Fitzwilliam Darcy," said Darcy.

Captain Merriweather took her hand and kissed it lightly.

"I'm delighted to make your acquaintance, ma'am," he said.

"As I am yours, sir. This is indeed a splendid ship."

He smiled, pleased at the compliment. "I like to think so, ma'am, though I own I may be prejudiced. My wife tells me I pay more attention to this vessel than I do her or my children."

Colonel Fitzwilliam laughed, and the two men greeted each other with respect.

"You have every reason to be proud, Captain," said Elizabeth, looking around her.

Once on board, she found the ship was even finer than she had thought. As Darcy continued with the introductions, her eyes wandered over the masts and wheel, to the ship's crew and the barrels of provisions which were being rolled on board.

"And is this the last of your luggage?" asked Captain Merriweather, as trunks followed the Darcys.

"It is."

"Then I will see that it is stowed safely below. We will be leaving with the tide in the next hour, ladies and gentlemen," he said, as he left them to see to essential matters. "I must ask you to make all necessary preparations and say your good-byes before then."

He nodded to Darcy and marched off along the deck.

"How exciting it all is, Lizzy," said Mrs Bennet. "And what

a wonderful ship. Do you not think so, Lady Lucas?" She turned round. "Lady Lucas?"

But Lady Lucas, together with her husband and daughter, had already gone below.

"I daresay they are looking at Sophie's room," said Mrs Bennet, adding in an aggrieved tone of voice, "though why you had to invite Sophie Lucas when you have four perfectly good sisters of your own, I cannot imagine."

Elizabeth was glad that the Lucases were not there to hear such an uncharitable sentiment, and to distract her mother's thoughts, she said, "Let me show you our cabin."

One of the cabin boys was on hand to show them the way, and they followed him slowly down the spiral staircase. The accommodation was rather cramped after the spacious and luxurious surroundings of Darcy House as well as Pemberley, but nevertheless Elizabeth regarded it as part of the adventure. And besides, for shipboard accommodation it was unusually spacious. The Darcys had taken over an entire deck, and she could tell from her children's excited shrieks that they were delighted.

As well as quarters for the servants and tutors that they had brought with them, there was a master bedroom for herself and Darcy and a cabin for the boys, while the girls were sharing another. Edward had a cabin next to Mr Inkworthy. Since the two men had become somewhat cool toward one another, especially when in the company of Sophie, Elizabeth could only guess at how their relationship might progress during the journey. As for Sophie, she had been allocated a tiny little room all to herself, and Elizabeth heard murmurs of interest from the Lucases, who were examining it together.

"Mama, do come and look," shouted Laurence, running up to her. Taking her hand, he pulled her toward the cabin he was to share with his brothers. "The windows are round."

"They're called portholes, Laurence," William informed him disdainfully.

Laurence ignored him.

"And look, little beds on top of each other too."

William rolled his eyes. "Bunk beds," he said.

Laurence poked his tongue out at his older brother.

"Mama, I want to sleep on one of the top ones, but John and William won't let me."

"You must all take it in turns, my darling. That is what Papa and I will do."

"Mama, you do not have bunk beds in your room."

"Well then, you must let me take it in turns to share the top one with you!" Elizabeth replied, her eyes twinkling.

Just then Jane and Beth appeared, and both Elizabeth and Mrs Bennet were taken to admire the girls' cabin.

They were joined at length by Darcy, who made it clear in his polite but determined fashion that Mrs Bennet should join Sir William and Lady Lucas, who were now being shown back to the top deck by Sophie in order to disembark from the ship.

Fond farewells were exchanged, although Elizabeth could not help feeling guiltily relieved that Mrs Bennet would soon be on her way back to Meryton.

As Elizabeth began to accompany her mother up to the top deck, Beth appeared from the girls' cabin.

"Mama," she said in agitation, "do please come quickly. Jane says she is feeling sick."

After the way Jane had been eating sweetmeats, which had thoughtfully been provided for her by her grandmama, Elizabeth was not surprised. She looked at her mother accusingly for a moment, but Mrs Bennet returned her gaze innocently and said, "It is the motion of the ship, no doubt, all this bobbing about on the water. Be off with you, Lizzy; pray do not worry about me. I am sure I can find my own way to shore."

Elizabeth embraced her mother and wished her a fond fare-well, then followed Beth to find Jane lying on one of the bunks and looking very green. The motion of the ship was not helping matters, nor was the rather stale air below.

Being a great believer in fresh air herself, Elizabeth first admonished her daughter for eating too many sweetmeats and then, holding out her hand, led Jane up onto the deck.

A fresh breeze was blowing, and in a few minutes Jane was starting to look a little better. The activity all about them was good for her, too, as it took her mind off her ills. Sir William and Lady Lucas were hurrying down the gangplank, while the sailors waited impatiently for them to reach the dock so that they could cast off. The boys were leaning eagerly over the ship's rail, watching all the activity.

The last of the guests having departed, the sailors loosed the thick rope that secured the ship then sprang lightly aboard, pulling up the gangplank as the ship rolled on the waves and began to pull away from land. On the dock, the Lucases turned to wave to Sophie, and Colonel Fitzwilliam saluted the passen-gers, giving a special smile to John.

From his specially chosen vantage point on board, Paul Inkworthy made rapid sketches of the sailors, the port, the passengers, the ship, and the seascape, while Edward enquired after Sophie's comfort, wondering if he could bring her a shawl or anything else she might require. Sophie, still looking wan but with some animation, said that she would appreciate her shawl, and Edward hurried off to get it.

"Well, we are off," said Darcy, coming up behind Elizabeth and offering her his arm.

She took it gladly, her eyes bright. "We are indeed. Let us hope the rest of our journey goes so smoothly."

"Is there anything wrong with Jane?" asked Darcy, as he noticed that his daughter was quieter than usual.

"No, only a stomachache. Mama has been feeding her sweetmeats."

"That is one danger we will no longer have to worry about!" said Darcy with a laugh.

"No. Much as I love my family, I…"

Her voice trailed away and a look of horror spread over her face.

Darcy looked at her curiously. "Is anything wrong?" he asked.

"Tell me I am dreaming. Tell me it is a trick of the light or a hallucination," said Elizabeth faintly.

He followed her gaze and saw… Mrs Bennet, coming up from below!

"Oh dear," said Mrs Bennet blithely. "What a catastrophe! I must have taken a wrong turn down below. And I was so sure I knew my way onto the deck. But I found myself in a storeroom with a lot of barrels, and then I found myself in another room with boxes and trunks, and somehow I could not find my way back to the gangplank," she said with an unconvincing sigh.

"And now the ship has sailed. It seems I must come to Egypt with you after all."

"No!" said Elizabeth, horrified. "That is, I am sure there is still time for you to disembark."

But the captain looked at her regretfully and said, "I am afraid that all who are aboard must stay aboard, Mrs Darcy. The tide waits for no one, ma'am."

Chapter 5

THE FIRST FEW WEEKS at sea were a new experience for the whole party. To begin with, they all suffered from the perils of the ocean to a greater or lesser degree. William, Laurence, Jane, and Margaret were laid low, and even John looked decidedly pale, while Sophie could walk nowhere without falling over. Elizabeth spent most of her time at the front of the ship, where no one could see how green she was looking, and Darcy spent a great deal of time with the captain, trying to take his mind off his ills by learning about their voyage. Edward remained in his cabin, from where groans emerged periodically, and Paul found himself a few choice spots from which to observe, sketch, and paint. Since neither he nor Beth suffered any great ill effects from the motion of the ship, they were often together, with Paul taking a kindly interest in her talented drawings and Beth regarding him with adoration.

By and by they all adjusted to the motion of the ship. Even Mrs Bennet, whose early elation at being one of the party had disappeared when she had felt the first wave of nausea, began to like the voyage.

And indeed, there was much to enjoy: the sound of the sails flapping in the breeze; the creaking of the ropes; the variety of the blues and greens of the ocean; the ever changing waves; the clean tang of salt; the sightings of unusual sea birds; the joy of seeing great schools of fish; the exciting and colourful ports at which they called to pick up fresh supplies; and the pleasure of finding letters from friends and relatives waiting for them in every port.

For Darcy there was also the joy of seeing his family adjusting so well to shipboard life. He felt a swell of pride as he walked onto deck one morning and saw John swarming up the rigging, finally climbing into the crow's nest; for while the rest of the party had been content to continue their normal pursuits on board, John had availed himself of every opportunity for activity and new experiences. Whenever his studies had allowed—and the children were often occupied with their tutors—he learned how to set sails, tie knots, and even take the wheel. Darcy stood for a moment, delighted to see his eager and energetic son enjoying himself.

"That is quite a boy you have there," said the captain, as John helped to unfurl a sail which had become caught in the rigging. "He tells me he intends to go into the army, but it is a loss for the navy. I would have been glad of him on my naval ship before I left to pursue civilian life, and any captain would feel the same. The boy is bold and adventurous, but he does not take any unnecessary risks, and he tempers his adventurous spirit with intelligence."

Darcy's heart swelled even further with paternal pride at this. But then, all of a sudden, the realisation hit him that John was growing up. He had always known it, but he had envisaged John merely a year or two in the future. Now he saw that soon John would become a man—a fine man, but one who would no longer need him. He was suddenly aware of a feeling of emptiness and loss and he understood how Elizabeth felt when she did not want her youngest son to be sent away to school. He had a wish to seize the moment and hold on to it, to stretch it out so that it would never end. It was captured in all its detail, with the sound of the gulls and the crack of the sails and the concentration on his son's face. And then John swarmed down the rigging and ran up to show him a new knot he had just learned to tie, and Darcy saw him as a ten-year-old boy once more and let the moment move on.

Laurence, meanwhile, was playing around his grandmama's skirts. He had at first wanted to join in his older brother's activities, but he lacked John's nimbleness and unfailing courage and so was content at last to run around the deck and bedevil his indulgent grandmama.

William, always immaculately dressed and walking with the unconscious arrogance of a Darcy as he moved about the ship, pursued his studies. His one concession to his location was that he pursued them on the deck, not below, and was presently looking through a telescope out to sea.

The girls, too, were enjoying their new venture, and while Beth sketched and painted, Jane was often to be found running round her grandmama, while it was common to see Margaret with Sophie.

The two were together now and as John ran off to help fold a sail, Darcy smiled to see them. His youngest daughter was often overlooked, especially by her grandmama, who preferred the more boisterous older children, but Sophie had taken the little girl under her wing and Darcy felt very glad they had brought Miss Lucas with them. She was looking very pretty in a summer dress with a light spencer jacket, the sun playing on her fair hair and the breeze catching at the feather in her bonnet.

He went over to her and complimented her on her embroidery, then praised Margaret's sampler, which was covered in shapes that resembled hieroglyphs.

"That is an unusual pattern," he said.

"It's Egyptian writing," said Margaret seriously.

"Margaret designed her sampler herself," said Sophie, looking fondly at the little girl.

"And what does it say?" Darcy asked his daughter teasingly, for not even Edward could unlock the secrets of the strange pictorial writing, though he spent the greater part of every day trying.

"It says, 'Aahotep *nefer*,' which means 'Aahotep the beautiful,'" said Margaret gravely.

Darcy was surprised at her imagination, which had never been in evidence before. But ever since she had discovered the doll it had been developing, and he found himself wondering if his youngest daughter might follow in the footsteps of Fanny Burney and become a novelist; although, if the things he had overheard her saying to her doll were anything to go by, she would be more likely to write Gothic horrors and become a second Mrs Radcliffe.

John a soldier, Meg a novelist, William the heir of Pemberley, Beth an artist... and what would Laurence and Jane become when they grew up? he wondered.

His thoughts were brought back to the present by the sight of Elizabeth standing at the prow of the ship. Her face was turned into the fresh breeze and her hair was blowing loose of its pins, dancing across her neck in a tantalising manner. He went to join her. He put his arms around her waist, and she turned at the feel of him, smiling up into his eyes. He thought how lucky he was, knowing himself to be as much in love with her as he had been on the day they married.

"Is it not exhilarating?" she said, her eyes sparkling.

He kissed her cheek lovingly. "It is. Ah, you mean the voyage!"

She laughed and put her arms over his.

"I was on the point of regretting the voyage when we were all afflicted with seasickness, but now I find myself wishing it would never end," she said. "There is something invigorating about a life on the water."

"This is just the start of things," said Darcy. "Only a few more weeks, and we will be in Egypt."

"Today it is all water, then it will be all sand!"

"And I have something to show you when we arrive."

"Oh? And what might that be?"

He took evident satisfaction in her curiosity.

"Let us just say it is a surprise."

While the others amused themselves on deck, Edward was in his cabin, poring over a print of the Rosetta Stone. He had been obsessed with its translation when it had first been discovered at the start of the century, but his interest had waned, only to be reawakened when he had found the map.

He became thoughtful as he relived the memory.

His father's tales of Egypt had inspired him as a boy, and the thought of a map marking the spot of an undiscovered—and unplundered—tomb had fired his imagination. But his father had refused to let him examine the map, saying it was worthless and telling him not to waste his life on daydreams. So Edward had stopped talking to his father about Egypt, but he had not stopped visiting museums, reading about the latest findings, and collecting pottery.

And then, on a particularly rainy afternoon the previous winter, he had gone into the attic in search of a brace of pistols which had been taken there by mistake, and on a table in a wooden box he had found the map—or at least part of it, for it was incomplete. Nevertheless, there was enough to show that the tomb lay near a city and between two oases. His initial excitement had been dampened by the knowledge that Egypt was full of cities and oases and that his father had been unable to find the tomb despite a diligent search. He reminded himself that it would not be any different for him... until he saw that, along the top of the map, there were several rows of hieroglyphs. In his father's time, there had been no hope of translating them. But now, with the discovery of the Rosetta Stone, it seemed that such a translation might be possible; and then the fabled tomb, with its fabled treasure, would be within his grasp.

And so he had written to some of the learned men who were working on translating the hieroglyphs and discovered enough to know that the city on the map was Cairo and not Luxor. Knowing that Sir Matthew Rosen was engaged on a dig in that area, he had arranged the meeting in London, hoping that he might be able to persuade Sir Matthew to allow him to join the dig. To his great excitement, Sir Matthew had agreed to his proposal. And what had excited him more had been the discovery that Sir Matthew had in his possession a frieze showing the likeness of Aahotep. The frieze, the doll, and the tomb were all linked, for his father had believed that the tomb was that of the young bridal couple Aahotep had supposedly poisoned.

He thought of the story again. Aahotep had murdered a pair of lovers in a jealous rage and they had been buried in a hidden tomb, protected by magical spells to ensure they would rest undisturbed. Strip away the fantastic story of magicians and spells, so beloved by the ancient Egyptians, and what was left was a down-to-earth tale of two wealthy people buried together in an undiscovered tomb. And he had a map to the whereabouts of the tomb.

But most exciting of all was the knowledge that Sir Matthew had discovered the frieze in a souk near Cairo, confirming that Cairo was indeed the city on the map, and not Luxor, as his father had thought. No wonder his father's efforts to find it had been in vain!

For the first time, Edward felt he had a real chance of succeeding where his father had failed.

Visions of gold and jewels swam before his eyes... and then visions of himself bestowing them on Sophie Lucas. He had never met anyone like her. She was fragile and delicate and ethereal, and he thought her the most beautiful creature he had ever seen. When she spoke, he bent his head to listen, as if it was drawn to her by a string. Her deep sadness brought out all his chivalrous instincts and he found himself wanting to bring a smile to her beautiful face. And what better way to do it than to shower her with jewels and lay all his earthly possessions at her feet?

Pushing aside his books, he decided to take a turn on deck in the hope that Sophie might happen to be there as well.

Sophie was enjoying the open air and the Mediterranean sunshine. After a long, dark time, she was beginning to come to life again. The new sights and scents stimulated her, and the uncomplicated love of the Darcy children soothed her battered spirit, for although her own family had tried to help her, their constant attentions had depressed her spirits rather than otherwise. They had exhorted her to count her blessings, but this had only made her feel worse, because she then felt guilty for being ungrateful as well as feeling unhappy; they had told her to forget Mr Rotherham, which she had been unable to do; and they had reminded her that she must not leave it too long to return to the land of the living, for at the age of twenty-two she was in danger of becoming an old maid and could not delay her search for a husband. They had talked incessantly of her married sisters: Charlotte, with her comfortable rectory and three children, and Maria, with her handsome husband and her new baby. They had said that she must find the same—never realising that it was those very exhortations which had made her so vulnerable to the attentions of the handsome but fickle nephew of her father's old business partner, Mr Rotherham, in the first place.

A fresh breeze sprang up and a sudden gust caught her bonnet, diverting her thoughts to the immediate task of keeping it on her head. She put her hand on it, catching it before it was ripped away, but her feather was not so lucky. It was torn loose by the wind and danced along the deck, whirling and pirouetting as it was blown toward the rail.

Laughing at the comical sight, she sprang up to chase after it, but Paul Inkworthy was quicker. Putting aside his sketch, he leapt up and caught it, handing it to her with a laugh and a bow.

Sophie blushed as she took it, feeling suddenly awkward. Mr Inkworthy was not handsome, but his eyes were kind and intelligent and there was no denying the fact that his evident admiration had done much to restore her confidence in recent weeks. But still she did not have the courage to speak.

"Miss Lucas..." said Paul, and then he stopped.

She willed him to continue but was not surprised when he did not. What could a young man such as Mr Inkworthy—for he was a year younger than she—have to say to a woman of her age? His kindness and gentleness were indisputable, but his admiration, she told herself, was of an artistic kind. But still she could not bring herself to walk back across the deck to her embroidery. And so she looked at him, willing him to continue, for she wanted to talk to him, but she had grown tongue-tied.

He lapsed into silence again and she felt a certain empathy with him. He, too, was shy and, she suspected, uncomfortably aware of his situation. His position was a difficult one. He was not a friend of the family nor yet quite a servant, and so he was an outsider to both parties. As, in a way, was she. For although the Darcys had invited her as their guest, she was considerably younger than Elizabeth, who had been a friend of her older sister Charlotte rather than a particular friend of hers, and she did not have the wealth or the position of the Darcys. Then, too, it was not always easy for her to talk to older people. True, there was another young man on board, for Edward was more of an age with her, but she did not encourage her feelings for him, as she knew too well how vulnerable a woman made herself when she entertained feelings for a rich and handsome man.

The silence was becoming awkward and so she turned to go but, emboldened by her step toward departure, Paul said, "I have no right…"

She stopped and waited for him to continue.

"I have no right," he said again and then went on in a rush, "but I cannot bear to see you so sad. I know I should not talk of it, but I can think of nothing else to talk to you about, except commonplaces, and I do not want to bore you with my feeble attempts to talk about the weather. Something has happened to you, I can tell that, something which has robbed you of your happiness. I just wanted to know if there was anything I could do for you. If I might be of service to you in any way—even if it is only to listen—well, then, I would gladly do anything in my power to lighten your burden."

He spoke with such obvious sincerity that Sophie found herself wanting to confide in him. She had tried to speak to her siblings at the time, but they had been busy with their own affairs and inclined to dismiss the feelings of the youngest member of the family. Her parents had had time and interest aplenty but no way of understanding her.

"There was an unhappy love affair, I think," he said, not looking at her but instead looking over the sea.

It made it easier for her.

"There was someone…" she said, not knowing how to begin but nevertheless wanting to speak.

"In Hertfordshire?" he asked, looking back toward her. "That is where you are from, I think?"

She nodded. "Yes." And then she stopped, for she did not know how to go on.

"I have never been to Hertfordshire, but I hear it is very pretty."

He had said the right thing. Given something so harmless to discuss, Sophie began to speak at length. She told him of her town and spoke of her neighbours with affection, but what was left unsaid was as revealing as what was said. As the youngest daughter of a large family, it was soon clear that she had been made to understand, though not unkindly, that marriage was the only honourable means of keeping herself from want once her parents died and that her choices of husband would be limited, as her parents could not provide her with much in the way of a dowry. She had accepted her situation but had still hoped that she would be luckier than her oldest sister, Charlotte, whose marriage to Mr Collins, it soon became clear, she could never view as anything other than a sham.

"Your choices are not so limited, I am sure," he said, looking at her with unconcealed admiration.

But it became clear from her halting sentences that her fragile beauty had been largely unremarked upon in the environs of her parents' house and that even the kindest neighbours had tended to see it as a waste in a child whose prospects depended more on fortune than merit.

"And that is when I met Mr Rotherham," she said softly.

Paul waited, saying nothing, giving her the opportunity to

order her thoughts and express them in a way she had not been able to before.

"He was very good to me," she said, speaking of Francis Rotherham with a mixture of wistfulness and pain, telling him of the way Mr Rotherham had made much of her during the summer balls and assemblies. "He laughed with me and danced with me and made me feel that I was special."

"And so you are," said Paul sincerely.

She shook her head. "No. For not long after such hopeful scenes, Mr Rotherham abandoned me at a lakeside picnic in order to pursue..."

"A wealthy young woman?" he hazarded.

She dropped her eyes, unable to meet his gaze as she remembered the rich young lady who had arrived from London—remembered, too, how Mr Rotherham had transferred his allegiances publicly, with no thought for her feelings or the hurt and shame she must feel. At his callous treatment, her heart had shrivelled, and when she had recovered a little, she vowed never to give her heart to a man she did not fully know, and fully trust, again.

She felt Paul's silent sympathy, even as her eyes came to rest on his hands. Paul Inkworthy had none of the artifices of Mr Rotherham. She had only to look at his paint-stained fingers and then lift her eyes a little to his rather worn shirt to see he cared little for society manners. The only time she had seen him animated was when he had discussed chiaroscuro one afternoon with Beth. It was art which stirred his passions, not fortunes. Even so, she knew very little about him, and although his admiration was gratifying, it was not enough to make her seek a romantic attachment again.

She made an effort to shake away the gloomy memories which were threatening to engulf her and reminded herself that she was lucky to have such good friends and to have been invited on such an interesting trip. She pushed her thoughts deliberately outward and, turning the feather in her hands, she said, "The wind is very strong."

"Yes, it is," he said, with a fervour which reflected his willingness to allow her to return to the safety of commonplaces, rather than the brilliance of her comment.

She smiled at his evident goodwill and, looking up, said, "It catches the sails as forcefully as it caught my feather."

"Yes, it does," he said, returning her smile.

"I do not know how the sailors can climb the masts in such a wind, but they know no fear."

"No."

Her eyes fell to the deck, where she caught sight of one of his sketches. It had caught the sailors' activity admirably. She picked it up to study it further and remarked that he had caught their vitality with brilliance; and he explained, with no false modesty, how he had done it. Before long, they were deep in a conversation about art, and all the awkwardness of their former conversation was lost. It was one subject on which he knew no hesitancy or reticence, and she found his enthusiasm contagious.

"I wish I could catch the feel of the wind in the sails, but I am afraid I am no artist," she said.

"It is easy when you know how," he said. "Here." He put a pencil into her hand. Then, putting his arm around her so that he could guide her, he took hold of her hand and sketched a few vital lines.

"Do you feel the flow of it?" he asked.

"Yes," said Sophie.

She felt something else as well, a warmth and tingling at his nearness. She could feel the sweetness of his breath on the back of her neck, and the strength of his hand was exhilarating. She was just about to make another line on the paper when a cheery voice called out behind her, "Miss Lucas, how do you like the journey so far?" and she turned, startled, to see Mr Darcy's cousin Edward coming toward them.

Unlike Paul, his wardrobe was immaculate, and his cuffs pristine white and innocent of a seamstress's darns. But his face—she sprang away from Paul at once, but not before she had registered the surprise and disapproval in Edward's eyes at her closeness to Mr Inkworthy.

Oh, why do men have to be so difficult, she thought, with a sudden flare of irritation with Edward and with men in general, for in one way or another they seemed to be forever disturbing her calm.

Edward simply bowed stiffly and moved on to speak to the captain, while Paul returned to his sketches.

Sophie returned to her seat to find that Meg had been joined by Elizabeth and that mercifully there were no men anywhere near. The little girl was regaling her mother with stories of Aahotep.

"My goodness, Aahotep had a very eventful life," Elizabeth was saying, while Meg nodded before carrying on with her embroidery.

Sophie sat down and Elizabeth, turning to welcome her, said in surprise, "You are angry. What about?"

"You are mistaken," said Sophie. "I am not angry."

"Yes, you are. And I am glad," said Elizabeth with satisfaction.

"It is far better than seeing you looking so listless all the time. It is good to know that your spirit is returning; a little anger is a healthy thing. Was it something Edward said?"

Sophie shook her head. "No, not really. It is just that... oh, why are men so difficult?" she burst out. "You are lucky; you found Mr Darcy, but other men..."

"Believe me, my husband is just as difficult as the rest," said Elizabeth, laughing.

"But you are happily married, whereas I..."

"Have that joy yet to come," said Elizabeth firmly.

"I wish it might be so," said Sophie, sitting beside her. "But after last year..."

"I understand. After your unfortunate experiences with Mr Rotherham, you feel that you do not want anything to do with men ever again. Believe me, I know how you feel. Did you really love him?" asked Elizabeth sympathetically.

Sophie said with a sigh, "I do not know. I thought I did, but now I am not so sure. I am not sure I know what love is."

Elizabeth nodded thoughtfully. "Would you like to find him in Meryton when you get home? Would it make you happy if he came back for you?"

"No," said Sophie without hesitation. And, after a minute's thought, she added, "And in any case he would not do so."

"Mr Bingley came back for Jane," Elizabeth reminded her.

"But that was not the same."

"How so?"

"Because Mr Bingley loved Jane. And she loved him."

"And in your case it is different?" Elizabeth asked.

"It is a strange thing, but now that you put it like that, I can see that it is. I have spent so long regretting him that I did not think to ask myself if I really loved him. I was flattered by his attentions and I was excited at the thought of him proposing, and I was relieved that my family would not have the burden of an unwanted female on their hands. And so I thought I was in love with him. And then when he humiliated me by withdrawing his attentions, and in such a public way, I was too hurt to know what I really felt. But now that it is all over, and I am many miles away, I can see things more clearly. Perhaps I never loved him after all."

"Affairs of the heart are never easy," said Elizabeth. "I made a lot of mistakes when I was about your age. I judged my husband on an overheard conversation, and from that moment on I set out to tease and plague him because he had slighted my charms. I was so pleased with my own cleverness that I was blind to his good points and exaggerated his bad points, never stopping to ask myself if I was being fair or just. I am ashamed when I remember it. And not only was I wrong about my husband, I was wrong about George Wickham. He seemed handsome and charming, and he seemed to be suffering. I believed everything he told me without once seeking confirmation elsewhere, and all the time he was deceiving me. It was a bitter time for me when I discovered my mistake. I was devastated. I truly thought I would never be happy again. But love is so complicated that mistakes are inevitable, and you should not be afraid of making them. They are a necessary part of falling in love."

"Thank you," said Sophie. "It is comforting to know I am not the only person who has been foolish."

"You must not let it worry you," said Elizabeth kindly. She

paused and then said, "Tell me, what do you think of the two young men on board? They are both decent men, I think, and they both seem very taken with you."

"I am flattered, I cannot deny," she said honestly. "But this morning I felt that I was nothing but a bone for them to fight over. Although…"

"Yes?" prompted Elizabeth.

"I do not think that P… Mr Inkworthy regards me in that light."

"Our holiday is only just beginning. We have not yet reached Malta, and from there it is another month to Egypt. You will have plenty of time to get to know them both better by the time we arrive."

Chapter 6

BY THE TIME THE ship docked in Malta, they were all glad to have the opportunity to go ashore. Mrs Bennet, who had inveigled her way onto the ship without an invitation, had been the loudest in her lamentations about the trials of the journey. But a few hours of wandering around the port and buying presents for her children and grandchildren back in England restored her to happiness.

Elizabeth and Darcy took the opportunity of teaching the children something of the history of the island, and John, who had been reading about Napoleon's campaign, enthusiastically told his brothers and sisters that Napoleon's army had stationed a garrison there at the end of the previous century.

"But Nelson set up a blockade and drove the French out, and then Malta became part of our empire," he finished.

"Malta was very useful to us, helping us to protect Egypt," said William, not to be outdone. "One of our ambassadors, I forget which one, called it the Watchtower of Egypt. And then we needed Egypt to protect India, and we needed to keep India safe because of all our trading there."

"What clever children they are!" said Mrs Bennet. "I do believe they are the cleverest children to ever draw breath."

Elizabeth privately agreed, although she did not say so for fear of making them complacent.

As William continued to tell them about the island, she had to resist an urge to ruffle his hair, for although she was proud of his learning, she had a momentary wish that he was still six years old so that she could tell him to run along and play. But play had never been a part of William's character. He even took his sports seriously and pursued them with a gravity that said everything about his consciousness of his position as a Darcy and nothing about a desire to win a game. Indeed, for William it was very true that it was taking part which was important; winning or losing was irrelevant to him. Perhaps it was because he had already won, she reflected, for in the game of life, despite his young age, he had everything anyone could wish for—at least until he started to wish for a wife! And then no matter how large his fortune or how impressive his estate, he would have to prove himself to any woman who was worth winning.

Jane and Laurence ran past, whooping in delight. They were enjoying the freedom of dry land after the confines of the ship.

Margaret told them off as they knocked her when they ran past and then continued pointing out places of interest to her doll.

"How long is it until we reach Egypt?" she asked her mother. "Aahotep was wondering."

"About another month," said Elizabeth, and Margaret dutifully relayed the information to her doll.

Paul took the opportunity to buy some art supplies, and Darcy said to Elizabeth, "It was an excellent choice to bring him with us. The portrait of you standing at the prow of the ship with the wind catching your hair is the most lifelike thing I have ever seen. He has caught you beautifully. I am intending to give it pride of place when we return to Pemberley. And some of his pictures of the children are superb. There is an oil painting of John climbing the rigging which is so full of life it could almost be real. And the little watercolour of Beth is exquisite."

"I agree," said Elizabeth, twirling her parasol as they strolled along. "And let us not forget the portrait of you with Malta in the background. Although it is only half-finished, he has caught your expression exactly. The paintings will serve as a constant reminder of our travels."

"This is very different from a trip to the Lakes," said Darcy.

Elizabeth laughed.

"Indeed. If we were in the Lakes, I would be twirling an umbrella and not a parasol!"

"And speaking of parasols, the sun has faded the silk," said Darcy, studying her parasol critically. "I think I must buy you a new one."

They were passing a variety of interesting shops, and Elizabeth had all the fun of choosing a new parasol, which she decided to use straightaway.

"Oh, what a good idea. I am sure I need a new parasol, too," said Mrs Bennet.

Darcy obliged his mother-in-law.

Edward then took Elizabeth aside and said in low voice, "I would like to buy a parasol for Sophie, but it would be impossible for her to accept such a gift from me. I will gladly reimburse you, Lizzy, if you will buy one for her."

Elizabeth agreed but told him that no reimbursement was necessary, saying, "You are right; such a gift cannot come from a young man, but from another woman there can be no harm in it."

Sophie was delighted with the gift, and her blush and smile made it clear she knew from where the thought had originated.

By the time they left the shop, they had bought so many parasols—for Elizabeth decided Jane would like one, and then Kitty and Mary and Lydia must have one too—that the shopkeeper was left with a beatific smile on his face.

"And now we must return to the ship," said Darcy. "We are dining with the British Consul tonight, and I have some letters to write before we meet him. If you have any letters to write, make sure they are ready by the time we leave for the consulate and he will make sure they are posted for us."

Once back at the ship, the party split up. The boys were claimed by their tutors, who were using the present location as a springboard for lessons in history, geography, science, and mathematics. Darcy went below to write his letters. Elizabeth and Sophie stayed on deck with the girls, taking out their embroidery.

Edward returned to his cabin, intending to work some more on attempting to decipher the hieroglyphic text, but as he approached the door he stopped when he heard noises coming from inside. He had half a mind to return to the deck, so that his servant could finish cleaning and tidying the small space undisturbed, when his desire to work overcame him and he went in. But instead of finding that his cabin was being cleaned, as he expected, he found that one of the sailors was rifling through his trunk. The sailor looked up, startled, and backed away from the trunk while all the time saying, "I wasn't doing nothing, honest." But Edward, with the evidence of his own eyes before him, was incensed and grappled with the man as he tried to make good his escape.

There was a scuffle, but the outcome was never really in any doubt, and Edward ended the wrestling match with a well-placed blow.

He hauled the dazed sailor to his feet and marched him off to the captain's cabin. He knocked on the door and went in. Captain Merriweather looked up in surprise.

"I came back to my cabin unexpectedly and found this dog rifling through my things," said Edward in disgust.

"I never did," said the sailor in a surly voice, though he evidently did not think he would convince anyone.

Captain Merriweather was grave and very apologetic.

"This is a very serious matter," he said, "and I am sorry you have been inconvenienced. Most of the crew are known to me and have sailed with me many times before, but this man is on my ship for the first—and last—time."

He ordered a flogging to take place that evening, and Edward, leaving the sailor in the captain's custody, returned to his cabin. But the incident had unsettled him and he could not work. Instead, he repacked his trunk, thinking how stupid the sailor had been, for there was nothing of value in it. But no doubt the small trinkets it contained would have been sold in the port before they sailed, and the sailor must have relied upon the theft not being discovered until they were under way again, by which time there would have been nothing to connect him to the crime.

News of the incident quickly spread round the ship.

Elizabeth, fetching a shawl from her cabin, was initially sympathetic toward Edward, but when she heard of the proposed flogging she was horrified.

"This cannot be," she said to her husband. "Think of the children."

Darcy, too, was unhappy. He opened his mouth to say that they could not protect the children from the world in which they lived, no matter how much they might wish to do so, and that John would see worse in the army. But realising, just in time, that this would awaken all Elizabeth's maternal fears and protective instincts, he changed his mind.

Instead he said, "Shipboard discipline must be maintained, my love, and the captain has every right to do what he must in order to achieve that end."

Elizabeth, however, was adamant that the man should not be flogged aboard any ship that carried her children as passengers, and finding herself at an impasse with her husband, she went herself to the captain. Captain Merriweather was obviously unhappy at her interference, but Elizabeth carried her point, and it was agreed at last that the man should be spared a flogging but that he should be discharged and set ashore at once. Satisfied that she had acted for the best, Elizabeth retired to her cabin to dress for dinner.

Her maid had just finished fastening the last button on Elizabeth's favourite amber silk gown when the door opened and Darcy entered. Seeing the anger in his eyes, she dismissed her maid, saying, "Thank you, Hester, that will be all."

Her maid bobbed a curtsey and left.

"What a pleasant time we had looking round the port," said Elizabeth, determined not to argue with him, for now that she had gained her point, no further arguments were necessary. "I am sure my sisters will be pleased with their presents. The only disappointment was that I could not find a new doll for Margaret. She carries that ugly little Egyptian doll everywhere, and it is so old and battered that I would rather she had something new."

"I did not come here to talk about a doll," he said. "I have just spoken to Captain Merriweather and discovered that, despite what I said this afternoon, you saw fit to disregard my wishes and insisted on having your own way."

"I am sorry if it upsets you, but I will not have my children subjected to such brutality."

"The children would not have been subjected to it. I had intended to arrange with Merriweather that it would take place when they were ashore tomorrow. But they cannot be shielded from all the unpleasantness in the world, Elizabeth, and you had no right to tell the captain how to run his ship. Aboard this vessel, his word is law."

"I do not notice it being law when you have a request to make," Elizabeth said, growing angry despite herself. "You have often asked him to change things to suit your fancy. I, at least, had a good reason to ask him to change his mind—which he was happy to do, I might add."

"A request is one thing, but you did not *request* that he should reconsider the punishment; you demanded it, and since he did not wish to offend the wife of his employer, he had little choice but to acquiesce. I told you we must not interfere…"

"Am I your servant, then, to always do as I am told?"

"No, you are my wife," he said, his eyes darkening at the interruption, "and when I tell you not to interfere, I expect you to obey me. I believe that is what you agreed to do on our wedding day."

"And you agreed to honour me, but I do not see much honouring at the moment. No, say nothing more," she said, brushing her hair savagely. "On this we must agree to differ."

She turned to the mirror and, in the absence of her maid, began to dress her own hair.

"We have not finished," he said. "Do I have your promise that you will not disobey me in this way again?"

"Where the welfare of my children is concerned, all I can promise you is that I will always do that which I think right."

"Then perhaps tomorrow, madam, you should consider returning to England. Immediately."

He spoke the words in a low growl, and though Elizabeth felt the blood drain from her face, she refused to let her fear show.

"Perhaps I will," she said equally coldly.

"Very well. And you can make arrangements to take your mother with you."

Elizabeth rose from her seat. "I see you wish to be rid of all the Bennet women then, sir," she said with as much dignity as she could muster.

He scowled. "Only those whose behaviour offends me."

And with that he left the cabin, the door banging behind him.

Elizabeth stumbled against the stool, almost unable to believe what had just happened. She and Darcy disagreed often but argued rarely and never to such lengths. It seemed impossible that they had just exchanged such harsh words. It was almost as if some malign force had seized hold of them and driven them on.

She clutched at the table, forcing herself not to collapse on the floor in a flood of tears. For several minutes she stood immobile before moving toward the open porthole and taking in great gulps of bracing salty air.

Gradually, she felt sense return to her thoughts. And as she replayed the scene in her mind she could not discount the uncomfortable feeling that he had, in part, been right—that she should not have gone behind his back. Darcy had never been the kind of man who demanded unquestioning slavish obedience; she would not have married him if he had. And the fact that he had intended to make an alternative arrangement for their children during the punishment showed he agreed with her. If she had shown a little more faith in her husband's judgement, this would not have happened.

She finished dressing, then went up on deck, where she saw her mother gossiping with Sophie—though Mrs Bennet was doing all the talking and Sophie was doing all the listening—and where the children were engaged in their various activities. Beth waved to her but then turned back to Mr Inkworthy. They were bending over a tablet of paper, and it was clear that he was instructing the girl in the finer points of sketching and that Beth did not wish to be disturbed. The boys were with the first mate, who was demonstrating how to use a sextant. No one, it seemed, had heard their argument. Relieved, Elizabeth looked round for Darcy.

It took her some time to find him but at last she saw him, standing at the prow of the ship, his coat slung over the side and his white ruffled shirt billowing in the breeze. His hair stirred, too, and she longed to touch it. She could not bear to be out of sorts with him, and so she walked over to him.

"Darcy…" she began hesitantly. He turned round and looked at her, his eyes no longer dark with anger. "I should not have gone behind your back; you were right to be angry," she said. "I should have talked to you about it again, and we should have come to some agreement."

"Yes, you should," he said, adding with a smile, "but then you would not be Elizabeth. I did not marry a meek woman, and I have no right to complain that you do not behave like one after fifteen years of marriage. And you were right, too. It was a difficult situation and one which needed careful handling, but I am glad you are so protective of the children. They are still young and the girls especially should not be subject to such things, particularly Margaret. She has a very vivid imagination, and I think this journey is already sending it down rather macabre channels. Egypt is a strange and unknown place, and the ancient Egyptians were in many ways a gruesome people. Laurence has been regaling her with stories of murderous crocodiles, and Jane has been telling her of musty tombs and ancient curses. Then, too, she has heard us talking. It is perhaps no wonder that she tells so many grisly stories to her doll."

"She does seem to talk to it rather a lot," said Elizabeth.

"Do you think we ought to take it away from her?" asked Darcy.

"No," said Elizabeth, after a moment's thought. "It would only provoke a storm of tears. Better to let her tire of the thing herself, as she soon will. On board ship she has little to amuse her, but once we reach Cairo there will be more for her to see, and I will make a special effort to find her a suitable replacement. In fact, I believe I will buy her one even if nothing special catches my eye. Then we can quietly remove Aahotep."

"I defer to your counsel, my love," he said and she smiled at him.

"Then you do not wish to be rid of me?"

"I never wish that. I cannot believe I ever said it. Do not, even for one moment, ever think that I do," he said taking her in his arms and kissing her. She returned his embraces, glad that they were hidden from the rest of the ship by the billowing sails.

"I feared that tomorrow I would have to find a ship to return home," she whispered.

"I feared that I would have to continue without you." He nuzzled her ear, before drawing back. "Your mother, however…"

Elizabeth laughed as she shook her head.

"I'm afraid there is no hope, my dear. Mama will not move from my side if there is a chance of new adventures. Come, you must dress or we will be late for dinner with the Consul." Taking his hand she led him back toward the ship's cabins.

"We could offer her a new wardrobe and a trip through Italy. I'm sure the Consul must know of some genteel companion who would be pleased to escort an elderly English lady back home in style and comfort."

"By all means, suggest it," Elizabeth said, wanting to laugh even louder at the hopeful look on his face. "But don't be surprised when she says no!"

From her seat on the aft deck, Sophie watched Darcy and Elizabeth longingly. She had been looking for just that sort of love and companionship all her life but had despaired of ever finding it. And yet, perhaps… She looked at her new parasol, which lay furled on the deck beside her. It was very pretty, but it was more valuable to her because of its origins. She knew that Edward had asked Elizabeth to buy it for her and thought it was typical of his chivalry. She bent down to pick it up, for although it was early evening, the sun was stronger than she had expected and it was hot on the back of her neck. But as she reached down she gave a start and her blood ran cold. Margaret's doll was lying there, and she could have sworn she saw it turn its head to look at Darcy and Elizabeth as they walked past on the way to their cabin. And she could have equally sworn that its eyes were glowing brilliantly with undisguised malevolence.

She drew back in shock.

"Is anything the matter?" came a voice beside her.

Looking up, she saw Edward.

"No, of course not," she said, more to reassure herself than him, thinking, *It could not be. It is impossible.*

"Are you sure? You are shaking," he said, his voice full of concern. "A touch of heatstroke, perhaps?"

"Ah, yes, that must be it," she said, grasping at the idea with gratitude. "I have had too much sun. I have been sitting here without a head covering, and I have been seeing things."

"It is not to be wondered at. You should use your parasol at all times, or at least wear a bonnet. Sunstroke is not to be taken lightly. Would you like me to escort you to your cabin? Perhaps you will feel better after an hour lying down."

"Yes, I think I will," she said, for she was still feeling shaken.

He offered her his arm, and she was about to take it when she remembered Margaret.

"Have no fear. Here is Miss Margaret's grandmama."

He hailed Mrs Bennet, who was looking for somewhere to hide from Laurence in a boisterous game of hide-and-seek.

Mrs Bennet drew the little girl to her, saying, "Quiet, Margaret, we must not let Laurence find us."

Margaret snatched up her doll, and Sophie was relieved to see that it was just a doll, wooden and lifeless, with pieces of coloured glass for its eyes.

Margaret tucked herself behind a suitable barrel with Mrs Bennet, and Sophie, putting her hand to her head, for she did feel rather faint, allowed Edward to escort her to her cabin.

Elizabeth and Darcy returned to the ship tired but in good spirits. Although their evening had started so turbulently, they had resolved their differences, and besides it had been good to get off the ship and new company was always stimulating.

They were greeted by the captain, and as Darcy stayed to talk to him, Elizabeth excused herself, for she was tired, and went below. But as she descended the stairs, she saw the door to their cabin was open. For a moment she had a pang of alarm and wondered if this was another untrustworthy crewmember trying to steal from them, but as she reached the threshold she saw what had happened. The two tiny portholes in the cabin had been left open, and although the sea was relatively calm, it must not have been that way all evening, for there must have been enough of a swell to cause seawater to come through. Elizabeth could not help crying out in despair. Their beds were ruined, as were several books and all their writing equipment. Then she saw her new parasol, which had been standing in the corner. It was soaked through and beyond repair.

"Oh, Lizzy," said Mrs Bennet, hearing her cry and rushing in behind her. "Whatever has happened?"

"Someone inadvertently left the portholes open and water has come in, Mama," Elizabeth replied, trying to sound light-hearted. "It appears that you were right to mistrust my enthusiasm for fresh air."

"Oh dear, and your lovely new parasol is ruined."

Elizabeth's maid appeared with a mop and bucket and soon everyone was busy trying to repair the damage done to the cabin. As they worked, no one noticed Margaret slip away to her own cabin. The little girl crawled onto her bed, her cheeks flushed and her eyes heavy with fatigue.

"You shouldn't have done that, Aahotep," she whispered to the doll that travelled everywhere with her. "Papa bought the parasol as a present for Mama. She will be very sad now."

She held the doll close to her ear as though she expected a reply, but none was forthcoming and eventually her eyes closed tight and she fell asleep.

Leaving Malta behind them, they set sail with the tide. It was a beautiful morning with a sea like glass, and Elizabeth left the portholes of her cabin wide open to finish drying everything and then went up on deck to give her daughters their daily lessons. Although Darcy had insisted on tutors and governesses for the children, who were all well qualified for their roles, Elizabeth still liked to give the girls some lessons herself. She had scrambled her way into an education as a girl, and she now enjoyed helping her little girls scramble their way into one as well, encouraging them to follow their enthusiasms and learn in a less formal fashion than with their governess.

As she joined them on deck, she saw Margaret carefully laying her doll out on the deck in a bright pool of sunshine. As the sun beat down on it, Elizabeth was surprised to see steam waft gently from the wooden toy.

"Goodness me, Meg," she said, picking the doll up. "Poor Aahotep is quite damp. Did you drop her in your wash bowl this morning?"

"No, Mama," said Margaret.

"Well, she has somehow become much the worse for wear," said Elizabeth. "You will have to play with one of your other toys instead."

"No!" said Margaret, taking the figurine from her mother in distress and clutching it tightly. The outburst disturbed Elizabeth although she could not quite say why.

"Very well, but you cannot play with Aahotep until she is dry."

Margaret consulted the doll and then said, "Yes, Aahotep wants to go back in the sun."

"I am very pleased to hear it," said Elizabeth, smiling at her daughter's drollery.

She watched Margaret put the doll back down in its previous sunny spot, viewing it with distaste. It really was an odd thing, and she could not understand why Margaret had such a liking for it. She picked it up. Most of the coloured glass was gone now and it was just a rather dirty wooden figure. But as Elizabeth examined it, she noticed a peculiar odour to it. She put it to her nose and sniffed. It smelled distinctly of seawater. How did the doll smell of seawater?

Uncomfortably, she placed it back down in the sun again. Then she gave her attention to Beth, who was asking her how long it would now take them to reach Egypt, and the queer little doll was forgotten.

Chapter 7

ELIZABETH SAT UP, STARTLED by the eerie wailing which had awakened her. It was a sound she had never heard before. The searing heat was confusing as well, despite the fact that dawn was only just beginning to creep across the horizon. The windows were wide open.

"It's the muezzin," came a sleepy voice beside her.

"The what?"

"The muezzin." Darcy repeated. "Had you forgotten? We arrived in Egypt last night and the wailing is the muezzin calling the faithful to prayer. Potheroe said we would get used to it. He said after a couple of days we wouldn't even notice it anymore."

"Ah! I remember," said Elizabeth.

She lay down in his arms and listened to the muezzin. Now that she was awake, the sound was not so disturbing. In fact there was something quite hypnotic about it.

They had arrived at the port of Alexandria late the night before. Even so late, the harbour had been teeming with people, and as Darcy and Captain Merriweather organised odd carriages called caleches to convey them to their rented house, Elizabeth and Sophie had watched with amazement as copper-skinned people swarmed up to them laden with strange fruits and little cups of tea, chattering in a language none of them could understand. Even Mrs Bennet had been stunned into silence, and Beth, William, and John had stood close to their mother, mouths open in astonishment. The three younger children had slept through it all.

Elizabeth lay quietly for a while, trying to reconcile herself to her exotic surroundings. But to her surprise, she found that now she was wide-awake. Gently she moved away from Darcy and, pulling on a wrapper, she moved across to the window.

The sun was taking more of a hold on the day, and she could see figures move about in the grey light, although they were still dim and shapeless. Up closer to the window, the noises of the day were more apparent. Donkeys began to bray as they were laden down with wares, and from the kitchen below someone laughed.

"You are awake now, my love?"

She turned to see Darcy behind her. He put an arm around her shoulders and they watched Alexandria come to life.

"It seems I am. Is it too early for breakfast?"

"I fear it is. However, since we are both awake..."

"Yes?"

"Perhaps we might use our time in a different way?"

Elizabeth smiled and agreed.

All the household rose early; excitement and the heat drove them from their beds, and although Elizabeth and Darcy were the first to arrive downstairs for breakfast, soon all their children appeared with Sophie and Edward.

"Good morning, Mama, good morning, Papa," Beth greeted them, looking cool and fresh in a white linen gown decorated with damask rose ribbons. She took her place at the table, with William and John following behind her. Laurence and Jane sat together as always, and Margaret slipped into a seat next to Sophie. The look of disappointment on Edward's face was not lost on either Elizabeth or Darcy, as he had to take a seat farther down the table.

"Where is Grandmama?" Elizabeth asked William, who was examining some round, flat bread rolls with interest.

"She bade us come to breakfast without her, Mama. She said the heat was too ferocious, and she could not leave her bed."

Sophie looked up in concern. "Should I go to her, Elizabeth?" she enquired, but Elizabeth merely shook her head.

"No, sit down and eat your breakfast. I will go to her presently."

"Make sure you eat well, children," Darcy continued, determined that his mother-in-law would not monopolise the proceedings. "We have a busy day ahead of us."

But he need not have been so concerned. The table, laden with exotic food, was of far greater interest to his children than their grandmother was. Fortunately, the servant who supplied them with great jugs of juice and hot coffee spoke a little English and some French, and he was in great demand explaining the names of the different fruits. Watermelons, figs, pomegranates, and apricots made up the unfamiliar meal, and the children were delighted.

After breakfast the children were dispatched to spend some time with their tutors, and the older members of the group discussed their plans. When organising the trip Darcy had decided that they should relax for a few days in Alexandria before undertaking the next stage of their journey to Cairo. The sea voyage had been exciting but arduous, and the journey to Cairo would take at least five days; it was important for the household to keep a reasonable equilibrium if they were to get the most from their travels.

"What are your plans this morning, Edward?" Darcy asked, finishing the last of the thick black tea they had been served in tiny cups.

"I thought I would visit the site of the ancient lighthouse to begin with…"

"I thought the lighthouse was no longer there?" said Darcy.

"You are right, but I want to imagine it as it was. And then I want to visit the acropolis and see its monument to Diocletian and the Serapeum and the catacombs—" He paused, seeing the look of amusement in Darcy's eyes. "Forgive me. As you can see I have much to occupy myself with today. I want to see as much as possible before we meet up with Sir Matthew in Cairo. I do not want him to think that I have been wasting my time!"

"Will you postpone at least one of those visits until this afternoon when the children will be with us? You know so much more than the rest of us, and I know they will be delighted."

"Of course," said Edward good-naturedly. "In that case I shall make a visit to the bazaar by the port instead this morning. It is renowned for its variety, and perhaps I can pick up some interesting items to show Sir Matthew."

"I am looking forward to visiting the bazaar myself," said Elizabeth. "Might we join you?"

"I would be enchanted. And perhaps Miss Lucas could be persuaded to accompany us as well."

"It sounds very pleasant, but perhaps we should see if Mr Inkworthy would care to join us also…?" said Sophie.

Elizabeth admired Sophie's efforts to protect her reputation by making it clear that she did not have a favourite, and she was amused by the deflated look in Edward's eye, which quickly disappeared when Darcy said, "Mr Inkworthy left very early this morning before you arrived to breakfast with us. It seems he needs some new watercolours or pastels, and he could not spare a moment without them."

"Then let us all meet in half an hour and set out together."

Once they were alone, Darcy said to Elizabeth, "It seems that Sophie has not made up her mind between the two men. Sometimes I think she favours one, and sometimes another. And sometimes, like today, I think she favours neither."

"She is certainly anxious to make it seem that way, though more in an effort to protect herself than anything else, I think," said Elizabeth.

"Do you know if she has any strong feelings for either of them?"

"At the moment, she enjoys their company in different ways. Their attentions have lifted her out of her melancholy and she likes Edward's enthusiasms and chivalry, while she appreciates Paul's quieter kindnesses. But as to anything serious, no, I do not think so, at least not yet, although I must confess that I do not fully know her thoughts. She confides in me a little, but of her deepest feelings I know nothing. I suspect she does not understand them herself."

Darcy nodded thoughtfully.

"It will perhaps be as well if she enjoys an agreeable flirtation with both of them and then forgets them when the trip is over," Elizabeth continued. "But life is seldom convenient, and I am watching her progress with interest."

By nine o'clock they were all sitting in a caleche and driving slowly through the crowded streets. The white walls of the buildings, designed to keep the heat at bay, were blinding in the sun. Every few minutes they came upon a market square with tiny stalls set up wherever there was a space. People shouted in shrill tones, advertising their wares, and all four travellers were entranced by the flowing white robes and rolled-up headdresses worn by the men. Donkeys brayed on every corner and each time they stopped, small boys appeared as if from nowhere entreating them to buy sticky brown dates and succulent figs.

At last they arrived at the entrance to a bazaar. The circular architecture with its sweeping domes was enough to set Edward off on a lecture about the mingling of French, English, and Arabic cultures. The bazaar was cooler inside thanks to the high ceiling and the thick stone of which it was built. As soon as they alighted from the caleche, Elizabeth and Sophie were drawn to an area given over to jewellery and brightly coloured fabrics.

All four wandered together at first, examining the stalls for their wares, but they separated naturally into two couples and finally they agreed to meet near the entrance in two hours' time. Since Sophie and Edward were to remain in sight there was no danger of impropriety, and they soon wandered off to follow their own interests.

Elizabeth and Darcy spent a happy morning, trying to compete with the market holders in their game of haggling, until at last, exhausted, they made their way back to the entrance. In one corner they found a coffeehouse with seats that looked out onto the scene. It advertised refreshments in French, English, and German as well as Arabic, and they sank down gratefully onto the beautifully embroidered seats.

"Good day to you, *effendi*," said the waiter, immediately spotting them. "How may I serve you? We have tea, coffee, many fruit juices, and many pastries."

"Coffee, please," said Darcy, and the young man bowed and slipped away as quickly as he had come.

"Are you satisfied with your purchases, my love?" Darcy asked with amusement. Elizabeth was surrounded by packages containing fabrics, toys and trinkets for the children, as well as gifts for friends and family at home.

"I am. I know Beth will love this cloth," she said, taking out a length of fabric in purple and red, entranced again by its cool silkiness. "And I have remembered the Egyptian cotton for my sister Jane. As for her namesake, I have bought this. I am sure she will adore it."

"It is very colourful," Darcy agreed, laughing as he saw the sequined headdress Elizabeth had bought for their daughter. It was clinked with metals of different shapes and patterns, and he could only too easily imagine how thrilled she would be.

"Do not laugh," said Elizabeth severely. "She has an eye for the unusual."

"I bow to your superior wisdom, my dear. But I must confess, I prefer the boys' presents."

Elizabeth nodded, equally as pleased with these purchases. She had found a book for William of Arabic myths and legends, which some enterprising writer had decorated with Arabic words and pictures; a set of toy soldiers in Napoleonic uniform, which she knew would soon be seeing battle in John's ever-increasing toy armies; and a small wooden sword for Laurence. As the waiter returned, she searched for the last present.

"*Shukran*," said Darcy, proudly displaying his one word in Arabic and receiving a wide smile from the waiter in return. He placed a glass jug on their table, intricately painted in blue and green and red, and beside it set down two tiny cups of the same design. A bowl of sugar completed the set. Elizabeth lifted the lid of the jug and the rich aroma of coffee revived her almost immediately.

"And I think Margaret will love this," she said, pointing to a soft felt doll in full Arab dress.

"Ah, you found one," said Darcy, turning it over and examining the different textures on the dress and turban. "Let us hope it diverts some of her attention from her other, unpleasant doll. I must say…"

"Yes."

He smiled a little shamefacedly. "I was going to say that there is something disturbing about Aahotep's features. In a dim light I could almost think she were alive and plotting some new atrocities. I am surprised that Meg is so devoted to her—it," he corrected himself.

Elizabeth poured out the steaming brew into the miniature cups and added sugar.

"It is strange you should say that. On board the ship, Sophie was telling me much the same thing. She said she fancied the doll actually turned its head of its own accord… though she was forced to admit that she had been sitting in the sun without a hat or a parasol at the time! But she says she keeps taking it away from Margaret when she is asleep, yet somehow it always seems to end up in her bed again."

"I think that is more likely to be Meg's determination not to be parted from it, rather than supernatural powers on the part of the doll!" said Darcy. "Even so, I am glad you have bought her a new one. I am sure that Meg will abandon the old one, as you predicted, when she sees how much better this one is. Are you hungry? I see the waiter is serving some pastries to that couple over there. Perhaps we should try some."

He signalled to the waiter to return and in no time at all, they had a plate piled high with cakes that were a mixture of European and Arabic cuisines. Neither spoke again about Margaret's odd doll. Instead, while waiting for Sophie and Edward to return they diverted themselves discussing the exotic habits of the Egyptians. Elizabeth was intrigued by the long water pipes prevalent in the cafés around the bazaar. Wherever one looked, one could see old men sucking contentedly as they played against each other at chess. The waiter told them these pipes were known as *sheeshas* and offered Darcy a chance to try it, but he declined, although it occurred to him that when Elizabeth and Sophie were engaged with Mrs Bennet in finding new clothes later on, he and Edward might test the experience.

After eating a delicious honey cake covered in sticky nuts Elizabeth declared her spirits restored. She looked about her, taking an interest in their fellows.

"Do you know, Darcy, it occurs to me that we are not the only English people here, and there are many French and German travellers here, too."

"It is true," said Darcy, looking round the bazaar. Now that they had become more accustomed to the scene, he found he too could pick out European fashions as well as Arabic robes. "Napoleon could not have guessed, when he forced his way here years ago, that he would make this place such a fashionable spot. The people over there, I would say, are French," he added, pointing to a young couple admiring the rugs on a stall.

"And those over there, German," said Elizabeth, joining in the game. "And perhaps those people by the jewellery stand are Italian."

"No, I would say Spanish. What do you think of that group?"

"Most definitely English, my dear."

"Agreed. And over there—oh!"

Darcy stopped and stared at a stall in the distance where two Alexandrians in full white robes were arguing ferociously. Seeing his face, Elizabeth leaned forward.

"What is it, Darcy?"

"The most extraordinary thing," he replied, still searching the bazaar with his eyes. "Just for a moment I could have sworn I saw George Wickham."

Sophie and Edward had stopped at every stall in the huge bazaar, and still it seemed Edward had not yet had his fill of the place.

At last Sophie halted by a coffeehouse tucked in the corner of the market. The smell of coffee and sweet, sticky cakes made her almost faint with hunger. It seemed to have been a long time since breakfast.

"Forgive me," said Edward apologetically, noticing her glance at the café. "I have indulged myself too much at your expense. Come, let us sit down and rest for a while."

Gratefully, Sophie nodded and they sat down by a rather rickety table. The waiter who served them spoke no other language than Arabic, and so Edward found himself forced to try his hand at the few words he knew and a great deal of sign language. Eventually two cups of coffee appeared, along with two glasses of what looked like milk.

"*Laban,*" the waiter kept repeating in response to their expressions of puzzlement before walking away in disgust.

Edward smiled wryly.

"I am not sure exactly what I asked for," he admitted, picking up the glass and examining it warily. "It seems to be milk, but perhaps it would be wise not to take the risk."

Taking his lead, Sophie picked up the other glass.

"If we both took a little sip, it couldn't do us much harm, could it?" she said. "After all, what is the point of travelling if one does not take a chance occasionally?"

Edward looked at her with admiration. "Bravo, Miss Lucas, you are quite right. Shall we?"

He lifted his own glass in a toast and after a slight hesitation, Sophie nodded and they each took a small sip.

"It is milk," Sophie said. "Only very sweet, with a flavour I do not recognise."

"And thicker than milk should be. Do you know? I recall reading somewhere that a French king in the sixteenth century was miraculously cured of some disease after eating a fermented milk drink sent to him by an Arabic doctor. Perhaps this is it. However," he added, as Sophie took another sip, "I would counsel some caution. This is only our first day here; we should be prudent in our experiments."

Sophie agreed and turned instead to the tiny cup of steaming black coffee in front of her. It was rich and thick, copiously sweetened, and very refreshing. "Most invigorating," she said.

"I am glad you are enjoying yourself."

"How could I not?" she said. "It is hard to believe that only a few short months ago I was languishing in Meryton, and all I had to look forward to was decorating the church with Mama for the harvest festival. It was a good notion of yours to come to Egypt."

"I have dreamed of this trip all my life," he said, and all his enthusiasm and natural good spirits were in evidence. "And now I am here, I am determined not to waste one single moment. There is so much to do and see that at times I almost feel overwhelmed by the thought of it all. When I woke this morning and smelled the jasmine in the air and heard the strange chatter in the streets below, I could scarcely believe that I was at last here. And this adventure has barely started for me. When we arrive in Cairo, there will be much to see and do. You will be entranced, S... Miss Lucas. There are the pyramids, and then there is the sphinx, which is a wonder to behold—or so I am told. And after that the beauty of the Nile and then down into the Valley of the Kings with all its splendour—" He stopped, suddenly aware that he was monopolising the conversation. "Forgive me, Miss Lucas,

I am afraid that when I start talking about Egypt I find it hard to stop, but I know not everyone finds it as fascinating as I do. How are you feeling now? If you are rested, we should perhaps continue with our shopping."

He was making a special effort to drag himself away from the topic which intrigued him, and Sophie smiled.

"I have spent so much of my life listening to my brothers talk of nothing but hunting and shooting and my father talking of his presentation at St James's that it is a pleasure to hear a man talk of something more interesting for a change. And you speak this strange language, too, which is something most of us have not even considered."

"Only a few words," Edward said, but Sophie shook her head.

"Nevertheless, we would not have managed without you today. Perhaps when we return to the hotel you might teach me some phrases."

"It would be my pleasure, Miss Lucas," he said warmly, looking at her with new respect. For a moment neither of them spoke—then Edward stood up. Leaving what he hoped was enough money on the table, he leaned forward to take Sophie's hand. "We really should be joining Elizabeth and Darcy now."

They began to gather up their purchases as the waiter came over to them. When he saw the small fortune that had been left, he was almost in paroxysms of delight.

"There, Mr Fitzwilliam," said Sophie, her eyes twinkling with amusement as the waiter showered them with "Allahs." "You have made a new friend at this coffeehouse today."

He looked at her warmly and said, "I hope I have made two."

She smiled in answer. He offered her his arm, and as they set off toward Elizabeth and Darcy she felt lucky she had discovered that there was more to life than deciding on which hymn to practise for the Sunday service and that feckless young men did not have the right to destroy her life. There were other young men in the world, interesting and courteous and chivalrous young men, who, perhaps in time, might be trusted. And then, who knew what might happen?

Paul Inkworthy looked at the camel driver in front of him. He tried to keep his mind on his subject as he sketched the man's long, flowing robe and characterful face, instead of letting his thoughts wander to the far more interesting subject of Miss Sophie Lucas.

Sophie had come to occupy his mind far more than was wise over the past few weeks. It had been impossible to escape her on the sea voyage, despite his noble intentions to stay away from her, as he knew full well that a poverty-stricken artist had nothing to offer a woman whose father was a knight. But now that they had arrived in Alexandria he knew that he must gradually withdraw his attentions, which had been more marked than they should have been, given that he was not in a position to support a wife. And so he had set out early that morning in order to remove himself from temptation.

Reminding himself that he was on the trip as the Darcys' artist, he forced himself to pay attention to his work. He had promised Mr Darcy a faithful representation of all the varied scenes of Alexandria: the boats coming and going along the river, the little boys driving donkeys, the camels with water jugs on their backs, the men with their copper faces and their long robes, the women with their black hair and eyes—all the noise and confusion of a busy Egyptian port.

He finished the sketch of the camel driver and then flicked back through his sketchbook, marvelling at the opportunities that had come his way since setting out from England.

The earliest sketches were of the Darcys in their London home: Darcy standing in front of the fireplace; Elizabeth walking in the garden, with the wind whipping her skirt about her ankles; the children at work and play. But these soon gave way to a collection of drawings and paintings of the sea voyage, which had provided him with a chance to produce character sketches of the sailors as well. It had also given him an unprecedented opportunity to perfect his rendering of tall sailing ships as well as to capture an endless array of seascapes, from calm to storm. In addition, the ports they had visited had given him a chance to sketch places as varied as Southampton and Malta.

And now he was in Alexandria, where the light effects alone would provide him with a year's study as he sought to capture the way the air shimmered in the heat and the way the water dazzled under the full glare of the sun.

He picked up a half-finished painting and put it on his easel, returning to the scene he had abandoned half an hour earlier and, newly inspired, captured the heat haze that had defeated him before.

He stood back to look at his painting when he was done, squinting against the bright Egyptian sun.

"Exceptional," came a voice at his shoulder. "I have seen many artists at work here, and they have all captured the scene in front of them to great effect. But you have caught the wind in the sails, the movement of the water, the bray of the camels, and the scent of the spices. I have long been searching for an artist to record my travels and I have been on the point of making arrangements with three of them, but something always held me back. I was looking for something more, though I didn't know what that something was. But now I know. Whereas other artists will bring Egypt into my living room, you, dear sir, will transport my living room to Egypt."

Paul turned to see an English gentleman who was well dressed and whose attire made no concessions to the heat. He was wearing a tight tailcoat and breeches together with a frilled shirt and a starched cravat. On his head was a tall hat, and he carried a cane.

"Allow me to introduce myself," said the gentleman. "Here, my card."

He handed it to Paul, and Paul felt the quality of it even as he read the name, *Sir Mark Bellingham, Bart.*

"Of the Shropshire Bellinghams," said Sir Mark.

"I don't know the Shropshire Bellinghams," said Paul awkwardly, feeling his lack of status.

"My dear sir, I would be surprised if you did," said Sir Mark, amused. "But you will, I hope, become further acquainted with this one. I am looking for an artist to travel with me through Egypt, making a record of my journey and providing me with a number of finished paintings to hang on my wall when I return to England. You have just the talent... no," he said, looking again at the paintings clustered haphazardly round Paul's feet, "the genius I am looking for."

Paul was flattered by the praise and the offer of employment, but he said, "I am already engaged."

"Whatever your patron is paying, I will double it," said Sir Mark, unconcerned.

"I think you would regret the offer if you knew the cost," said Paul with a sudden smile. "Besides, I cannot abandon my current patron in the middle of his journey."

"I admire your loyalty, if regretting its consequences. But can we not share you? If you will accept a commission for three paintings of Alexandria from me—"

Paul shook his head.

"We will only be in Alexandria for a few days. After that, we travel to Cairo."

"That is no difficulty," said Sir Mark, waving away the problem. "I will be going to Cairo myself next week."

"But we will not be long there, either," said Paul. "We will be travelling down the Nile shortly afterward."

"I, too, will be sailing down the Nile," said Sir Mark. "Whereabouts will you be staying?"

"We will be joining Sir Matthew Rosen's dig."

"Ah," said Sir Mark. For the first time he acknowledged the problem.

"I believe Mr Darcy had a certain amount of difficulty in persuading Sir Matthew to accept his presence," said Paul. "I am not sure Sir Matthew would welcome another…"

"Dilettante?" suggested Sir Mark. "Well, perhaps not. But you will not be working for Mr Darcy forever. Perhaps you will be good enough to keep me informed of your progress, and when your present patron announces his intention of returning to England, you will find another patron waiting for you."

"That is very good of you," said Paul. The thought of

continuing employment was very welcome. "But I believe I must return to England with the Darcys."

"Must you?" asked Sir Mark. "But why?" His eye, which had been travelling over Paul's collection of sketches and paintings, came to rest on a portrait of Elizabeth. "Ah!" he said. "It seems there is a lady in the case. Your patron has a daughter, and a very lovely one. I understand now your reluctance to leave him."

"That is not his daughter; it is his wife," said Paul.

"Indeed," said Sir Mark with a quick glance at Paul. "A beautiful woman."

"Yes, she is," said Paul.

Sir Mark looked at him appraisingly for a moment then looked again at his paintings, letting his gaze wander over them until they came to rest on a sketch of Sophie.

"And who is this?" he asked.

"That is Miss Lucas, a friend of the Darcys," said Paul, blushing as he said it.

Sir Mark smiled.

"I see. A family friend. A young lady who is well-connected and therefore above a poverty-stricken artist with his way to make in the world. But not above an artist with a wealthy patron and a handsome income, I think. Keep me informed of your whereabouts, young man. True artists are hard to find, and I believe you could make my reputation as a serious patron of the arts. In return, I could make your fortune."

With that, he tipped his hat and walked away.

Paul watched him go and then turned the card over in his hand again. Sir Mark Bellingham. A wealthy baronet with a love of art.

Visions of a rosy future opened up in front of Paul. He saw himself paying court to Sophie, winning her hand, and then settling in some splendid home, thanks to Sir Mark. There would be London exhibitions, fame, fortune, success…

A camel bumped into his easel and the painting fell, still wet, toward the sand. Leaping into action, Paul managed to catch it before it hit the ground, while the camel driver shouted at him in rich, colourful language and the passing throng laughed, brought together by the comical scene, before moving on.

Paul began to pack up his belongings, laughing at himself wryly for his daydreams. It was too hot now to paint and he wanted to return to his room, where in the relative cool he could ponder the morning's events.

The man who had introduced himself as Sir Mark Bellingham returned to his lodgings with no less to ponder. He had learned a lot about the movements of the Darcys and had confirmed what he already knew, as well as giving himself the advantage of an informant in Darcy's camp, for he did not doubt that the artist would apprise him of his movements, particularly if there should be any change to the Darcys' plan.

He went into the walled house, with its refuse-strewn courtyard, and up the crumbling flight of steps to the large room beyond. His wife was there, surrounded by a host of colourful items: shawls and scarves and earthenware pots. She looked up as he entered the room.

"La, George, where have you been?" she asked. "I have been wanting to go out this last half hour, but it is not safe for a woman to go out unaccompanied here. I set my foot out of the door and nearly had it shot off by a soldier of some kind. The men here are not what they are at home."

"And so I told you before we arrived," he said.

"I wish you would tell me what we are doing here. You told me it would be an adventure, but all it has been so far is seasickness and dysentery," Lydia said discontentedly.

"You did nothing but flirt with the sailors on the various ships that brought us here, and as for dysentery, you have the strongest stomach I have ever come across in a woman," said her husband without sympathy.

"La, George, ever since Mama told us that Lizzy was going to Egypt you have been acting very strange. I am sure I had no objection to leaving England, seeing as how our creditors were pressing us close, but I wish you would tell me what we are doing here. And what are these cards for?" she asked, picking up one of the calling cards he had lately given to Paul Inkworthy. "Who is Sir Mark Bellingham?"

"For the moment, I am," said George.

"Oh, another scheme," said Lydia. "You are always hatching some plan or other."

"This one will make our fortune," said Wickham.

"How will coming to Egypt make our fortune?" said Lydia. "And why did we have to come by ourselves instead of travelling with Lizzy and Darcy? We could have travelled in comfort, instead of taking passage on a variety of cheap old tubs, setting off before Lizzy and arriving after her."

"Because no one must know we are here, least of all Darcy." He had no particular wish to take her into his confidence, but she gave him no peace until at last he rapped out, "If he knows we are here, he will know we are after the treasure."

"Treasure?" said Lydia, stopping in midsentence. "What treasure? There is something you are not telling me, George. Very well, if you will not tell me, I will ask Mr Darcy. I am sure it will not be hard to find out where he is staying."

Wickham scowled, but seeing that she would not be satis-fied unless he told her everything, he said, "You know that my father was a friend of Darcy's father? And a friend of Edward Fitzwilliam's father, too, for that matter."

"I know he was old Mr Darcy's steward," said Lydia unhelpfully.

"He should have never been a steward," said Wickham, a flash of anger breaking through his crocodile charm. "He should have been a wealthy man and in a position to employ a steward himself, not become one. He saved old Mr Darcy's life, and for that, old Mr Darcy rewarded him by making him his servant! My father was not born to be a servant. He was the son of a gentleman. He should have been a wealthy landowner. Then he would have left his estate to me. And he would have been, had old Mr Darcy valued the service my father did for him, saving his miserable existence."

"I never heard he saved old Mr Darcy's life," said Lydia, her interest aroused.

"It was in Egypt, many years ago," said Wickham. "When my father was a young man, before he met George Darcy, he was left a small inheritance and he used it to finance a Grand Tour. He visited France and Italy then he travelled on to Malta, where he met Charles Fitzwilliam and George Darcy. The three of them became friends and travelled on to Egypt together. They sailed down the Nile, stopping every now and then to explore half-visible temples which rose out of the mountains of sand. When they were returning from one such expedition, they found a man in the middle of the desert. He was lying in the full sun, collapsed, more dead than alive. He begged them to take him back to Luxor and promised them a reward if they did so.

"The reward meant nothing to them, but they did as he asked. However, by the time they arrived at Luxor he was so weak that he died. They paid for his funeral and afterward were surprised to find that he had left his few worldly possessions to them in his will, namely three pieces of a map and a curious Egyptian doll. He left a piece of the map to each of them, with the assurance that it pointed the way to an unplundered tomb. It showed various landmarks and had an inscription in hieroglyphic writing. They did not believe him, as the tombs thereabouts had been plundered many times, but nevertheless they were curious and they set out to find it.

"But they never did, and their search came to an abrupt end when they had a terrifying experience, becoming trapped in a cave by a landslide. My father was on the outside at the time and he dug them out with his bare hands, working until they were bleeding and raw. And what happened once he had rescued them? They returned to Luxor and thence to England to resume their lives.

"Charles Fitzwilliam returned to his estate in Cumbria, George Darcy returned to Pemberley in Derbyshire, but my father had nowhere to go. He had spent his small inheritance on his Grand Tour and did not know what to do. Instead of rewarding him handsomely for saving his life, George Darcy offered my father a job as his steward."

"But what does that have to do with any treasure?" asked Lydia.

"I think that Charles Fitzwilliam's son Edward has discovered the map and knows where to find the tomb," said George. "Once your mother told us he was going to Egypt, I made some enquiries and discovered that ever since last winter, he has been in constant contact with various men who are engaged in trying to decipher the Egyptian hieroglyphs found on the Rosetta Stone. And when I found that he was intending to travel to Egypt, I was sure. There are men here who are experts and whose help will be invaluable to him, and when he finds out where the tomb is hidden, he will be in the right place to look for it. The fact that Darcy is with him confirms it. They are trying to find the treasure, and they are doing it without me. They have two parts of the map and they must feel that, with the new clues revealed by the hieroglyphs, they do not need the third."

"But you have the third part?" said Lydia.

"Alas, no, I do not have it. It was destroyed, which is a pity, as it was the section of the map which marked the exact spot. But no matter. I have something better than the map. I have a plan."

"And when we have found the tomb, will all the treasure make us rich?"

"Very rich," said George.

"Rich enough to buy a home of our own?"

Wickham smiled, and restored to good humour, he picked his wife up and kissed her. "Rich enough to buy us a palace."

Chapter 8

THE DARCY PARTY SET out for Cairo a few days later. The intervening time had been spent seeing the Alexandrian sights, with Edward conducting them around a series of marvels, helped by a hired interpreter.

The morning of their departure dawned hot and clear. There was much excitement as they boarded the low, flat boats. The triangular sails billowed out in the breeze and the boats pulled out into the river. The water was a clear turquoise and the fertile banks were green with bushes, while farther off the greenery gave way to the golden sands of the desert.

Beth found a shady spot and took out her sketchbook, producing a creditable drawing of the river. Paul went over to look and suggested some ways in which she could improve upon it and Beth thanked him with a faint blush.

Elizabeth, watching from the other side of the boat, realised with a start that this was not just hero worship.

Darcy, coming over to her, said, "What is it?"

"Beth," said Elizabeth. "I think she has developed a *tendre* for Mr Inkworthy."

"Nonsense," said Darcy. "She is just a child, far too young to be developing a *tendre* for anyone."

"She is nearly fourteen," said Elizabeth. "When I was her age, I became infatuated with the Meryton curate. Other girls become infatuated with their dancing masters. It is not uncommon."

"She cannot marry an artist," said Darcy.

"My dear, she has no intention of marrying him, only of worshipping from afar and hoping he will notice her, as he does occasionally. Fortunately he is a kind young man and he will not play on her feelings, despite the fact that she is an heiress."

"No," said Darcy, "I believe he is the sort of man who would never be tempted by money, for if he was, her age would not protect her for long. Georgiana was only fifteen when Wickham attempted to run away with her."

"But Wickham is a very different man than Paul Inkworthy. I think we are fortunate that Beth has picked him for her first infatuation. She will come to no harm with him."

"You are right, my love," said Darcy, putting his arm round her waist.

She detected something wistful about the gesture and asked him if anything was wrong.

"No, not really," he said. "Only... we are losing them, aren't we?"

Elizabeth leaned her head on his shoulder.

"Ever so slowly, yes," she said. "It has to happen, you know. You told me so yourself."

"Yes, I did, did I not? Only this feels different. To lose the boys to school is one thing, but to lose Beth herself is another. She is changing before our eyes. What will we do when she grows up? When they all grow up?"

Elizabeth gave a sigh.

"I do not know. But we have not lost them yet," she said, rallying.

"No," said Darcy, rallying too. "And when we do, there will be compensations. We will have more time to spend by ourselves. And speaking of more time to ourselves, when we land I will be taking you on the first stage of your surprise. You have not forgotten I promised it to you?"

She was immediately curious but he would say no more. She teased him about it until they finally landed and continued to tease him as they left the boats behind and covered the short distance to Cairo, passing cultivated fields in which oxen worked, but he was infuriatingly silent on the subject.

Once they had settled into their new lodgings on the outskirts of Cairo, however, he said to her, "When would you like your surprise? Today? Or, if you are too tired, we can wait until tomorrow."

She assured him that she was not at all tired and he said, "Then we will set out after dinner."

"After dinner? Set out? But if we are going somewhere, will it not be better to wait until the morning?"

"This particular surprise will not allow it," he said.

She tried to contain her impatience throughout dinner but when it was over and they had informed the others of their proposed absence, she could contain it no longer.

"Dress warmly," Darcy said. "We are going to spend the night at the base of one of the pyramids."

"It seems a very strange thing to do. If you want to show me the pyramids, I will see them better in daylight."

"There is a reason for it," he said.

He would say no more, and so, having dressed herself warmly, for the nights were cool, she told him she was ready.

Darcy, too, was dressed for the Egyptian night. He wore a caped greatcoat over his coat and breeches, and on his feet he wore boots.

They left the house by the light of the moon and outside they were joined by their guards, who followed them at a discreet distance as they walked through the deserted streets. Elizabeth took Darcy's arm and relished the silence. Gone was all the raucous noise of daytime: the souk sellers crying their wares, the sound of copper pans being beaten, the braying of donkeys, the snorting of camels, and the incessant babble of voices, rising and falling like a tide rising and falling against the shore. Instead, there was a peaceful silence, broken only by the chirrup of insects.

They went on foot and Elizabeth felt her body relax. This was the exercise she preferred, away from the jolting of a donkey or camel and without the rise and fall of a boat. Instead, there was only the feel of the cool air against her cheek and the comforting feel of solid earth beneath her feet. She relished the exercise and squeezed Darcy's arm, enjoying the wonder of it all. The light was intriguing, with dark shadows falling across their path as they walked past the houses that blocked the light, becoming brighter as they emerged into full moonlight. Here and there a minaret glinted as they wound their way through the narrow streets, and the stars glittered in the black sky.

They walked at first through the outskirts of the city, but

soon they left it behind and found themselves on the edge of the vast desert. The dunes were eerily lovely, their great ridges sculpting the landscape with different shades of brown and black as they caught the diaphanous starlight or dropped down into blackest shadow where no light could reach.

And on the horizon loomed the pyramids, beautiful and mysterious in the moonlight.

Darcy placed his hand over Elizabeth's arm and she looked up at him, wondering how she had been so lucky as to find herself here in this magical place with the man who had made her whole life magical. True, he could be infuriating at times and their life together had not been without its arguments, but she knew she could never have married anyone else. He had brightened every day with his presence and he still, after all these years, managed to excite and surprise her, as he was doing now by taking her on a midnight walk across the desert.

As they emerged from the fronded shadow of a palm tree and set foot on the desert, she felt the sand shift beneath her feet and shivered with pleasure. This was what she had wanted. An adventure! A wonderful chance to experience life anew and to feel again all the excitement of new places and the unforeseeable delights they might bring.

"I thought of having camels ready, but I know how you love to walk and it is not too far. Although it will not be easy walking, I have seen you walk much farther and on much worse ground at home."

"You know me well!" said Elizabeth.

"I should, by now," he said with a smile, dimly visible in the soft light.

"And that is why you wanted us to set out so late, I suppose, so that we could walk in the cool of the evening."

Darcy did not reply.

Elizabeth's eyes, accustomed now to the moon and starlight, took in the full splendour of the pyramids. They loomed ever larger as she and Darcy walked toward them, moving as briskly as the soft sand and stones beneath their feet would allow.

"To think, the great pyramid has been here for four thousand years," said Elizabeth, adding, "You see, I have been listening to William. He has been reading all about it. I think he almost knows as much about Egypt now as Edward does!"

"I am not surprised. He spends his life with his books. But I intend to make sure he spends more time away from them now that we are on dry land."

"It will do him good," said Elizabeth.

They talked quietly as they walked onward until at last Elizabeth saw a small camp ahead of them. Several black wool tents were set up at the base of the great pyramid and in front of them was a campfire. The smell of roast mutton filled the air as it turned on a spit over the fire.

"I sent some men on ahead," said Darcy by way of explanation.

Elizabeth was glad of it. She had enjoyed the walk but she was tired and the appetising smell revived her, as did the warmth of the fire. She sat down gladly beside it. The footmen who had set up the camp withdrew to a second set of tents some way off, and the guards withdrew to a discreet distance.

Darcy sat down beside her and they warmed their hands at the fire, until at last Elizabeth felt able to remove her cloak and Darcy his coat. He began to carve slices of the roasted mutton and he handed it to Elizabeth, together with the rice and other foodstuffs that had been brought from Cairo, on a china plate.

"I never knew you had a desire to sleep in a tent and eat from a campfire," Elizabeth teased him. "Although it is rather an elegant form of making camp," she added, as she took the china plate.

"Ordinarily, nothing could be further from my thoughts, but we are here for a reason, as you will see, and I could not let you starve in the desert, now could I?"

She began to eat, the hot food refreshing her. After they had eaten their fill of the mutton, Darcy set it to one side and then took some small cakes out of a box. Elizabeth savoured the sweet, honey-laden taste of them, and when they were done they sat companionably by the fire, which had died down and looked like a glowworm in the dark.

"This is perfect," said Elizabeth, with a final glance at the stars when at last they retired to their tent.

Darcy took her hand. "The best is yet to come."

Elizabeth was awakened early the following morning before it was light by Darcy kissing her cheek and shaking her gently, saying, "Wake up."

She opened her eyes and then closed them again.

"It is still dark!" she murmured, turning over and starting to go back to sleep.

"It is time to get up all the same. I want to show you something. It is time for your surprise."

She roused herself with difficulty and said, "You mean it was not sleeping out here under the stars?"

"No, it is something different, but I cannot show it to you until you get up."

She rubbed her eyes and reluctantly sat up, pushing her hair out of her face and yawning. It was very early and she was still tired. To her surprise, she saw that Darcy was not only up, he was already dressed. He disappeared through the tent's opening and returned a few moments later with a cup of hot coffee, which he handed to her, together with some small cakes and dates.

"Here," he said. "You will feel better when you have had something to eat and drink."

"Am I allowed to know what the surprise is?" she asked, as she took a sip of the hot coffee.

"No. Not yet," he said. "But I will tell you why you are having it today, or at least, I will remind you. Do you know what day it is today? Or, I should say, date?"

"The twelfth. Oh!" she said with a broad smile. "The twelfth of October."

"Yes, the twelfth of October. The day we met. Sixteen years ago, we were at the Meryton assembly in Hertfordshire, and little did we know it but our lives were about to change. I was feeling irritable because Bingley had dragged me there against my wishes, and I was not in a mood to enjoy a country entertainment..."

"...or to give consequence to a young woman who had been slighted by other men!" said Elizabeth.

"No, I was not," he said with a rueful smile.

"And I was not feeling very cordial toward you for disdaining my charms. No woman likes to think she is not handsome enough to tempt a man to dance, though I managed to laugh about it with my friends."

"What a fool I was," he said, kissing her. "To think I almost missed the best part of my life because of my pride, my arrogance, and my conceit. But fortunately, I realised what a fool I had been before it was too late and claimed you as my own. And now I want to give you something to celebrate our first meeting. I have given it a great deal of thought, because I wanted it to be something different, not the usual gifts of jewels—"

"Although the Pemberley jewels are magnificent," said Elizabeth appreciatively.

"—but something unique. I was hoping we would arrive here in time for this day and knew that we would if all our plans went well. And now that we have, we can celebrate in a special way."

Elizabeth put down her cup, closed her eyes, and held out her hand for the gift.

"Oh, no," he said with a laugh. "It is not so easy this time, no small box I can hand to you, nor even a horse waiting outside for you when you draw back the curtains."

She smiled, remembered one of his larger gifts, and opened her eyes again.

"This time, you cannot just receive it, you have to work to get it."

She was intrigued but could not resist teasing him. "Ah, I see how it is. I knew you would tire of me in the end. Now I am to work for my presents; how long before you send me out to work for my pin money? Perhaps Lady Catherine would let me scrub the floors at Rosings!"

He kissed her on the tip of her nose and said, "Get up."

She pushed the covers back and climbed out of the make-shift bed. There was already water in the bowl standing beside it, a luxury in the desert, and one which she knew must have taken some trouble to arrange. She washed gratefully in the cool water and then dressed, throwing a cloak around her shoulders and settling a bonnet on her head before venturing out of the tent.

The guards' silhouettes could be seen not far away, but everything was peaceful, with no threat of disturbance.

"Where are we going?" she said. She looked into the distance. "Is it far?"

"Not in terms of length, but in terms of height," he said. "We are going up."

"Up?"

She craned her neck and looked up at the towering pyramid, at whose base they had made camp, and then back at him.

"Yes. We are going to climb the pyramid."

"We are?" she asked, a shade doubtfully.

"We are," he said firmly. "Unless it is too much for you?"

Elizabeth could not resist the challenge and took his arm as together they walked to the base of the pyramid. The sides were made of great blocks of stone, arranged in a steplike pattern leading to the top, but once again she looked at it somewhat doubtfully, for each block was almost as high as her waist. Nevertheless, she was beginning to catch Darcy's enthusiasm, and mingled in with it was an enthusiasm of her own. What a chance to do something different! And what a view they would have from the top. And then she realised… "Oh!" she said ecstatically. "We are going to watch the sun rise."

She felt a surge of pure joy at the thought. Her tiredness was forgotten as she took his hand and together they began to climb the pyramid.

"Now I know how the children felt when they were toddlers and they tried to climb the staircase at Pemberley!" she joked as she put her hands on the next step and managed to scramble her way up by dint of jumping and pulling herself up with her arms at the same time.

Darcy reached down his hand and helped her up the next stepped level.

"How did the ancient workmen manage to build such a thing?" she asked.

"It took a lot of labour and a lot of rollers. I have been talking to Sir Matthew," he said, "and he has made a study of it. Luckily we do not have to build it, only to climb it!"

"And that is difficult enough," said Elizabeth.

But she was not complaining. She found the exercise exhilarating, and the knowledge that she was climbing farther and farther to the top spurred her on.

They stopped to look about them and enjoy the beauty of the scene as the darkness gradually lessened and became less impenetrable. The desert lost its amorphous look and began to reveal its contours, and the outlines of the buildings in Cairo were dimly visible in the waning moonlight, their minarets showing as black silhouettes against the sky.

Having caught their breath, they set off again for the summit. The air began to grow warmer and Elizabeth climbed with renewed vigor when she saw that the top was within reach. With a burst of effort, she climbed the last few blocks and stood upright at the apex. She felt a huge sense of achievement and was flooded with a sense of wonder as she realised that dawn was on its way.

She spun slowly, drinking in the wonderful view. She could see for miles, and she came to rest again facing the east. There was a mist over the plains, but it could not obscure the spectacular sight as the sun began to rise. Bands of orange light suffused the sky, warming the diaphanous clouds, and at their centre was the very top of the sun's molten disk as it began to rise above the horizon. It seemed to grow as she watched it, and the light intensified as it spread its rays ever wider, illuminating the desert and driving the chill from the air. She turned again, slowly, as the mist began to clear, unveiling a majestic view. To the south she could see a collection of smaller pyramids, their sand-coloured sides warming to tawny in the orange light, and to the west was the endless desert, its billowing dunes turning golden before her eyes. She turned slowly again to the north and looked out across fertile lands, with the Nile descending toward the sea. And turning again to the east she saw Cairo sparkling in the strengthening sunlight, the gold light of morning gleaming on its numerous minarets. Beyond Cairo lay the plains, lushly populated with groves of palm trees, and far off in the distance were the mountains.

"Well?" he asked softly. "Was it worth it?"

"Oh, yes," she nodded, glancing at him before looking back at the wondrous view. "A thousand times yes. We will remember this for the rest of our lives."

He put his arms around her waist and she turned to face him, and they kissed in the early morning sunlight as if it was the first time.

In Cairo, the rest of the party was having a more conventional start to the day. With the children soon whisked away by their tutors and Mrs Bennet declaring that she had had enough of the sun and that she intended to write some letters, Sophie suddenly found herself with nothing to occupy her. This was such an unusual state of affairs that she could not, to begin with, think what to do about it. At home she was constantly in demand either by her parents, her married brothers and sisters, or the vicar and his wife, since everyone thought that an unmarried woman could have no plans of her own and would be glad of any occupation.

Elizabeth and Darcy were far more courteous to her, but she had found that there was always something for her to do and, eager to repay their hospitality, she had done it. And so she had not realised until now that she had barely had a moment to herself. She was either helping Elizabeth share the burden of Mrs Bennet or she was amusing Margaret and trying to distract her from her rather horrid doll or she was performing a hundred other little tasks that needed doing. The prospect of a free morning was unsettling for a moment—then it was liberating.

Unlike Mrs Bennet, Sophie did not feel the need to go and hide from the sun. Indeed, Cairo in October was little hotter than a high summer's day in England, and their journey had taken them through lands with much fiercer heat than that which they were now experiencing. She decided to take a leisurely stroll around the grounds of the house and perhaps rest in the shade of a palm tree with a book. So, armed with the latest edition of poems by Lord Byron, she set out for a quiet place to read.

The house was situated near the river, and as Sophie walked down the sloping hill that looked out onto the Nile, she was delighted to see the white sails of the feluccas, the Egyptian Nile boats, floating gracefully up and down the water. For a moment she stood and admired their beauty against the deep blue of the sky; then she realised she was not alone. Someone else was standing in the shade of the trees, an easel in front of him. With a start Sophie saw it was Mr Inkworthy.

She was aware of conflicting emotions where the young men were concerned. Despite her best efforts not to encourage either one of them, she took pleasure in their company and it was obvious they took pleasure in hers.

During the long sea voyage she had perforce seen much of both of them and found much to like in each. She liked Edward's bright spirits and lively nature, but she also liked Paul's quieter, more serious character and she had found his grave, courteous attention pleasant. She liked the way he encouraged the children to paint and had found something good to say about each attempt, even those from Laurence and Jane, whose restless spirits had found it the hardest to practise the patience and stillness that all artists require. She enjoyed his company and she thought he enjoyed hers too, but ever since they had landed in Alexandria he seemed to be avoiding her. Six months ago such behaviour would have driven her back into her shell again, but she was not the same girl who had boarded the ship at Southampton and she was glad of an opportunity to speak to him, for she liked his company.

"Mr Inkworthy!" she called. "Is it not a beautiful day?"

"Yes… indeed, yes."

"May I see what you are painting?"

"Oh... I... of course."

He moved back slightly from the easel. Since it was hot and he had assumed he would not be disturbed, he had thrown off his frock coat and stood now in a thin lawn chemise with the sleeves turned back. His arms were tanned and he looked a romantic figure, with his golden arms and neck, and his hair stirring slightly in the breeze. He reminded her of Lord Byron, whose person no less than his poetry drove the women in London wild. But whereas she had seen Lord Byron and not been impressed, she could not help her feelings stir at such a sight.

She realised that she was staring and, with a blush, turned her attention to the painting he was working on. It was a scene of the family near the river. Mr Darcy and Elizabeth were in the centre, the children playing around them. William was reading a book, while John, Laurence, and Jane were running after a surprised monkey which had just leapt into a tree for shelter. Their mischievous expressions were so lifelike that Sophie could not help but smile. Beth was next to her mother showing her some embroidery and looking very grown-up. Slightly to the edge of the painting was Margaret, with her doll, and an attractive, elegant-looking woman in a pale blue gown was seated beside her, listening intently to something the little girl was saying. The dress looked familiar to Sophie and she frowned trying to remember where she had seen it before. Then, suddenly, in a flash, she realised it was one of hers and that she, in fact, was the woman in the picture. She flushed.

"It is a striking painting," she said.

"Striking? Perhaps, but I fancy I haven't quite managed to

replicate the vivid colours of the flowers or the way the sunlight plays on the water. I thought if I came out here I would be able to capture it more realistically."

"I am disturbing you. I should leave."

"No. Please don't," he said impulsively.

She felt she should go back to the house, but she was unable to tear herself away.

"You have caught the children's characters extremely well," she said, feeling it was safer to speak of painting than anything else. "Beth is very well done; she looks charming, but I fear you've romanticised Margaret's doll."

He laughed, sounding more comfortable. "It is rather ugly, is it not? I did not wish to scare my employers too much, and so I have softened its malevolent features."

"I confess I like it better that way. And you've been far too flattering to me. I scarcely recognise myself."

He looked at her more gravely. "I am afraid I cannot agree with you there. I have painted what I see."

Sophie suddenly felt uncomfortable and yet happy at the same time. She realised at last that he had not been avoiding her because he found her company dull; indeed, his motivation was the exact opposite. To cover her confusion, she looked more closely at the painting.

"How cleverly you have drawn together the whole family in such an exotic setting. And the expression in the eyes is very realistic. Whenever I try to draw, my subjects look lifeless and doll-like."

"It is a skill that can be taught."

"I am sure it cannot. One has to have talent."

"Of course. But even talent has to be nurtured or it will wither and die. I taught you how to draw the wind in the sails on our voyage, did I not? Now let me show you how to catch the expression lines of a face."

He took the painting off the easel and placed it carefully in the shade of the wide-leaved tree before putting some blank paper in its place; then he began to explain to Sophie how to bring figures to life on the canvas. Soon she was engrossed in the lesson, and when he offered her the use of a chair and the rough drawing board he had brought out with him, so that she might practise the techniques he had suggested, she accepted with alacrity, Byron and his poems forgotten. Both of them lost track of time as he put his arm around her and covered her hand with his as he guided her pencil strokes, showing her how to suggest an expression with a few lines. She liked the feel of his closeness and the firm grip of his hand. She liked, too, the feel of his breath on the back of her neck, and when he stood up and rested his hand on her shoulder, she liked the warmth that radiated outward from his hand.

So engrossed did she become that she did not notice time passing. It was not until Laurence and Jane came roaring and galloping down the slope with a message from Mrs Bennet, saying, "Mama and Papa are back!" that she realised how late it was.

Paul stepped away from her, saying, "You have promise, Miss Lucas. I hope you do not waste it."

Then John and Margaret appeared, and they found they had many willing young hands to help them disassemble their artistic paraphernalia and carry it up the hill in time for a late luncheon.

Elizabeth and Darcy returned to the house refreshed and revitalised after their romantic sojourn. It was a good thing, as they were met with a variety of complaints on their return: John declared that Laurence had taken some of his soldiers, and Laurence declared that he had never touched the things; William said that Jane had drawn in one of his books, which Jane denied; Beth said she was sure she ought to be wearing her hair up as she would soon be fourteen and would be a laughingstock if she continued to wear it tumbling around her shoulders; and Mrs Bennet complained that Margaret would not let go of her old Egyptian doll.

"I cannot think why, when she has a lovely, new doll to play with," said Mrs Bennet. She held out the new doll enticingly. "See, my lamb, this is so much prettier than that horrid creature covered in smudges. See how the headdress sparkles on this one. Ouch. And that nasty thing is covered in splinters!"

"Thank you very much, Grandmama, but I like Aahotep best," said Meg gravely. "She talks to me."

"Oh, how I remember my dolls all talking to me. There was a toy soldier of my brother's, I remember, who used to ask me all the time to dance! But he was a nice, clean doll in a red coat, not a nasty, dirty thing. Just look at your new doll's dress, Margaret. She will talk to you too if you give her the chance."

Margaret looked disdainful, saying, "How can she, Grandmama? She is only a toy."

"Only a toy?" asked Mrs Bennet. "Only a toy? Why, she is an Egyptian princess."

"No," said Margaret firmly, clutching Aahotep tightly and looking scathingly at the offered treasure.

"If I had spoken to my grandmama like that when I was a little girl…" Mrs Bennet began.

Knowing that Mrs Bennet's tales of *when I was a girl* could last for hours, Elizabeth and Darcy exchanged glances.

"Meg, my darling, time to go to the schoolroom," Darcy said, holding out a hand to Margaret, who took it happily, and the other children accompanied them—all but Beth and William, who were now old enough to eat with the adults. Meanwhile, Elizabeth put her arm through her mother's.

"Come, Mama, let us go in to luncheon," she said, leading her mother firmly away from the children.

"I cannot think why Meg is so enamored of that ugly thing," said Mrs Bennet.

"All children have their foibles, as you well know," said Elizabeth.

"I am sure I would never have allowed you to have something like that," said Mrs Bennet. "When you were children…"

Elizabeth sought to distract her mother's attention, for tales of Mrs Bennet's exemplary maternal achievements were almost as frequent as her tales of *when I was a girl*. Luckily, Elizabeth did not have far to look, for Edward had met Sir Matthew Rosen that morning by arrangement at a local souk and had brought him back for luncheon.

"I hope I am not intruding," said Sir Matthew, rising to greet them.

"Not at all," said Elizabeth. "We are delighted to see you. How are things at the dig?"

"They are improving all the time. I have just secured the services of a physician, who will be joining us at the camp shortly.

There are always minor injuries and illnesses on such a dig, and now that our numbers are growing, a physician is a useful man to have about the place."

As they took their places round the table, Sir Matthew continued to tell them of the conditions in the camp, the progress that had been made, and the small treasures found, making sure to thank Edward for his patronage and to stress how vital his continued support would be to the continuation of the dig. He regaled them also with an account of some of the difficulties: the problems of hiring reliable workmen, the heat, and the ever encroaching sand.

"I cannot wait to see it for myself," said Edward.

"Why do you not all come?" asked Sir Matthew.

Sophie brightened at once, while Darcy glanced at Elizabeth, his eyes saying, *Sir Matthew is hoping for further investment in his work.*

Elizabeth knew that this was Sir Matthew's motive, but despite this, she found herself stimulated by the idea. It had been their intention to remain in Cairo, where it was relatively civilised, while Edward went on to the dig, but the lure of the desert had taken hold of her and she found herself longing to explore.

"Yes. Why not?" said Elizabeth, looking at Darcy.

"Because life on a dig is very hard," said Darcy.

"Our dig is bigger than most," said Sir Matthew. "We have almost a small village of tents, with easy access to the river and a wealth of interesting tombs in the vicinity. We have several renowned scholars working there, men with international reputations. It would be educational for the children, and of course this kind of opportunity does not come along very often. There are many discoveries to be made, not only of treasures but also of scholarship. Just think if we find another Rosetta Stone. We could name it the Darcy Tablet."

Darcy laughed. "You know how to flatter your patrons."

"But why not?" asked Sir Matthew. "Discoveries have to be given some name, and the name of the generous patron is surely the best one to give."

"I think my cousin will be disappointed if I steal his thunder," said Darcy.

"Not at all," said Edward robustly. "You may have the privilege of giving your name to any significant historical or archaeological finds, while I will content myself with the treasure."

"You still believe you will find your tomb?" asked Sir Matthew.

"I am certain of it."

"Treasure?" said Mrs Bennet. "Oh, yes, I do hope we find some treasure. I would like a new necklace, for Mrs Long was wearing a diamond necklace before we left and crowing about how valuable it was. I am sure we will find something better here, or what was the point of coming all this way?"

Elizabeth forbore to mention to her mama that she had not been invited but had taken it upon herself without so much as an invitation.

"Well?" said Sir Matthew, looking at Darcy.

Darcy turned his glass in his hand. "When do you leave?" he asked.

"I was planning to return tomorrow, but if you will join me, I will wait for you and travel onward at your convenience."

"And my expense?" asked Darcy good-naturedly.

"Naturally," said Sir Matthew. "Further patronage is always welcome."

Elizabeth glanced at Darcy with unmistakable enthusiasm.

"I can see that my wife will give me no peace if I refuse her this opportunity to live in a tent, where all her possessions will be covered in sand and where she will have nothing to entertain her but a hole in the ground, and so I accept. And as my wife will not consent to leave the children behind, we will all accompany you when you return to the dig."

Sir Matthew bowed. "As to the patronage…" he began.

Elizabeth took her cue and stood up. She gathered the ladies with her eye and led them from the room, leaving the gentlemen to discuss the financial implications and the practical necessities of their onward journey. The ladies made their way to the cool, airy chamber they had claimed as their sitting room. While Mrs Bennet enthused about the portrait Mr Inkworthy was painting of her, Beth picked up her sketchbook and Elizabeth and Sophie turned their attention to writing some letters.

"It is about time I had my portrait painted," said Mrs Bennet. "Your father would never commission one, though I asked him to time after time. I am looking forward to hanging it in the drawing room at Longbourn. How green Mrs Long will be."

Mrs Bennet continued to relish the faces of her neighbours while the others worked at their appointed tasks.

"At least sand is one thing we are never short of in Egypt!" said Sophie as she sanded her letter. "Although the ink dries so quickly here it is not really necessary."

"But it is hard to break the habit," Elizabeth agreed. "Have you written to everyone? Once we set off down the Nile, there will be no more opportunity to post a letter until we return. I am sure the dig site is very primitive, despite Sir Matthew's boast, and he only sends to Cairo once a month for letters and supplies."

"Yes. I have written to Mama and my sisters," said Sophie. "I have told them all about our stay in Cairo, but by the time I write the next letter, there will be something even more exotic to talk about."

She wandered over to one of the windows and looked out over the desert.

"It is strange to think that a mighty civilisation flourished here but that it is now covered in sand," she said. "Whole temples have been buried beneath the desert. I am glad we are going to join Sir Matthew at his dig. I never thought about the wider world before; indeed, I never thought about anything outside Meryton, but now my eyes have been opened and it is all thanks to you, Elizabeth."

"My dear Sophie, we were only too glad to bring you with us."

"Do you think Mr Fitzwilliam will really find an undiscovered tomb, with all its treasures?" asked Sophie.

"He certainly hopes so."

"The pyramids, the tombs... they make me wonder about the people who made them. And yet it shows the insignificance of men, do you not think, that their most triumphant works can be buried so easily by nature?"

"But they are still there," said Elizabeth, "not destroyed, only lost. And that which is lost can be found."

Sophie paused, much struck. "Yes, it can." Her voice took on a musing tone. "I thought I had lost something forever..."

"Mr Rotherham?" asked Elizabeth gently.

"No, not Mr Rotherham, but something more important, my joy in life. I thought he had destroyed it. But he had only buried it, and I believe I am finding it again."

"It is lucky that Edward is so adept at archaeology," said Elizabeth innocently.

"Elizabeth!" said Sophie, blushing.

"Well it is he, is it not, who has reawakened your joy in living?" said Elizabeth teasingly. "Unless it is Mr Inkworthy?"

Sophie's colour subsided slightly, although not completely, and a faint flush could still be seen beneath her tanned skin.

"I confess I like him, too. He is very different from Edward, more serious perhaps and not as confident, but he is an interesting person. He is no less passionate in his own way."

"And his looks, although not handsome, have a way of growing on one," said Elizabeth.

"Yes, they do."

Elizabeth paused for a minute and then said, "Sophie, you have no mother with you and so I will say to you what my aunt said to me, many years ago, when I thought I was on the way to being in love with George Wickham. I have been very happy to see you coming back to life, and a light flirtation with Mr Inkworthy is an agreeable thing, but I want you to be on your guard. Anything more serious would be imprudent because of a want to fortune on both sides. I have nothing to say against him; he is a most interesting young man, but I think you must not let your fancy run away with you. I hope I am not offending you by speaking so openly?"

"No, not at all. But you must not take it too hard if I cannot follow your excellent advice. Oh, I do not mean that

I am in love with Mr Inkworthy—far from it—only that you did not allow a matter of fortune to sway you in your marriage, for I believe you would have married Mr Darcy if he had been a pauper. And how can I promise to be wiser than you and so many of my fellow creatures if I am tempted, or how am I even to know that it would be wisdom to resist? All that I can promise you is that I will do my best."

Elizabeth laughed.

"And now you have answered me as I answered my aunt. Well, I can ask for no more than that. Now, I had better instruct the servants, there will be plenty to do over the next few days. If we can complete our journey down the Nile without Jane falling overboard or Laurence bartering his grandmama for a camel, then I will think myself fortunate indeed."

Chapter 9

THE REMAINING FEW DAYS in Cairo passed quickly. Paul travelled out to Giza to sketch the head of the sphinx and returned with a tale of having accepted a camel ride back to Cairo, only to be taken deeper into the desert by the camel's owner, who demanded money of him and threatened to leave him if he did not pay. He returned to the house chastened, and it was a reminder to all of them that they needed to be aware of the dangers all around them and properly prepared for their journey. But at last all the preparations were made, and they embarked on the flat-bottomed boat that would carry them down the Nile.

Their journey was enjoyable, and Elizabeth regretted it when the last night on board arrived. She was dressed in a loose muslin gown. A large hat was shading her face and protecting her eyes from the low rays of the sun. They were all lingering on deck, eager to make the most of it—all but Jane and Margaret, who, tired, had been put to bed.

Elizabeth and Darcy were sitting apart from the others at the back of the boat. As they watched the sun sinking into the water, Darcy dropped soft kisses on her hair. Elizabeth leaned back against his chest, enjoying the view. The graceful palm trees on the banks made intricate silhouettes against the rapidly darkening sky.

"First a sunrise and now a sunset. We have seen some magnificent skies in Egypt," she said. "It is strange to think of other people watching this same sight, going back for thousands of years."

"Strange and also humbling to think of other lovers watching the sun go down, even as we are doing now."

"Yes, love is the one thing that never changes," agreed Elizabeth as she basked in Darcy's love and the beauty of the evening. "Although people themselves do. Those lovers in earlier times did not know why the sun sank beneath the horizon every evening. They thought it happened because the sun god, Ra, left the heavens to travel through the underworld, where he would fight the serpent Apophis before emerging again, triumphant, the following morning, bringing with him the new day."

"I see that Edward has been telling you about the Egyptian myths."

"Yes, he has. And I am not the only one," said Elizabeth, looking toward the front of the boat, where Edward was entertaining the children with an Egyptian tale, while Sir Matthew looked on with a kindly air. Edward's words drifted through the still, calm air toward them:

"...the king did not want to go to war, as it meant leaving all his treasure behind. But at last he had no choice, and so he left his treasure on the island of Elephantine, which was guarded by a powerful magician. As soon as the king left, his relatives tried to claim the treasure for their own—"

"He should have passed a law forbidding anyone to touch it," said William.

"He should have left some soldiers behind to guard it," said John.

"He didn't need to; he had the magician to guard it," said Laurence. "No one would be able to steal it if it had a magician guarding it; it would be safe."

"Unfortunately not," said Edward. "They slew the magician—"

"Then the king should have chosen a better magician," said Laurence. "He wasn't very powerful if he got killed so easily."

"He was a very powerful magician," said Edward, "for he rose from the dead, turning into an enormous serpent who ate them all. And there the serpent remains to this day, guarding the treasure."

"How are we going to kill him then?" asked Laurence.

"It's only a story," said William.

"We are not going to the island of Elephantine," said Beth. "We are going to a dig in the desert; it is not the same thing."

"Quite right, Miss Darcy," said Sir Matthew. "A real dig, not a fairy tale."

"But some bold adventurer might steal the treasure one day," said Laurence, ignoring them.

"The serpent is too powerful, with a light on his head which blinds all who see it," said Edward.

"Yes, but sometimes it leaves its cave and goes down to the river to drink; you said so yourself," remarked John thoughtfully. "If I had a sword and a party of good men, I could take the treasure in its absence and then lie in wait for it in the back of the cave. I would tie a cravat round my eyes to protect them and then my men and I would kill it when it returned."

"I wouldn't need a sword and a party of men to get the treasure," said Laurence with contempt. "If the stupid serpent has been guarding the treasure for thousands of years without realising the king must be dead, it will be easy to outwit. If I ever find the island, I will just close my eyes and feel my way up to the serpent, pretending to be a beggar. I will tell the serpent the king has sent for it, and then steal the treasure when the serpent slithers away."

Darcy laughed.

"Our youngest son is nothing if not enterprising."

Elizabeth laughed with him. "Whatever problems they face in life, our sons will always deal with them in their own individual ways. William will legislate for the problem, John will fight it, and Laurence will trick the problem into solving itself."

"Whereas Beth will charm it and Jane will torment it, while Margaret…"

He stopped suddenly. Elizabeth turned her head slightly to see what he was looking at and saw that Margaret had appeared on deck, dressed in her nightgown.

"Is she sleepwalking?" Darcy asked.

"I am not sure," said Elizabeth.

The little girl appeared to be looking at something on the bank.

"Margaret?" asked Elizabeth, rising to her feet.

Her daughter ignored her and padded softly toward the railings, her eyes fixed steadfastly on a point beyond their sight. Her plump cheeks were flushed in a way that Elizabeth was beginning to recognise. In her hands was the doll.

"Meg," said Darcy, reaching her before Elizabeth and bending down to speak to her. "What is it? Could you not sleep?"

But still Margaret showed no sign of being aware of them.

"She *is* asleep, Darcy," Elizabeth whispered. "Take care not to startle her."

Just then Margaret's eyelids fluttered open.

"Mama, Papa," she said and put her arms around her father's neck.

"What is it, my darling? Did you have a nightmare?"

Margaret rubbed at her eyes with one chubby hand.

"No, but Aahotep wanted to come upstairs. She's feeling happier now she's nearly home. She told me she's missed the sand under her feet." The little girl giggled. "She went for a run without any shoes on."

"Aahotep should remember she needs lots of sleep," said Elizabeth shortly. "Come back to bed now."

Margaret rubbed her eyes again and nodded. Darcy picked her up and she lay her head against his shoulder.

"Mama," she said as they began to walk along the deck back to the cabins. "Aahotep is sorry about your parasol."

"My parasol, darling?"

"Yes. She was angry with you before because you said you were going to take her away from me, so she made the sea ruin it. But I told her off. I said it was your favourite and you would never steal her from me anyway."

"Of course not, my dear." Elizabeth and Darcy exchanged worried glances at this statement.

"She is sorry, really," the little girl insisted. "She told me she does things like that without thinking and then realises afterward that she was wrong. I told her she should count to ten before she does something and then think about it again, and she said she will try. She also said to tell you your dresses are very pretty and suit you even though you are quite old and our clothes are funny shapes."

"How kind," Elizabeth said, unsure how to reply to such a queer statement from her youngest daughter, which did not sound like Margaret's usual language at all.

Margaret yawned.

"Aahotep wants to be kind; she's just not very good at it. She did something very bad once and she's been punished for a very long time over it, and now she's sorry and she's tired and she wants to go home."

They had reached the cabins where the girls were sleeping now. Jane was fast asleep in her narrow little bed, and Darcy and Elizabeth crept in silently so as not to disturb her. They slipped their youngest daughter under the netting they had strung up to deter mosquitoes and tucked her in.

Elizabeth kissed her daughter and suddenly asked, "Meg, what was it Aahotep did that was so bad?"

"Aahotep won't tell me. She says it is not for the ears of the young and innocent." As she drifted off to sleep, it was almost as though they could hear the words coming from older lips.

Elizabeth and Darcy waited until Margaret's breathing was light and regular and then they slipped out of the cabin and back onto the deck again. It was now completely dark; stars glittered against the deep velvet black of the mysterious Egyptian night sky, and the moon was visible in all her ghostly white splendour, full and heavy, with the faint outlines of a face grinning at them. Despite the heat Elizabeth shivered.

"Are you cold, my love?" asked Darcy.

"No, but that was… disturbing, was it not?" Elizabeth said to him. "Just for a moment I wondered if Aahotep really spoke to Meg."

As soon as she said it, she felt foolish. What was she thinking? That the doll was somehow alive? What nonsense! She would find herself believing Edward's stories about serpents next.

"It was nothing but a bad dream," said Darcy reassuringly.

Of course, she thought, *what else could it have been?*

"I wonder if it was even prompted by a guilty conscience," Darcy went on. "You know how Meg loves to come into our room in the mornings. Perhaps she went into our cabin and opened the portholes for some fresh air, and then forgot about them and felt guilty when the water came in and ruined your parasol. You know how she loved to play with it. And you said yourself that her doll was wet. It was—"

Before he could finish his sentence, there was the sound of muted argument from the servants' quarters. They turned to see the boat's captain, the *reis*, berating his staff roundly. Chastened, the men slunk off.

"What is it?" Darcy enquired.

The *reis* turned to them.

"Nothing, just some foolish peasants who know no better. They have been telling each other ghost stories, and now one of them swears he has just seen a real ghost. They are stupid, not like we educated people," he said, sticking out his chest with pride. "They believe the old stories about gods sailing the skies in their ships and wicked magicians and evil spirits. They think there are ghosts everywhere."

"They were probably dazzled by the moonlight," Elizabeth

said, though she had the curious feeling she was trying to reassure herself and not the *reis*.

"You are very gracious."

"What did he see?" Darcy asked curiously.

The *reis* laughed.

"He imagined he saw a woman running along the bank in the clothes of long ago, with the sand firm beneath her bare feet. She was laughing, he said. And then she disappeared in front of his eyes. No doubt she was being pursued by a powerful magician and was beautiful and rich too. These peasants and their tales! Good night, *effendi*," he said and walked off to continue his duties on the boat.

Darcy and Elizabeth looked at each other.

"It is coincidence, nothing more," said Darcy at last.

Elizabeth nodded her head vigorously. But even as they returned to their seats on the deck and Elizabeth lay her head once more against Darcy's shoulder, she could not help but remember Margaret's words about Aahotep running with delight along the riverbank. Also, unbidden and unwelcome, a line from Edward's story, told to them in England, echoed in her memory: "…to this day, one can see a mad woman fleeing along the riverbank when the moon is full."

"Darcy, I think the time has come for us to take the doll away from Meg."

"You surely cannot believe this folklore and superstition?" he asked.

"I am not sure what I believe," said Elizabeth. "Out here in the desert anything seems possible. And besides, whatever else, this attachment to the doll cannot be healthy."

Darcy was about to protest when the memory of his youngest daughter standing by the railings in her thin white shift rose in his mind. It had no doubt been nothing more than a trick of the moonlight, but she had seemed to take on an otherworldly form.

"Very well," he said. "When we land, we will make sure the doll does not go ashore with us."

And then he surprised himself by thinking grimly, *Whatever sins you may have committed, Madam Aahotep, you will have to find someone else to help you make amends.*

Chapter 10

"This is it," said Edward, the following morning. "This is where we leave the boats and venture into the desert. Is it not magnificent? An endless stretch of golden dunes, stretching as far as the eye can see, and buried beneath it, fabled treasures just there for the taking."

Darcy made arrangements for the boats to remain close by for the duration of their stay; he wanted to be able to take his family back to Cairo without delay if for any reason their adventure proved unsuitable for his wife and children.

While he was speaking to the *reis*, Elizabeth arranged for many of their own possessions, including cooking implements, bedding, and other necessaries, to be left on board until they should be needed, for although Sir Matthew had assured her that the camp was well equipped, she suspected that an archaeologist's idea of "well equipped" would not match her own.

And embedded securely within a pile of sheets was Aahotep.

Leaving behind some of the guards they had hired to protect the boats from any passing thieves who might otherwise prey on them, and to make sure that the *reis* did not decide to remove his boats without their permission, the Darcy party disembarked. All around them were the *fellahs* who had been engaged to work for them, unloading their less precious possessions and then putting them onto the backs of camels and donkeys.

"Well, Elizabeth?" said Darcy as he saw his wife eyeing one of the beasts. "What is it to be, a camel or a donkey?"

"Mama, Mama, look at me!" shouted Laurence enthusiastically, as he balanced precariously on top of a camel which rose unsteadily to its feet.

Paul rapidly sketched the sight, catching Laurence's expression of triumph perfectly—as well as the camel's placid gaze, the undulation of the sand dunes, and the exotic dress of the camel driver, whose long robe was tied in the middle with a rope belt and who wore a rusty red turban wound around his head.

"I can hardly do less than my son," said Elizabeth.

She accepted the camel driver's hand and he helped her to mount another beast, which was kneeling before her. It looked placid enough, but its teeth were large and its smell was appalling. It was, nevertheless, an exhilarating experience when the camel stood up and she found herself high above the riverbank, looking down at Sophie and Edward.

Sir Matthew, William, and John were already astride camels, while Jane was perched in front of Laurence. Beth had decided, like Sophie and Edward, to ride on a donkey. Margaret stood by, placidly watching them all and clutching her new doll.

There had been tears when Aahotep could not be found, but her nursemaid had consoled her by saying that Aahotep had no doubt been packed in one of the cases and would be unpacked when they reached the dig, and in the meantime there was her new doll, which her mama had kindly bought for her on a shopping expedition...

So Margaret had unwillingly accepted the substitute, which had come as a relief to Elizabeth and Darcy, and the nasty little doll was left behind.

Darcy climbed onto a camel and scooped his youngest daughter up in his arms, setting her down in front of him, and the caravan began to move away from the lush, fertile banks of the Nile toward the endless sand dunes that lay not far beyond. Their camels sailed along, stepping sure-footedly in the shifting sands, and once Elizabeth had become accustomed to the strange rolling sensation and to being so high above the ground, she found she was enjoying herself. The sun shone down from a cloudless sky, and the party was in cheerful mood. It was not too hot, the year being advanced, and they stopped once at an oasis, where they rested in the shade of the palm trees and drank from the cool waters of the pool. Ferns grew there and a surprising number of wild flowers.

"We will return here later, just you and I," murmured Darcy. "We will come one morning for a picnic, without our entourage."

"I should like that very much," said Elizabeth.

After another few hours' ride they began to see signs of activity, which was a welcome change after the vast emptiness of the desert. *Fellahs* in loose robes and colourful headdresses were leading strings of heavily laden donkeys toward a campsite in the distance.

It was for this site they headed. Elizabeth was surprised to see how well organised it was. They passed an area which served as a stable, where donkeys were being unloaded, and then rode through an archway into a courtyard. The courtyard was surrounded on all sides by a long, low building, which was alive with bustle. Men came and went through open doors, and in the middle of the courtyard there sat a group of small boys washing bits of pottery, some of it broken and all of it colourful.

"You did not believe me when I told you it was almost as large as a village," said Sir Matthew, seeing her face.

"No, I must confess I did not. I thought…"

"You thought I was saying what I must in order to persuade you to visit and finance further work," he said, "but as you can see, I spoke nothing but the truth. It was very much smaller at the start of the year, but with the help of my patrons I have been able to extend it to a useful size."

"I am glad to see your trip to London was so profitable!" Elizabeth returned, as her camel knelt and Sir Matthew helped her down.

"It has enabled me to continue my work, and do so in some comfort," said Sir Matthew. "You will be hot after your journey, but once you have had time to wash and eat, you must let me give you a tour."

They were all ready for a meal eaten in the shade, and once they had refreshed themselves, Sir Matthew himself showed them round the camp.

"On this side of the courtyard we have the bedrooms," he said. "Rooms have been made ready for you. They are simple, but I think you will not find them too uncomfortable."

Elizabeth looked round at the bare walls, but noticed with pleasure the rug on the floor.

"A mixture of goat, sheep, and camel wool," said Sir Matthew, following Elizabeth's gaze. "Not as fine as the rugs you have at home, I am sure, but colourful and attractive in their own way."

There was a bed and a washstand with a bowl and jug and space for hanging clothes. It was indeed sparse when compared to Pemberley, but Elizabeth glanced at Darcy and knew she could be happy with him anywhere. She caught his gaze and knew that he was thinking the same.

Sir Matthew led them on, showing them the rooms where the finds were kept. Most of them were pieces of pottery, but here and there were small daggers and the like, and the glint of gold.

"We found these in the desert not long since," said Sir Matthew, picking up one of the necklaces. "A pretty trinket, no more. The tomb it came from had been plundered many times and only a few, small pieces remained."

The passed through into another room, which housed an easel and various artistic equipment.

"Mr Waite, our artist. He makes a pictorial record of every object found."

Elizabeth was amused to see the two artists eyeing each other, but after a short conversation, when it became apparent that Sir Matthew's artist had no interest in portraiture or landscapes—indeed, regarded them as frippery wastes of time—the two men seemed content to take their own similar, but different, places in the expedition.

"And then there are the bones," said Sir Matthew.

"Bones?" asked Laurence, his attention caught.

"Yes, bones. I thought that might interest you, young

sir. We have found a great many bones, and we have found mummies as well."

Laurence's eyes grew wide with delight.

"Would you like to see them?" asked Sir Matthew.

The girls declined, but Laurence looked as though the world held no greater pleasure, and Sir Matthew dispatched the boys with a trusted assistant to view the grisly remains.

Beth and Jane soon tired of the adults' conversation and began to run about, glad to be able to stretch their legs after their long hours of riding. Elizabeth looked affectionately after them, her pleasure in the sight bittersweet, as she knew that Beth was already leaving such pleasures behind and that, before long, her eldest daughter would regard it as beneath her to play in such a carefree manner. Already, much of the time, Beth was conscious of her dignity and refused to play with the younger children, but there were still moments when she reverted to her childish ways and Elizabeth relished them, knowing they would soon be gone.

Only Meg remained with the adults. She had fallen asleep and was now being carried in Darcy's arms.

Soon Mrs Bennet, too, tired of the conversation. As they went into the courtyard she sat down in the shade and wafted herself with her hand, too hot to speak. Another of Sir Matthew's colleagues, with Egyptian features but wearing English dress, saw her perspiring brow and brought her a fan made of palm leaves. She was about to take it, but he shook his head with a smile and wafted it to and fro himself. Mrs Bennet, never slow to appreciate a handsome young man, flirted with him in a way which would have made Lydia proud.

Elizabeth and Darcy exchanged long-suffering glances and

then, with Edward, they followed Sir Matthew round the rest of the site as he showed them what a difference their patronage had made.

"Having such well-connected sponsors has helped me to attract many more, and now, as you can see, we are well provided for here, with all the necessary tools and with plenty of space to store our findings," he said, showing them a simple, but well-organised, room of tools. Then they moved on. "In this room we examine our finds and decide which to keep for further study and which to send back to England. I have already shipped three crates of artefacts to the British Museum since seeing you last, and now, with your further help," he said, bowing to Edward and Darcy, "I intend to send them many more."

"We are all looking forward to seeing your Egyptian room at the museum when it is finished. It seems a long time since we saw you there," Elizabeth said, recalling the gloomy room into which they had stumbled in the spring.

"You would scarcely recognise it; it is already taking shape, thanks to your generosity. Several funerary urns and statuettes have already joined the frieze of Aahotep." He turned to Edward. "Are you still determined to look for her fabled tomb, young man, or have you accepted that the real treasures are the artefacts which show us how the ancient Egyptians lived? The map you have is nothing more than a madman's delusion, I assure you, and if you continue to believe in it you will be disappointed. These maps of undisturbed tombs are found everywhere in the bazaars of Egypt, always marking the location of a fabulous treasure and always being sold to the unwary for a fabulous price."

"Map?" asked Darcy, looking at Edward intently. "You did not tell me about the map."

Edward looked uncomfortable.

"Ah," said Sir Matthew. "It seems I have made a *faux pas*. I thought you knew."

"Knew what?" asked Elizabeth.

"That your cousin is not just here to learn more about ancient Egypt; he is here for a purpose," said Sir Matthew. "But I have said enough."

"Edward?" asked Darcy, setting Margaret down gently on a chair, for she had started to stir. "Is there anything you would like to tell us?"

"Nothing at all," said Edward, though he looked even more uncomfortable as he said it.

"You are not really thinking of searching for the tomb our fathers tried to find?" asked Darcy.

"And what if I am? Is it not worth finding?" he demanded.

"That map is meaningless. Believing in it broke our fathers' health, and it will break yours, too."

"No," said Edward. "Because I know something our fathers did not. I know the meaning of some of the hieroglyphs that decorate the map, thanks to the work of Thomas Young and his like—I have been in correspondence with them—and thanks, too, to my own endeavours. I have already discovered that the city marked on the map is Cairo and not Luxor, as our fathers thought, and so when I found that Sir Matthew was already excavating in the area, I went to see him in London and enlisted his help."

"Which I gave you on the understanding you would

not place too much reliance on the thought of finding an undisturbed tomb, and on the veracity of your map," said Sir Matthew uneasily.

"Then you *have* found the map," said Darcy. "And all this time you have said nothing about it. But where did you come across it?"

"It was in the attic, along with a portrait of our fathers, and the queer little doll that Margaret so loves."

"That map claimed a year of our fathers' time, and it very nearly claimed their lives," said Darcy. "They searched for the tomb repeatedly but found nothing except illness and accident."

"If you only knew what I know you would think differently," Edward said, his enthusiasm overcoming his embarrassment. "Look!"

He took a piece of parchment out of the pocket of his jacket, which he had worn throughout their long, hot journey from Cairo. When he spread it on the table they could see the markings on it.

"Here is an oasis, and here the river," said Edward, pointing out the landmarks. "Exactly as we have found them."

"An oasis and a river," said Darcy. "Egypt is full of spots like that. And even if you were certain, the map is not clear enough to be of any use. The last third is missing, and it is the last third which pinpointed the exact spot of this supposed tomb."

"I am sure it is here," said Edward doggedly. "It is not only the map; it is everything else as well. When I heard Sir Matthew's frieze of Aahotep was found near here, I was certain it was significant, as that was the name of the doll our fathers brought home. The frieze, the doll, and the map are all connected. Do you not see? I am convinced she is somehow connected to the undiscovered tomb, and in all probability it is the tomb of the wealthy people she murdered."

"I see nothing of the kind," said Darcy. "It is a tenuous connection at best, and at worst it is madness, the same sort of madness which infected our fathers. I am sorry now I agreed to help you."

"You will not be sorry when we find the tomb and fill Pemberley full of its marvels," said Edward. "Or when there is a Darcy collection at the British Museum. Only think what we will be giving to the world, as well as…" He trailed away.

"As well as?" Darcy prompted him.

"Oh, well…" Edward gave an awkward laugh. "As well as the treasures we will collect for ourselves. I know you do not need treasure, Darcy, but it is different for me. I have an allowance, of course, and it does very well for the moment, but I am a younger son, and a younger son must make his way in the world. He is so positioned that he has expensive tastes but not the means of satisfying them."

"I seem to remember your brother saying something similar at Rosings many years ago," said Elizabeth.

"I am not surprised. But he was lucky in the end. He fell in love with Anne, and Anne had enough fortune for the two of them. But S—" He stopped suddenly.

"But Sophie does not?" asked Elizabeth. "That is what you were going to say, is it not?"

He could not deny it.

"Are your feelings for her serious, then? You are not simply amusing yourself with her or trying to raise her spirits after her unhappy love affair?"

"No, I am not simply amusing myself, and yes, my feelings are serious," he admitted. "There is something about Sophie," he said, glancing toward her as she played with the children. "It is not just that she is pretty, although she is very, very pretty, nor just her sweet nature. There is something about her that makes me want to spend my time with her more than anyone else. When we are together, I feel differently about everything. The world seems better and brighter, and so do I. She is the only woman in the world I want to marry."

"You know that she likes Mr Inkworthy?"

"I do," said Edward, sounding glum, then he brightened. "But, fortunately, Inkworthy is not in a position to marry any more than I am. But when I find the tomb—"

"*If* you find the tomb," said Darcy.

"Very well, *if* I find the tomb. But why should I not? Sir Matthew has found some promising signs of a tomb located nearby." He turned to Sir Matthew. "Now that you cannot deny."

"No, I cannot," said Sir Matthew.

"It is there somewhere, Darcy; I can feel it."

Elizabeth was growing fatigued by the heat and sat down. Sir Matthew, noticing it, said, "Gentlemen, might I suggest some refreshments before you continue your discussion?"

"A good idea," said Darcy.

Elizabeth gratefully accepted. Turning to her daughter, who had wandered over to the map and was studying it intently, she said, "Come, Margaret, let us find something to drink."

Margaret seemed not to hear her. Instead, she leaned over the map and studied it with even more innocent intensity. Sir Matthew smiled, charmed by her interest.

"Do you like the pictures, my dear?" he asked kindly.

Margaret looked up, a stern expression on her face. "They're not pictures; they're writing."

"Indeed they are. We call them hieroglyphs and many great men have spent years trying to decipher their meanings."

Margaret nodded almost casually. "That's Ammon and that's Husn. We're here at last. Aahotep is very pleased."

Sir Matthew looked at her curiously.

"What did you say, my dear?" he asked.

"This is the place where Ammon and Husn are. Aahotep is very happy you're all here." She yawned suddenly.

Elizabeth was disappointed that thoughts of Aahotep had not been left behind, even if the doll had not travelled with them, but reasoned that it would take some days, or even weeks, for Margaret to forget the doll entirely.

"Meg is tired after her long journey," Elizabeth said.

"I have no doubt that is true, Mrs Darcy," Sir Matthew replied. "Nevertheless, I would very much like to know where she heard those words."

"Why? Do they mean anything to you?" asked Elizabeth. "I confess, they mean nothing to me."

"They are names. Egyptian names."

Edward, whose finger still traced the hieroglyphs, said, "It could be the meaning of these hieroglyphs here. Some of the pictures we have already deciphered fit in with those names. But there is no way Margaret could have known."

He looked at her with a perplexed frown.

"Tell me, where did you hear those names, my dear?" asked Sir Matthew.

"It was Aahotep," said Margaret, holding up her doll. "She told me."

Elizabeth blanched. The doll Margaret was holding up was not her new doll, but Aahotep.

She tried to catch Darcy's eye, but he was looking at the map, and she was glad, a moment later, that she had not been able to catch it, for of course there was an innocent explanation for the unsettling occurrence: one of the maids must have come across the doll in the case of things to be left behind and, thinking it was a mistake, had repacked it in the things to go with them instead. But even so, it had given her a nasty turn. And now she was left with the problem of extricating it from Margaret all over again.

"Aahotep?" said Edward with a frown. He turned to Sir Matthew. "You do not think...?"

"Nonsense," said Sir Matthew robustly. "We must not allow ourselves to get carried away by folktales. I must have mentioned the names when we all met in the British Museum, that is all, and the delightful Miss Margaret has remembered them." He smiled benignly at Margaret. "What a clever girl you are."

"Aahotep doesn't think you're very clever," said Margaret without animosity. "She says you're very stupid."

"Margaret!" Elizabeth exclaimed.

"Dear me, does she?" asked Sir Matthew. "And why does she think that?"

"Because you haven't found the tomb. She keeps telling people where it is and still no one has found it."

"And where is it, Margaret?" asked Edward before suddenly looking ashamed of himself as he realised he was treating Margaret's fantasy as if it were real.

"Out there," said Margaret, pointing.

"Out there, in the desert?" asked Sir Matthew.

"Yes," said Margaret, "buried in the sand."

Elizabeth heaved a sigh of relief. For a moment she had expected her daughter to give them explicit instructions, relayed from the long-dead Aahotep. But "out there, buried in the sand" were the sort of vague directions any little girl would give.

"Well, we will just have to unbury it then, will we not?" said Sir Matthew.

Margaret nodded gravely.

"But not today," said Elizabeth. She added meaningfully, "I think someone needs her sleep."

And taking Margaret firmly by the hand, she allowed one of the *fellahs* to show her to the Darcy sleeping quarters.

"Margaret," said Elizabeth, as she undressed her daughter and put her to bed for a nap. "You must not speak to other people that way. It is not polite."

"It wasn't me; it was Aahotep. I like Sir Matthew," said Margaret with a sweet smile. "It is only Aahotep who thinks he is stupid."

Then she gave a huge yawn and closed her eyes, falling quickly into a slumber.

Taking her opportunity, Elizabeth lifted Aahotep out of the bed and replaced it with the new doll. Then she kissed her daughter on the forehead and went to find Darcy. He was sitting for Paul, who was busily sketching him, and Elizabeth did not like to disturb them. She listened instead to John's information about fighting in deserts and the difficulties of everything from supply lines to walking in sand, and she humoured her mother as

Mrs Bennet told her how wonderful the young men in the camp were and how she had invited several of them to England.

"For I am sure your papa would be delighted to have them all at Longbourn," said Mrs Bennet.

Elizabeth could just imagine her father's face if half a dozen handsome Egyptians invaded his home, and that face was not one of delight! But there was no use remonstrating with her mother, and so she relied on the language barrier to protect Mr Bennet from an invasion.

As soon as Darcy was free, Elizabeth went over to him and took his arm, steering him away from the others and toward the edge of the camp where they could talk in peace.

"I suppose we cannot persuade Edward out of the search for this tomb?" she asked.

"Unfortunately not," said Darcy.

Elizabeth shivered.

"I cannot like it," she said.

"Come now, it is just because you are tired. Or are you really regretting coming? We can always return to the boats if you wish."

"No," she said, reassured by his matter-of-fact tone. "As you say, I am just tired—and hot and thirsty. I am allowing my fancies to run away with me. There are many marvels in the desert and I want to experience them while I can. But all the same, I hope Edward either finds the tomb or realises it is not out there. One way or another, I would like his obsession to come to an end."

"On that we are agreed. It is not just his obsession that worries me; it is the deceit. It is all the more unsettling because I have never known Edward to be deceitful before. He has his faults, as do we all—"

"Really, my dear? I did not know that you had any!" she teased him.

"I have kept one or two, for the sole purpose of allowing you the pleasure of correcting them!" he said, kissing her on the tip of her nose. "But if I had known that Edward had found the map… and yet he kept it from me." His tone darkened. "It makes me wonder what other secrets he is keeping."

Chapter 11

THE NEXT DAY EDWARD was up early, stirred by his enthusiasm to find the tomb. The sun had barely begun to show its face above the horizon as he moved around the camp, loading the equipment he meant to take with him onto the camels, who stood placidly in the dawn light, oblivious to his nervous energy.

Disturbed by the noise, Sophie stirred. For a while she struggled to wake, exhausted by the exertions of the day before, then finally she washed and dressed in a loose muslin gown and tiptoed out of the tent she was sharing with the girls to find out what the commotion was.

"Edward, do you mean to leave us?" she enquired as she sleepily took in the sight of the camels and *fellahs* in their long white robes.

"Only for a while," he said, gratified by the note of disappointment he fancied he heard in her voice. "The desert is vast, but I'm sure there are great treasures still to be found, and I mean to find some."

"Bring me back a diamond," she said, smiling.

"At the very least." He hesitated and then moved closer to her. "Sophie, you know that although I am the son of an earl, my fortune is not great."

"I believe I can match you in that regard," she said.

"I would not wish to marry for money." He hesitated and then continued. "If my prospects were better I would hope—"

Just then one of the camels, less tolerant than its fellows, began braying and kicking at a *fellah* who had tightened the girths too tightly, and some of Edward's papers began to fall to the ground. He glanced quickly at Sophie.

"We will speak more when I return," he said.

Sophie watched him in the dawn's half-light, before drawing her shawl round her shoulders and returning to her tent.

Darcy and Elizabeth were also woken by the braying of the camel. Reaching for his robe, Darcy peered out of the tent.

"What is it?" Elizabeth enquired with a yawn.

"It appears Edward is making an early start," Darcy said. He came back into the tent. "Do you have any plans today, my love?"

"After such a long ride yesterday, I wish for nothing more than a long leisurely breakfast and then perhaps to see what Sir Matthew has uncovered."

"I think you are right," said Darcy with a wry smile. Then he sobered. "I think I had better accompany Edward today. Ever since he walked into our drawing room in London last spring, he has been subtly changed and I want to keep him from further mischief."

"Protecting him from himself?" asked Elizabeth.

"Yes, I do believe I am. It is not just his lack of openness; it is his unwavering belief he will find something. He has always been of an optimistic disposition but this is different. He seems unaware of the dangers to be found in the desert, blinded by his determination to succeed."

He reached for his shirt.

"I had better get up as well," said Elizabeth.

"There is no need for both of us to be disturbed so early," he said. He kissed her lightly on the forehead and dressed quickly before disappearing out into the heat of the day.

When he reached the cooking fire, Darcy realised that he was not the only person who intended to accompany Edward on his quest. Sir Matthew was also dressed, a cup of coffee in his hand. He smiled jovially when he saw Darcy.

"Ah, Darcy, your cousin means to make me look like a slugabed. He has already breakfasted and is eager to be off. If I did not know better, I would think he had meant to start without us."

Darcy cast an appraising look at Edward, who contrived to look guilty and unrepentant at the same time.

"It is the early bird who catches the worm, gentlemen," Edward said. "And I mean to catch a very juicy worm today if possible. Do you care to join me?"

"Allow me ten minutes to give some instructions to my people and then we'll strike out together," said Sir Matthew.

"I thought you did not believe in the tomb?" asked Edward.

"There are many secrets to be found in the desert besides your tomb. Mr Darcy, do you mean to come too?"

"I do."

Edward smiled. "Our fathers would be proud of us," he said, handing Darcy a cup of coffee.

Darcy said, "I wonder."

Elizabeth went back to sleep after Darcy left and did not awaken until a more civilised time. When she rose, she found the children were already up and that Paul was hard at work on an oil painting, taken partly from earlier sketches and partly from the scene before his eyes.

"I thought a painting of the children in the camp would be interesting and would remind them of their adventures," said Paul as Elizabeth approached.

"It is a good thing you have sketches to work from. Even in this heat, the children are never still." She looked at the painting and was pleased with its progress. "Is it difficult to work the paint in the heat?" she asked.

"It is certainly not the same as it is at home in the cold and the damp," he said, "but I believe I have mastered its use here. The paintings dry much more quickly here than they do at home."

Elizabeth left him hard at work and went over to her mother and Sophie, who were eating fruit in the shade of an awning.

"Mama!" said Laurence, running up to her. "Saeed has been telling us all about the tunnels. When can we go and look at them?"

Saeed was Sir Matthew's most trusted helper, and Sir Matthew had left him in charge. He had been explaining the principles of archaeology to the children and had been telling them of the tunnels and plundered tombs that had so far been excavated.

"You may go after breakfast," Elizabeth promised him.

"Saeed said there will be lots of rats," said Jane in excitement.

Beth, looking very pretty in a white muslin gown which had somehow managed to remain unspotted by dust or sand, said,

"I think I will stay here, Mama. I am sure Grandmama will stay with me."

"And so I will," said Mrs Bennet. "I cannot imagine why you want to spend the day in rat-infested tunnels."

"I would like to go with you, if I may," said Sophie.

The reason for her interest was not hard to find, for Paul was going to sketch them. *So you have not yet decided firmly against Paul*, Elizabeth thought. *And with Edward's obsession with the desert growing steadily stronger, it is perhaps small wonder. No woman likes to be ignored.* Out loud, she said, "We would be glad to have you with us." Adding, "Would we not, Mr Inkworthy?" as Paul, having left his painting to dry, joined them.

"We would be honoured," he said.

It was settled. Mrs Bennet would remain at the camp with Beth and Margaret, while the rest of the party would explore some of Sir Matthew's more recent excavations with Saeed as their guide.

The women put on their hats and pulled their veils down over their faces; then, donning their gloves and picking up their parasols, they declared themselves ready.

The sand had been trodden down into a path by the passing of many feet, and on the way they passed *fellahs* leading donkeys laden with sand and rubble. They came at last to a great hole in the ground and the children ran in and then out again, laughing and shivering at the same time, while Saeed smiled to see their horrified glee.

Elizabeth and Sophie folded their parasols and went down into the gaping hole, looking about them with interest, while Paul brought up the rear, his sketchbook never out of his hand.

Saeed told them about the excavation as they proceeded, and they spent an hour wandering through the damp darkness. Rats and mice scurried in horrid little corners, and Elizabeth was convinced she saw a bat once, although Saeed assured her there were no bats in the tunnels. They all carried a lamp, which thrilled Laurence. He kept swinging his backward and forward, insisting he could see ghosts and almost once setting fire to a workman's clothes. After that, Elizabeth had to insist he give up his lamp or be escorted back to the surface.

Paul was fascinated by the friezes that the workmen had uncovered, and he scribbled feverishly throughout their tour. Elizabeth could tell he was desperate to return when not encumbered by his employer's family. As he rushed to take as many notes as possible, covering his sketchbook with quick sketches and at the same time pointing out the colours and shapes of the ancient Egyptian artists, he did not neglect Sophie and he explained to her what he was doing and why he was doing it. Every now and then he ran his hand through his hair, rumpling it most attractively and flashed a smile at Sophie, who responded with a smile of her own.

Finally they returned to the surface, with Saeed promising Laurence he could return tomorrow and telling Paul he would arrange another visit with more lighting that evening, thankfully out of Laurence's earshot. They all blinked, finding the daylight too strong after the dark of the tunnels, but by and by their eyes adjusted and Paul offered Sophie his arm as they set off back to the camp.

Elizabeth changed for dinner and joined her mother and Sophie in the shade, where she listened with fond affection to an account of Beth and Margaret's day.

The sun was setting low on the horizon when John and Laurence came running toward Elizabeth with the news that they could see a caravan of camels heading for the camp: the men had finally returned. As soon as Elizabeth saw Darcy's face she knew the day had not gone well. Shepherding the children into her mother's care, Elizabeth joined him in their tent.

"You look tired, my love," she said by way of a greeting.

"I am," Darcy replied wearily. "We seemed to have covered hundreds of miles over endless dunes in search of nothing more substantial than mist, and yet still Edward insists the tomb exists. I wonder…"

"Yes?"

"Oh, nothing."

"Never mind, you have time to undress and rest before dinner. You seem to have brought most of the desert into the tent with you. What hope is there for Jane and Laurence when they have two such untidy parents!"

Coaxing and soothing him, she bade the servants bring cool water in a bowl, for once refusing the assistance of Darcy's manservant, and gradually, under her calm ministrations, his weariness faded. Finally he lay back on a rough canvas chair and smiled at her.

"Are you rested now, love?" she said, handing him a drink.

"Yes. You always know how to make me feel better."

"Not always," she said.

"When it counts. It is not your fault I have a young fool for a cousin, though luckily he is saddle sore and intends to remain in the camp tomorrow. Which means that you and I can return to the oasis and have the picnic I promised you."

By the following morning, Darcy's uneasiness over Edward's obsession had evaporated. The sky was blue, the air was clear, and Elizabeth was looking enchanting. Her spirits had bloomed with the novelty of their trip, and he had never seen her looking lovelier. Her somewhat jaded air of the previous winter had given way to a new vitality, and the splendid sights and sounds of the pyramids and oases had rejuvenated their marriage, giving them some welcome opportunities to be alone.

Leaving the rest of the camp sleeping, they set out for the oasis. Elizabeth felt the warmth of the early morning sun on her face and the strong presence of Darcy behind her as they left the camp, riding on a camel. She was now used to the strange gait of the animal and felt safe on its back, enjoying the view it gave her of the rolling sand dunes. In England it would probably be raining, and the colours would be a dreary green and an even drearier grey, but in Egypt the sun shone down from a bright blue sky, turning the sand to gold.

"This is the real treasure," she said as she looked about her. "I do not believe that any jewels could be better than this."

Darcy's arm tightened around her waist and he kissed the back of her neck.

"Or this," he said.

She leaned back against him, delighting in his nearness and in the feel of his breath blowing cool across her neck. When they had first married, they had often gone out alone, with Darcy delighting to show her the extensive grounds of Pemberley and then, later, the Derbyshire countryside. Together they had explored the wild moors, with their rocky outcrops and rough grasses—a countryside which was completely different from the pleasant Hertfordshire countryside where Elizabeth had grown up. They had ridden down small country lanes and climbed low, dry stone walls. They had walked across wide acres of turf, finally sinking down into swathes of glorious purple heather to kiss and caress and talk.

They had wound their way through woods full of bluebells and picked their way across bubbling streams, and they had climbed to the moors' summit and looked across at the vast spread of the landscape and then down at the small villages that nestled in the hollows.

But never had they been anywhere as entrancing as Egypt.

And yet, for all the strangeness of the landscape, Elizabeth felt something of the same sensations, for she was once more exploring an alien world with her husband, and only with her husband.

She put up her hand to stroke his cheek, revelling in the sensation of being alone with him. He took it and held it, kissing the back of it and then turning it over and kissing the palm. She leaned back against him and his arm went around her.

"I have missed this," she said to him. "At home, our lives are full of other people."

"Yes, they are," he agreed.

"It is not that I am not grateful. I know we could not run Pemberley without such a large staff or maintain the grounds without an army of gardeners, and I know how lucky we are to have such a large circle of friends and family, but..."

"But sometimes it seems as though we are caught up in a swirl of people from whom we cannot escape?" he asked.

"That is it exactly."

She thought of all their duties and responsibilities at home, most of which fell upon Darcy's shoulders, but many of which fell upon her own. She was the first lady of the neighbourhood, and scarcely a day went by without an appeal of some kind: someone asking her to speak to her husband about preferment for their son or nephew or brother or a woman in the village who needed her help. Always someone and something, so that sometimes she did not see Darcy from morning 'til night, at least not without a whole host of other people present.

But now here they were, alone, save for the guards who kept a distance so discreet as to be invisible.

The camel began to walk more quickly and Elizabeth sat up, the better to keep her balance. Up ahead, the unbroken sand dunes gave way to the blues and greens of the oasis, which shone like a sapphire nestling in its golden setting. It was surrounded by tall palms, whose branches swayed and rustled in the breeze. Beneath them was a surprising carpet of ferns and wild flowers, and the whole glowing scene was reflected in the water.

The camel came to a halt beneath one of the palm trees. Darcy dismounted as the animal knelt, and then helped Elizabeth down, before tethering the animal nearby.

Darcy took Elizabeth's hand and they walked to the far side of the pool, taking the picnic hamper with him and setting it down beside a luscious fern.

Elizabeth breathed in deeply. Away from the camel the air was sweet, far sweeter than it was at the dig, and the coolness of the water and the whisper of the palms was reviving.

Elizabeth sat down beneath one of the palm trees and Darcy sat beside her. They sat in the shade and remembered anew why they had fallen in love with one another, thinking how lucky they had been to find each other, for although Darcy was not always the easiest of husbands, Elizabeth knew he was the only man she could ever have married. She loved to see him like this, away from the cares of Pemberley and away from the responsibilities of his life in London—away from his young cousin, too, and away from the children, for much as she loved them, there were times when Elizabeth wanted Darcy to herself.

He sat with one knee up, in an attitude he would never adopt at home, with one arm resting negligently across it. His cravat had been discarded and his shirt was open at the neck. His dark hair was disordered by the breeze and his face was tanned by the sun, making his teeth show white against it. She put her hand up to his cheek, stroking her finger across his finely chiselled cheekbone and then leaned toward him and kissed him.

He took her chin in his hand and they kissed for long minutes. Time stood still. They lived for the moment and the pleasure of being together. At last their lips parted and they talked of their love for each other as Darcy stroked Elizabeth's hair and she rested her hand on his thigh, feeling the strong muscle beneath the fabric, and then they kissed again.

Beside them, the picnic hamper laid untouched and ignored.

But by and by, as the day progressed and the light began to fade, they found themselves growing hungry. At last they turned their attention to the selection of food they had brought with them. Elizabeth took a ripe fig from the hamper and shared it with Darcy, the succulent flesh tasting exotic against her tongue. Then they shared some little cakes, feeding each other with the delicacies, which were rich with the sweet taste of honey and pungent with the aroma of nuts.

The evening passed in lazy delight, with no one to please but themselves, as they kissed and ate and relaxed, happy in each other's company—now talking, now silent; now looking at the stars that began to appear in the darkening sky; now having eyes only for each other, refreshing their spirits with the beauty of the oasis, which provided a calm haven for them in the everyday bustle of their lives.

Elizabeth felt her eyelids drooping at last as the evening turned to night and she lay back against her husband, falling asleep against his chest. He smiled and kissed her hair, reaching out toward the hamper carefully so that he would not wake her and pulling out a blanket which he laid gently over her. Then his head, too, drooped, and he fell asleep, his head resting on hers and his arms around her, holding her safe.

Darkness had fallen back at the camp, too, and Edward sat alone by the dinner table listening to the night sounds. He had just bidden Sir Matthew good night and was considering retiring himself when he saw a figure make its way toward him by the dim light of a candle.

"I think I may have left my shawl here," said Sophie. "It is becoming cooler at night."

"Here let me help you look for it," Edward replied, springing up. They both searched around the table and chairs and eventually found it lying on the sand.

"Thank you," said Sophie. She hesitated. "It seemed strange not to have Elizabeth and Darcy with us tonight."

"Yes, it did. I especially missed Elizabeth. She has a way of dealing with Mrs Bennet… well, let us just say that Mrs Bennet is better when Elizabeth is here."

Edward was out of humour with Mrs Bennet, for she had spent the time since dinner making arch comments about Sophie and Paul, who had returned to the camp arm-in-arm, oblivious to the obvious discomfort of the parties concerned and oblivious to Edward's irritation. Worse still, Mrs Bennet had let drop that Paul had told her he had been approached by a wealthy patron in Cairo. She had said it as a means of self-aggrandisement, to show how important he was and therefore how important his portrait of her was, but it had affected Edward in a different way, for he knew that if Paul acquired a wealthy patron, one who intended to sponsor him for years, he would be in a position to take a wife. That thought had made Edward morose.

What does she really think of him? thought Edward, glancing at Sophie and trying to read the answer in her face. *Does she prefer him to me?*

Sophie blushed. "Mrs Bennet means well."

"No doubt," he said shortly.

Sophie turned to leave and he felt ashamed of his bad temper. He asked her forgiveness, saying, "I have not been very good company this evening, I fear."

Sophie hesitated. "I think something is troubling you. If you have a problem I hope that you feel you can speak to me—as a friend," she hastily added.

"As a friend," he said in a hollow tone. Then he rallied and said, "Very well, then, as a friend. Since you ask, the past few days have not gone as well for me as I had hoped. I sometimes wonder if Darcy is right and if my obsession is becoming unhealthy. I feel as if something has taken hold of me, something outside myself, something that is driving me on. I almost wonder…"

He stopped himself just before saying something ridiculous: that he almost wondered if the strange doll he had found in the attic had something to do with it. He had known a little of her story before leaving England, but a souk seller in Cairo had told him more: that Aahotep had been apprehended soon after her wicked deed by a powerful magician named Ptah, who had been hired by the family of the murdered lovers. Ptah had trapped her spirit on the mortal plane and doomed it to walk the earth, "where it will remain until she can find a way of making amends." Edward had smiled at the notion and asked, "And how is Aahotep to make amends for her crimes?" To which the souk seller had said, "In the usual way, of course; she must find some innocent to transport her to the tomb so that she can beg the forgiveness of the two lovers she so cruelly murdered, and then she will be allowed to rest."

It was nonsense, of course, but even so, Edward could not shake an uneasy feeling that Aahotep was indeed returning to the tomb of the murdered lovers and that both he and the innocent Margaret were helping her.

Shaking aside his strange thoughts, he said, "Darcy is not pleased with me."

"Are you surprised?" she asked, and Edward found himself forced to shake his head in agreement.

"No. No, I am not. I should have told him about the map. But I did not because I knew how he would view it. He would have told me that the map led my father astray and it would do the same to me."

Sophie sat down at the table again.

"And in a way I cannot fault him because he is right," he said. "Even so, I hoped… but yesterday was a disaster."

"Was it?"

"We spent all day in the desert, following the map and searching for the tomb in the missing portion of the map. I was so sure we would find it. But we found nothing," he said in a dejected voice.

Sophie reached out to him impulsively, but before she could touch him they were both distracted by a noise coming from the tents behind them. There was a white blur and Sophie let out a cry, then she laughed a little shamefacedly.

"Oh dear, I thought it was a ghost! But it is only Margaret. I believe she is sleepwalking again. Quietly, Edward; we must not disturb her in this condition."

They reached Margaret, whose eyes were wide open but clearly seeing nothing. She held the doll cuddled up to her face and seemed to be murmuring to it, and although her words seemed like nonsense, she moved with a purpose that belied her sleeping state. Edward and Sophie followed her a little way behind so they could catch her if she came in the way of any harm, but she walked round objects as though she were awake. It was only the blankness in her eyes that refuted this.

She moved away from the camp, out of the comforting circle of light cast by the lamps, and both Edward and Sophie began to grow concerned as they followed her deeper into the desert.

"Are you sure we should not wake her?" Edward asked. "She moves as though she means to walk all night."

"I am not sure," Sophie confessed.

"I do not think we should let her go much farther, Miss Lucas," Edward said uncertainly as Margaret ascended a sand dune and proceeded to slip down the other side. "Even if it means picking her up. I shall be as gentle as I can, but—"

Suddenly he realised Margaret had stopped and was now sitting cross-legged on the sand, her doll pressed close against her cheek—her wooden doll, which she had somehow managed to reclaim. Then she began to draw a wide circle around herself, all the while muttering something under her breath. Edward was close enough now to touch her and so he heard her words, softly spoken and almost immediately lost on the night breeze: "Ammon, Husn, Ammon, Husn."

She whispered them several times before sighing and closing her eyes. Then she dropped gently to the ground, fast asleep.

"Edward!" Sophie cried in alarm. "Is she all right?"

"There is nothing to be alarmed about; she is just sleeping," Edward replied, picking the little girl up in his arms and carrying her back over the dune. "She is exhausted no doubt by her midnight ramble."

He was nevertheless relieved when Sophie ran over to him and examined Margaret carefully.

"Well?" he asked.

"It is as you say," said Sophie, for Margaret was soundly sleeping, her breathing even and regular, her cheeks barely flushed with her exertions.

"Let us get her back to bed," Sophie said, taking the sleeping child and cradling her against her shoulder.

Edward nodded and then, on a sudden impulse, and with the memory of Margaret's whispered words in his ears, he took out his pocket watch and dropped it unobtrusively to mark the spot. Then he followed Sophie back to the camp, where she tucked Margaret once more into her little bed.

Sophie sat down beside her, and Edward's heart lurched at the tender sight.

"I do not think she has come to any harm," he said reassuringly.

"I will stay with her anyway," she said. "But thank you for helping me."

"I will always help you, whenever you need it. Sophie…"

"Yes, Edward?"

He hesitated, and in the silence a great deal passed between them. But he could not say the words he wanted to say and so at last he said, "Good night."

"Good night, Edward," Sophie said, but he was gone before the words left her mouth.

He walked about outside for some time, wondering how much it would cost to set up an establishment and if he could afford to offer a life to Sophie even if he never found any treasure. She did not need a great deal to live on, he was sure, but the thought of condemning her to a life of penury did not satisfy him, and that was what it would be, for his father would not approve the marriage and would not help him. So unless by some miracle he found the tomb…

He thought of his pocket watch, marking the spot at which Margaret had whispered, *Ammon, Husn,* and seized by an irresistible compulsion, he knew he had to go back straightaway and begin digging. With a determined air, he took a large shovel from the pile of tools in the tool store and walked out into the night.

It is nothing but a fantasy, he told himself as he walked. *There is no tomb… it is not intact… Margaret's words mean nothing…*

But it was no use. Something had taken hold of him and all he could think about was the eerie tomb awaiting him beneath the desert.

The night was cold and he walked briskly, guided by the starlight. To begin with, the going was easy, as he trod the paths which had been made firm by prolonged use. But by and by he passed into the desert proper and his feet began to sink into the soft sand. Walking became more difficult but it did not deter him. Quite the opposite. He walked with more determination, his eyes seeking the ground for the glint of metal that would tell him he was in the right place.

He walked for some time without seeing anything and he began to be afraid that the sands had already covered his watch, but then he caught sight of something metallic at a distance and hastened toward it. There, lying on the sand, was his watch.

He picked it up and put it in his pocket, then began to dig. He worked feverishly, feeling the sweat break out on his back as he threw the piles of fine golden sand to one side, digging a hole which grew ever deeper. When it was knee-deep he jumped into it and began to dig from the inside, piling the sand on all sides around him until it was shoulder high. And still he dug.

A breeze sprang up, and the fine sand began to drift, catching him in his nose and throat. He became aware of the dangers of his enterprise and wondered if he should have left word of his intentions, but it was too late for such thoughts.

He stopped to rest, the sweat drying on his back, and he felt cold. But he could not let go of his fantasy, and soon he began to dig again. And then his spade struck something hard. He stopped and probed gently. Yes, it was definitely something hard and solid.

Dropping to his knees, he began scrabbling at the sand with his hands, feeling his way around the obstruction as his excitement mounted. His fingers closed around a step and he sat back on his heels, laughing with joy. He had found it! The lost tomb! The tomb of Ammon and Husn! And on the breeze he caught an echo of laughter.

He began to dig again, but as the night wore on his excitement waned and he began to realise how exhausted he was. The huge mounds of sand all around him bore testament to his work and a glance at his watch showed him that he had been digging for hours. Already the sky was beginning to lighten. The work was not progressing fast enough. It was time to get help.

Taking out his compass, he took his bearings, and leaving the spade standing upright in the sand, he returned to camp as fast as his tired legs would take him.

There were already signs of life. The *fellahs* were untethering the donkeys and Sir Matthew, shrugging himself into his coat, was emerging from his tent, ready for a new day.

"I've found it," said Edward, stumbling forward with the last of his strength. "Bring every man in the camp. I've found the tomb."

Chapter 12

WHEN ELIZABETH AND DARCY rode into camp after their romantic night at the oasis, they found it a mass of shouting and confusion.

"What is it?" asked Elizabeth as she slid from the camel. "What has happened?"

"Oh, Lizzy, is it not exciting?" asked Mrs Bennet, rushing out to meet them. "Edward has found the tomb. What riches we shall have! Bracelets and necklaces and crowns, too, I should not wonder. What a wonderful young man he is! How unfortunate that all my daughters are married, and my granddaughters not yet old enough to be betrothed, for I am sure he would make an excellent addition to the family. Mrs Long will be green with envy when we return home."

"Is it true?" Elizabeth asked Sir Matthew, who was standing in the centre of the chaos and giving a string of clear, calm commands in Egyptian.

He broke off from directing affairs and said, "It is certainly true that he has found something. Exactly what remains to be seen. He was digging in the desert and his spade hit stone. Further excavation revealed that he had hit a flight of steps leading underground, which convinced him that he had found the entrance to a tomb. However, until we know more I would advise restraint. All too often, these early excitements give way to disappointment. The steps that seem to promise access to a burial chamber turn out to be an embellishment on the plinth of a statue or some such thing, and even if they do indeed prove to be something more, then all too often the tomb has been broken into by generations of grave robbers and there is nothing left inside but rubble and broken pottery."

"Even so… do you think it could be the tomb of Aahotep's lovers?" asked Elizabeth.

"It is certainly possible—the tomb is in the area missing on the map—but it is too early to say anything except that a few steps have been found."

"You have told Edward this?" asked Darcy.

"Of course, but youth…" Sir Matthew shrugged expressively.

"Youth is optimistic," said Elizabeth.

"I was going to say foolish, but you are kinder than I," said Sir Matthew. "I would advise you to remain here in the camp until we know more."

"Good advice," said Darcy.

"But like all good advice, destined to be ignored!" said Elizabeth. "I have a mind to see the tomb, if it is a tomb, uncovered. I do not suppose I will ever have a chance to participate in such a discovery again."

"Very well, if you wish," said Sir Matthew, with a resigned look which said *Wealthy patrons must be humoured.*

"Oh, yes," said Mrs Bennet. "What fun it will be."

"There will be nothing to see for hours or even days," said Darcy. "Would you not rather wait here until the tomb is revealed?"

"I do not see why I should have to stay behind," said Mrs Bennet in an aggrieved tone of voice.

Elizabeth, better used to managing her mother, said, "Of course you must come. A little sand in the mouth and nose will not put you off, and when we enter the tomb, I am sure you will not mind the foul air and the desiccated mummies. It is more exciting than staying here in the cool of the camp, with drinks close to hand and nothing to do but gossip until we return with the treasure."

Mrs Bennet paused, openmouthed, and then said, "But someone must stay behind and look after the children. I think, after all, I am the only person reliable enough to do it."

Matters thus being settled, Elizabeth and Darcy returned to their tent, where they readied themselves for the excavation. When Elizabeth emerged, she was swathed from head to foot in a long muslin gown. She was wearing a hat to which she had attached a muslin veil. It not only would serve to keep the hot sun off her face but also would act as a useful guard against the sand which would be filling the air. Darcy wore a muslin cravat which could be pulled up and used in a similar fashion when the occasion demanded.

They were just going to join Edward, when they saw that he was with Sophie, but their tact was misplaced, for Edward brushed Sophie aside in his eagerness to continue his exploration. After a moment of looking hurt, Sophie quickly rallied and turned away from him, making a remark to Paul instead. Then, seeing Elizabeth, she said, "Might I speak to you for a moment?"

"But of course," said Elizabeth, as Darcy excused himself to speak to Sir Matthew.

"I thought I should tell you that Margaret was sleepwalking again last night," said Sophie. "Luckily, Edward and I saw her, and because we did not like to wake her, we followed her until she lay down and passed into a natural sleep, then we brought her back to the camp. She does not seem to have taken any harm from her experience; in fact, she seems in good spirits today. She is less interested in her doll than usual. I know you took it away from her, but she managed to find it again and I could not pry it out of her fingers last night. But she has put it down several times of her own accord this morning, and in another day or two I think she will forget all about it altogether. She has been far more interested in playing with her brothers and sisters, which I cannot help but think is a good thing."

"I agree," said Elizabeth. "It is lucky you saw her. I will make sure her nurse or her governess is with her throughout the night from now on, in case it happens again, but I should not worry about it. Lydia used to walk in her sleep, I remember. Papa declared it was because she was too energetic to lie down for ten hours at a time! Perhaps Margaret is more active at night here because she takes more naps in the day."

"Yes, I expect that is it," said Sophie, relieved.

"Are you coming with us to see the tomb?" asked Elizabeth.

"I am not sure…"

"Your reluctance has nothing to do with Edward being brusque, has it?" asked Elizabeth.

"It has nothing to do with Edward at all," said Sophie, with a pride Elizabeth admired. "I will certainly join you."

"Well, I am glad. I think it will be interesting."

Elizabeth joined Darcy and Edward at the head of the procession of donkeys and camels. "I knew we would find the tomb. Did I not say so all along? Oh, I know what Sir Matthew says—it might all lead to nothing—but I am convinced, Darcy. It is the tomb our fathers searched for, and now we are about to enter it and make all their sacrifices worthwhile. Just think what this will mean for all of us!"

The procession made its way across the desert with Edward and Sir Matthew at its head. To begin with, Edward led the way confidently, guided by his compass, but as they progressed his camel went more slowly as he tried to remember exactly where the steps had been found.

They retraced their path several times and then he gave a cry of elation.

"Here!"

He slid down from his camel and ran over to the spot, his feet sinking in the sand as he did so. Sir Matthew followed at a more leisurely pace.

The *fellahs*, however, slowed their steps and at last came to a halt altogether, a hundred yards away from the site. The donkeys stopped beside them.

"What is it?" asked Elizabeth as a murmuring broke out.

"They say 'Very bad place,'" translated Saeed. "'Much magic here. Very, very bad place.'"

"Which means they want more money to go on," said Sir Matthew. "It is always the way."

"No, no, *effendi*; they say it is not money," said Saeed, translating the babbling of the *fellahs*, who were huddled together as if for protection. "This place is under the sway of a magician, a very powerful magician; he has put a curse on the tomb so that no one may enter it. If they do, something terrible will happen."

"What kind of terrible thing?" asked Sir Matthew, with a twinkle in his eye.

"Something terrible," said one of the *fellahs*, who spoke a little English.

"Come, come, now, if you know so much, you must know more. Tell us what will befall us if we enter the tomb. Will we be struck down by a plague? Or will we meet with a terrible accident perhaps? Or will some afrit of the air whirl us away, or some water demon deluge us with a flood?"

Saeed translated, then translated the man's reply: "These things are not a fit subject for laughing. The magician will take his revenge."

"And how much money would persuade the men that it is worth braving the magician's wrath?" asked Sir Matthew.

Saeed consulted with them.

"They would need much money, they say. They will be risking their lives and leaving their families destitute if the curse falls upon them. This is a very bad place, they say."

As the haggling continued, Edward impatiently sprang from his camel and unfastened a spade.

"If you wish to see anything before sunset, or indeed before next week's sunset, you might care to come with me," he said to his cousins, then waded through the sand to the top of the exposed steps.

Elizabeth and Darcy followed him, curious to see what had

been found. There were five steps uncovered, with piles of sand beside them.

Edward began to dig, and Darcy, returning to the camel for another spade, joined him.

Edward gave a lopsided grin.

"I knew you had the family obsession inside you somewhere," he said. "Admit it; it is exciting."

"It might be exciting, depending on what we uncover," said Darcy.

"Well, that is a start," said Edward.

As Elizabeth watched them, she felt her own excitement stirring. The steps were beautifully preserved, and as the two men dug deeper, more were uncovered, until at last Edward gave a cry.

"A door!"

Elizabeth ran down the steps and saw what had given rise to the cry. Climbing up from the bottommost step were two stone columns: doorposts.

Edward began to dig again and then, suddenly throwing down his spade, he hurried over to the workmen, who were still arguing and haggling for more money.

"Decide," he said curtly, speaking to the men in their own language. "Either start digging, or start walking. I have no use for men who will not work."

"The magician—"

"I know all about the magician and his curse," said Edward. "Either take my money and brave the curse, or go home empty-handed. I will not have idle men on my dig."

"*Effendi*—"

"Choose," said Edward, in a tone that brooked no dissent.

There were a few more protests that the magician would appear and curse them all with a plague, but they were no more than halfhearted gestures, and before long it had all been resolved to everyone's satisfaction. The *fellahs* had almost doubled their pay, and Edward had a small army to dig for him.

Work proceeded quickly. Sand was carried away in large baskets by the donkeys, and a palisade of palm wood was erected to prevent the sides falling back into the hole. As the doorway was gradually revealed, the sand around it was drenched with water from the Nile so that the sand would remain firm. The doorposts were decorated with hieroglyphs—"Powerful spells, *effendi*"—and between them stood an unbroken door.

"The seal is intact," said Edward reverently. "We have found it."

"There speaks the voice of inexperience," said Sir Matthew dryly. "All the evidence points to this being a false entrance. There are only eight steps leading down to the door, and it would be more usual to find fifteen or sixteen steps, placing the tomb much deeper underground."

But Edward was obstinate, saying, "This is Aahotep's tomb; I know it."

"If the stories are correct—and I will admit there is no reason why they should be—but if they are, then the tomb you are searching for is not the tomb of Aahotep but the tomb of the lovers she murdered," Sir Matthew corrected him.

One of the men murmured and Saeed translated, "A tomb protected by a mighty magician, hired by the lovers' families to guard them in death. Its desecration will bring down the wrath of the magician on our heads."

"We are not going to desecrate it," said Edward. "We are going to give Aahotep a chance to make amends."

They looked at him in surprise, and Edward looked surprised himself, then said, "By showing us the treasures, of course!"

"And what, might I ask, do you intend to do with the treasures?" Sir Matthew asked.

"Display them, so that the world at large might see them," said Edward.

"The world at large, or private collectors who are willing to pay handsomely for them?" enquired Sir Matthew.

But Edward was not listening. He was examining the hieroglyphs on the doors, brushing off the clinging sand with his fingers and revealing the intensity of the bright blues and reds and yellows. The beautiful and exotic markings were so brilliantly coloured that they might have been painted the previous day, not thousands of years before.

"Look!" he said. "The lovers are here! Their names are in the cartouches."

Elizabeth saw that Sir Matthew was not convinced, despite the presence of the names. Nevertheless, he waved Edward aside and set about making a small hole in the top corner of the door.

"Is it not easier to break the seal?" asked Darcy.

"I want to discover if the passage beyond is blocked. It will help me decide how we should open the door," Sir Matthew explained.

He gave a last chip with the chisel and broke a small hole in the plaster.

A murmur went up from the *fellahs*, who stumbled back as

if expecting a djinn to appear through the hole and whirl them away on a cyclone or burn them in a geyser of flame. But when nothing happened they took courage and pressed forward again.

Sir Matthew lit a flambeau and by its light he peered through the hole.

"Well?" demanded Edward.

"The passage behind the door is not blocked," said Sir Matthew.

"Then we will soon be inside," said Edward.

"You misunderstand," said Sir Matthew.

But Edward was not listening. He was already moving his hands toward the seal. Sir Matthew intervened, breaking it with care, and before long they were through. The stale air emanating from the gaping maw was enough to convince them that the door had not been opened recently, and indeed it smelled as if it had been there since the tomb was built.

Sir Matthew put a hand on Edward's arm and advised caution, saying, "The supposedly magical plagues which affect archaeologists are often no more than natural illnesses brought about by the foul air inside these places. I suggest we withdraw to a convenient distance and take some food while the *fellahs* make the entrance safe, then rest over the heat of the day and return when the air grows cooler. We will post a guard to see that nothing is disturbed."

"And will you trust your guard?" asked Elizabeth curiously.

"I will trust my own eyes, for I will not be so far away that I cannot see what goes on," said Sir Matthew.

This plan was agreed upon. Edward could hardly eat for excitement and three times suggested that the time had come for them to return, only giving way to the opinion of others with the greatest reluctance. He paced about, full of restless energy, while the others rested.

"You do not seem very excited," said Elizabeth to Sir Matthew, who ate without haste and with an air of calm. "Do you not think we have discovered the tomb?"

"No. As I tried to explain to your young cousin, the corridor behind the door is empty. If the tomb was of any importance then I would have expected it to be blocked with stones and rubble, in an effort to keep intruders out. I think what we have here is a false tomb, a small underground chamber designed to confuse grave robbers and make them give up in disgust."

"Edward will be very disappointed," said Elizabeth.

"Disappointment is the most common feeling when searching for buried treasure," said Sir Matthew philosophically.

When the sun had passed its zenith and the air began to cool, Sir Matthew said they should proceed. Edward was greatly excited and sprang to the steps, descending them eagerly. On reaching the bottom, he covered his face with his handkerchief, for although the air was far sweeter than it had been, still it was not pleasant. Taking up a flambeau, he disappeared from view.

"Are you sure you want to go inside?" said Darcy to Elizabeth.

"I am," she said, and she followed Edward through the doorway.

By the flickering light of the torch, she saw that she was in a small chamber and that the walls were covered with paintings of strangely flat-looking people whose bodies faced forward but whose heads and legs faced to the right. The men wore simple skirts, and their bronzed torsos gleamed nakedly in the red torchlight. The women wore white gowns. Their black hair reached to their shoulders and was cut square at the ends.

There were hunting scenes and various depictions of gods and goddesses, among whom Elizabeth recognised a painting of the sun god Ra, with his head like that of a falcon and the disk of the sun above his head. Paul sketched them all with a quick, sure hand.

Edward did not stop to look at the marvellous paintings, however, but proceeded to the back of the room and then walked slowly around the walls until he came again to the door.

"I must have missed something," he said.

"You have missed nothing," said Sir Matthew. "As I suspected, this is a false tomb."

"No!" said Edward.

"Alas, yes," said Sir Matthew. "These discoveries are not infrequent; it does not do to be too disappointed."

"But I was so sure," said Edward. "I am still sure the tomb is here somewhere; I can feel it."

"I think you are right," said Sir Matthew. "You have missed the point entirely, young man. The existence of the false tomb shows us that we are on the right track. It was built in order to demoralise would-be grave robbers. If I do not miss my guess, the real tomb will be close by."

Newly energised, Edward and Sir Matthew stayed in the desert with the *fellahs*, but the rest of the party announced their intention of returning to the camp.

"Are you going to come back with us, or are you going to stay a while longer?" Elizabeth asked Sophie.

Sophie was looking at Edward, but his back was turned to her and he took no notice of her, or of the question.

If he asked her to stay, she would, thought Elizabeth, seeing the expression on Sophie's face. *She would rather have Edward, but she is not the spiritless young woman who joined us in London and she will not allow another man to hurt her as Mr Rotherham did. Paul may win her yet.*

"I have seen all I need to see," said Sophie.

"Then might I give you my arm?" asked Paul.

As the two young people set off together, Elizabeth said in exasperation, "Edward is a young fool. He sees nothing but his tomb. It has been there for thousands of years and it will still be there tomorrow."

"Whereas Sophie will not?" asked Darcy.

"No, she will not. And who can blame her?" asked Elizabeth. "Especially when a personable young man is doing his best to make himself agreeable to her."

When they arrived back at the camp, the children and Mrs Bennet were still eating luncheon. Four more places were quickly set at the informal *al fresco* tables. The meal was simple but tasty with many of the unusual dishes they had learned to appreciate in the heat of the desert. Salads of cucumber, tomatoes, and chickpeas were a staple and the sweet stuffed peppers were quickly becoming a favourite with the children, as were melons and spiced oranges. Most of the conversation was taken up with the new discovery. Mrs Bennet at first expressed a wish to see it, but Elizabeth's graphic descriptions of the unpleasant interior made a deep impression on her and she decided she would rather remain in the relative comfort of the camp.

After they had eaten and rested during the hottest part of the day, Paul set up his easel in the shade, but instead of painting any of the marvels he had seen, he asked Sophie to sit for him.

She did so gladly, and as he painted in quick, assured strokes, they talked and smiled and laughed together and Paul was obviously enchanted.

When Elizabeth walked past the easel as afternoon turned to evening, she was not surprised to see an extraordinary portrait.

"When she sees that portrait, I fear Edward's fate is sealed," she said to Darcy.

"He has made his choice," said Darcy, "although I cannot help feeling... but he had a chance to stop her leaving this afternoon, and yet he could think only of the dead."

Elizabeth shivered.

"Cold?" he asked, shrugging out of his coat and putting it round her shoulders.

"Yes," she said. "It is growing late."

"Too late for a turn around the camp?" he asked, offering her his arm.

She took it willingly and they began to stroll in the pleasant cool of the evening. There was a breeze which ruffled her hair, blowing tendrils across her face, and he turned to face her, brushing the tendrils aside and looking down into her eyes with a tenderness that made her heart turn over.

"What fools these young people are," he said. "I would like to be superior and say that I was never the same, but unfortunately that would not be true. I turned away from you just as Edward is turning away from Sophie. I cannot even plead that I did it with better cause, for I was motivated by pride, which is surely a worse reason than a desire to discover a piece of history. I cannot believe how lucky I was to be given a second chance. I only hope that Edward is given the same."

"Are you motivated by partiality?" asked Elizabeth as they walked on again.

"No. I think she would be good for him, and he for her."

"Whereas she would not be good for Paul Inkworthy?"

"I think she would be good for any man, but I doubt if he would be good for her. I have had a chance to talk to him on many occasions, and it seems to me that he is already in love with his art. I pity any woman who had to compete with that for more than a few months. A beautiful face will attract him, but when he sees one more beautiful, and one he prefers to paint?"

"So you think his interest in her is only that of an artist?"

"I am not certain of it, but I think it might be the case, yes. Only time will tell."

Elizabeth was thoughtful. "It will be interesting to see how their tangled feelings unravel themselves. But of one thing I am certain: I am glad that I am not courting again. I remember thinking that no amount of future happiness could make up for the turmoil I endured when I did not know if you loved me and if you would ever propose again."

"And were you right? Has your future happiness fallen short?" he teased her.

"No!" she said with a laugh. "Even so, it was an uncomfortable time. I would much rather be here with you now, secure in your love and happy in my marriage."

"There are times when we argue, but with that I can only agree."

Sir Matthew's prophecy had been correct. After a few days' further searching, another set of steps was found about half a mile away from the original chamber. Sir Matthew, together with Edward and the *fellahs*, worked tirelessly to excavate the steps and promised to send word to the camp when the door was reached.

And that was not the only good news. As Elizabeth sat sunning herself early one morning, she was distracted by the sound of the children arguing beyond the tents. She was spared from pursuing the problem herself by the sight of Margaret running toward them.

"Mama, Papa, Laurence has hidden my doll and won't tell me where it is," she said.

"Your doll, Meg?" asked Darcy in surprise, noticing that she held the wooden doll—still sometimes in her possession, though less than before.

Margaret looked down at the rather grubby figure disdainfully.

"Not this one, Papa," she said and threw it on the sand. "Mama bought me a beautiful new doll in Cairo with a red and green dress and sparkling veil and black slippers, and I want to play with it and Laurence won't—"

"Come with me, darling," said Mrs Bennet, getting up and taking her granddaughter's hand. "I'm sure Laurence is only teasing you and when Grandmama explains how important your new dolly is to you, he will gladly return it…"

She led Margaret away.

For a moment Darcy and Elizabeth were speechless; then they both laughed at the same time.

"Well, at last Madam Aahotep has been ousted from her

spot as most favoured toy," said Darcy, picking up the discarded doll and brushing off a few specks of sand. "Do you know, just for a moment…"

He broke off.

"Just for a moment you thought the doll was alive, inhabited by the evil spirit of Aahotep?" asked Elizabeth.

Darcy looked embarrassed.

"You were not the only one. I must confess that, for a while, so did I. And Sophie, I think, has entertained similar notions. Even Edward has once or twice said something that has made me think he distrusted it, too. But it is nothing but a doll, after all."

"And one Margaret has finally tired of," said Darcy.

"Not before time," Elizabeth replied with relief. "Here, let me take it. I will put it in my embroidery basket. Out of sight means out of mind, and I think we should do everything we can to encourage Margaret's change of heart." So saying, she took the doll from Darcy's hand and buried it deep at the bottom of her workbasket, hiding it among many skeins of wool and silk.

"I agree. It will do Meg no harm at all to concentrate on her other toys. But I wonder why the sudden change." Without being aware of it, he looked across to the direction of the new campsites beyond the oasis. Elizabeth followed his gaze.

"You are thinking that because Edward and Sir Matthew have indeed found the tomb of the two lovers, Aahotep no longer needs our daughter?" she teased him.

"It is a fascinating thought," Darcy admitted.

Elizabeth leaned across and laid a cool hand on his cheek. She knew Margaret, as his youngest daughter, held a special place in his heart and seeing her sleepwalking had frightened him more than he would ever care to admit.

"It is coincidence, nothing more, my love," she said softly.

Darcy took her hand and kissed it.

"Let us see if the children would like to go for a camel ride."

Laughing, they set off in search of their family.

The second find proved more promising than the first, and when the entire set of steps had been revealed, a new excitement filled the camp. Darcy and Elizabeth were eager to see the new discovery, and the children were no less excited. Sophie, too, expressed an inclination to visit the excavations. There was a look of lingering longing on her face, and Elizabeth thought, *So it is Edward after all. She has her pride and will not let him see it, but it is still Edward she dreams about.*

They made the journey out into the desert in the early morning, when the sun was just rising and casting pink shadows over the dunes. The dig was visible from some distance and they quickened their step until they were at the scene. Sir Matthew came to meet them, his face wreathed in smiles.

"This will be much more worth your while to inspect," were his first words as they walked toward the tunnel, which was protected with awnings.

"It was all Sir Matthew's doing," said Edward with enthusiasm. "He seemed to know exactly where to go almost as though he could have done it blindfolded."

Sir Matthew looked pleased. "Many years of experience, my young friend. When you've seen as many tombs as I have, you gain an instinct for this kind of work. Perhaps Mr and Mrs Darcy would care to see what we have uncovered so far."

Mr and Mrs Darcy did and were thrilled by the hieroglyphs embedded in the steps already uncovered, as was Paul, who had been hard at work.

"We found a chest in the first chamber," Edward continued.

Sophie congratulated him, but he hurried into the gaping hole without a word of reply.

It was left to Sir Matthew to lead them across to the awnings by the new tomb. The fantastically coloured canvas stretched far beyond the mouth of the tomb and gave much needed shade to the entrance. They descended the steps, and at the bottom they saw the final steps give way to a vast portal through which the workmen streamed continuously, carrying baskets of stones and rubble.

"Sir Matthew was right, then, when he said the entrance to the true tomb would be blocked with rubble," Darcy remarked.

"Indeed, sir. Come, you should see what has been uncovered so far. Perhaps the children should remain behind at first," Paul added. "The tunnel is quite cramped and will admit only a few at a time."

Immediately John and Laurence began to complain, but it was clear to Darcy that there would not be enough room inside for the entire family, and it was promised to the children that they would be allowed to return later. Instead, Saeed offered to take them to the false tomb with many promises of gruesome drawings, and they left eagerly enough.

"This way," Sir Matthew said, lighting a torch near the entrance.

Slowly Darcy and Elizabeth made their way down the steps,

with Sophie and Paul close behind them. They stopped to stare at the doorway. It was covered with fabulous designs of bird-headed men and slaves carrying priceless possessions. Above it all was the golden face of the sun with rays spilling away and covering all around with its life force. Against the flickering of the torch it made an eerie picture, and Elizabeth could not suppress a shudder.

They could see straightaway that the workmen had been busy. The tunnel was long and dark, barely high enough to accommodate the average man and no more than four feet wide. As they followed Edward, squeezing continuously to the side to allow the workmen to pass by them with their baskets, they saw more drawings. These seemed more intimate in nature, depicting what were clearly a man and a woman hand in hand in some designs and seated opposite each other in several frames, on boats and on land. The smell was a curious mixture of damp earth and stale air.

At the end of the tunnel were several torches and they could see, and more importantly hear, Edward talking excitedly to his mentor. He turned as they caught up with him, his eyes feverish and his words very fast.

"Darcy and Elizabeth! Is this not wonderful? And you have arrived at the most opportune moment. Sir Matthew thinks we have reached the door to the tomb itself and I am sure—yes, I am sure—he is right!"

"Is this true, Sir Matthew?" Darcy asked.

But even as they reached their friends and Paul held up his torch, he could see that they were indeed looking at another door with even more fabulous exotic drawings. As Sir

Matthew nodded, the workmen removed the last few pieces of rubble and the doorway stood in front of them, at last ready to be breached.

"I am hopeful that we will find something of great historical interest here, gentlemen, ladies," he said as he examined the door seals, brushing specks of dirt away and tracing the designs reverently. "As you can see, the hieroglyphs are much more intricate and elegant than at the false tomb—and still intact, which strongly suggests no one has ever broken through. Well, well. Now let us see what is beyond."

He took a chisel and, working slowly and with infinite patience, began to break the seal. Behind him it was almost possible to see steam coming from Edward's ears as he fought to control his own impatience. But Sir Matthew seemed unaware of his young protégé's eagerness and continued to work with a calm unhurried air.

At last he had worked his way round the entire door, and they were ready to proceed. Darcy and Elizabeth moved back to allow the *fellahs*, along with Edward and Sir Matthew, to push against the door. It seemed to take a long time and Elizabeth thought the door would never budge, but finally there was a sound of stone moving against stone and Sir Matthew's eyes widened in surprise for a moment. Then they all felt it—a waft of hot air against their faces. The tomb was open.

The *fellahs* moved back, muttering to themselves, clearly not eager to be the first into the tomb in case of some potent curse. But Edward suffered no such inhibitions. He strained against the door one last time, pushing it wide open, then picked up a torch. At the last moment he hesitated a second, then with a glance at

Sir Matthew, who nodded, he put a foot past the doorway and disappeared from their sight.

"Mr Darcy, Mrs Darcy, wait here a second," Sir Matthew cautioned. "You too, young Inkworthy. I would like to…"

He got no further. There was a shout of unbridled pleasure from within the tomb and then Edward's face appeared round the door again, covered in cobwebs and eerily flushed in the flickering orange flames of the torch.

"It is fantastic!" he cried. "You must come see immediately. But take care, the flooring seems rotten in places and some of the Nile has crept in over the aeons. Do you see?"

He held up his left foot and they saw his boot was soaking wet well up to his ankles. He disappeared again almost immediately. More cautiously, the others followed. The workmen did not.

As Elizabeth and Darcy entered the tomb they could not help but give gasps of amazement. It was as unlike the false chamber as it was possible for two spaces to be, and they both understood straightaway why Sir Matthew had been so skeptical when he saw it. This new tomb was vast, cathedral-like in its dimensions, stretching what must have been fifty feet up above them and away beyond their sight. Their footsteps echoed along the walls and back again. And in between were vast stores of possessions—chests and boxes, all gaily bedecked in the most brilliant oranges and yellows and reds, all the colours of the rainbow. A boat stretched out across the centre of the room and as they turned and surveyed the tomb, the light from their torches constantly set off hundreds of thousands of twinkling lights from jewellery that littered the whole place. It was like an exotic fairyland.

But like all stories of fairyland, there was a sinister twist. As they moved farther in, unable to take their eyes off all the treasures in front of them, Edward lurched forward suddenly. He gave a sickening cry that set Elizabeth's heart racing and then seemed to disappear right before their eyes. At the last moment Darcy caught him by his arm and dragged him back to where they were standing. Sir Matthew and Paul swept their torches down to the floor and they all gasped. The entire chamber was ringed with a moat which was invisible to the naked eye in the gloom. It needed the merciless illumination of fire to make it detectable and as they peered into its depths, Paul's foot dislodged some stones which fell into the abyss. It was at least ten seconds before they heard the sound of the pebbles hitting the floor.

"And that, gentlemen, is how the ancients kept grave robbers on their toes," said Sir Matthew dryly. "My dear sir, you must take far greater care in here."

Edward said nothing. His face was parchment white, and for a moment the excitement that had been almost tangible in his face disappeared. Then he nodded and took hold of Darcy's arm.

"My profound thanks, cousin," he said, passing his hand over his eyes.

Darcy nodded in reply and gripped his cousin's arm tightly. Then he turned to Elizabeth.

"How are you, my love?"

"Very well, Darcy," she replied, only slightly disconcerted by the wobble in her voice. "But I fear we must disappoint the children. They cannot be allowed in here now."

"Indeed not," Darcy replied fervently. "In fact I do not see how anyone can get past this obstacle."

"I have heard of this device before, Mr Darcy," said Sir Matthew, walking slowly along the moat. "It merely needs the application of some sturdy walkways to act as a temporary bridge. The moats are deep but not usually very wide. I think we will be able to accommodate such needs and then we will be able to touch these sumptuous treasures. This is truly a magnificent find. Well done, young Fitzwilliam. I confess that when you first came to me back in London with your plans, I expected that I had heard nothing more than a colourful fairy tale. But this is outstanding." He shook Edward's hand vigorously, looking very pleased.

They spent a little more time examining the treasures that were tantalisingly out of reach, taking care to keep well away from the moat. Then gradually, curiosity overcoming their fears, the *fellahs* started coming in and soon the chamber was alive with the sound of human voices for the first time in thousands of years.

Chapter 13

THERE WAS MUCH REJOICING at the camp that night. The children were allowed to stay up late and even join in at dinner, and many toasts were made to Edward and Sir Matthew, and Ammon and Husn. Edward seemed to have lost some of his obsession now that the tomb had been found, and he paid Sophie several compliments. Mrs Bennet was beside herself with joy and became tipsy early on and had to be helped to bed by Elizabeth and Sophie.

"Well, my dear," Mrs Bennet said to Sophie as she removed her bonnet. "You must be very excited. Mr Fitzwilliam is a fine young man and he will be set for life with this magnificent find. Your dear mama will be very pleased." Try as she might, Mrs Bennet could not help but allow a little envy creep into her voice as she thought once more how tiresome it was that all her daughters were already married.

But Sophie looked uncomfortable at the intimation.

"Everyone will be pleased when they hear this," said Elizabeth. "Edward's parents as well, and I am glad. Edward has had to endure a deal of teasing over his passion for Egypt but now it has proved successful. I am glad that Sir Matthew thought to send messengers to the British Embassy straight-away. The sooner people at home know of Edward's good fortune, the better."

"Oh indeed," replied Mrs Bennet, yawning.

As they returned to the others, Elizabeth put a hand companionably through Sophie's arm.

"Take no notice of my mother," she said lightly. "She has spent so long conspiring for good marriages for her daughters that she cannot stop now. I daresay she will be the same before long with Beth and then Jane and Margaret."

"Your mother only said what was on her mind, Elizabeth, and in truth I cannot blame her for her curiosity. Sometimes I wonder myself what Edward's intentions are. I thought, at first, that he liked me, but ever since reaching the dig he has been so distracted he has barely spoken two words to me. I do not blame him," she said hurriedly. "Of course it is a wonderful find and I know that what you say is true—he *has* had to listen to a great deal of discouraging comments about his love of ancient Egypt. But even so... Sometimes on this trip he has been a charming and attentive companion and I have enjoyed his company a great deal—but at other times..."

She trailed off and Elizabeth nodded.

"At other times it has been as though you barely exist. And Paul is much more consistent in his attentions."

Sophie looked up at the inky black sky with its fabulous blanket of stars. A warm night breeze ruffled the curls of her blonde hair and she looked delightful.

"Paul is also very charming, and apart from a few awkward moments at first, he has never been unpredictable. And that is a virtue I find very attractive, Elizabeth. Perhaps it is because of my misadventures last summer, but I do not intend to let anyone use me so badly again. I will not give my heart to someone who treats it as a toy to be played with—to be picked up in an idle moment and put aside when something more interesting offers itself."

If Elizabeth had believed that Sophie felt more for Paul than Edward, then she would have said no more. But she was convinced it was Edward that Sophie really wanted.

"Well," she said, "now that he has found his treasure he will have more time to spend with the living, and once his obsession has burned itself out, you will be able to discover if he is of an inconstant disposition or if this was a once in a lifetime distraction. Come, let us return to the party. The night is not yet old, and I believe Sir Matthew has many more toasts in him!"

They both laughed and returned to the table in a merry mood to see that the younger children had been escorted to bed but that William and Beth had been accorded the privilege of staying up later. Elizabeth was pleased to see her two oldest children treated with this new dignity, especially Beth, who was looking very grown-up in a long dress, with her hair in a grown-up hairstyle. Paul was talking to her gravely now, his forehead wrinkled in concern, and Beth was nodding seriously too.

"You seem very solemn," Elizabeth said. "What can Mr Inkworthy be saying?"

"Forgive me, Mrs Darcy, I did not mean to bore Miss Darcy with my problems. I was simply explaining to her about the many sketches I have managed to make over the past few weeks. I did not expect there to be such an abundance of inspiration in an arid desert and now I am running out of paper. And yet there is still so much to document, especially when we return to the tomb tomorrow with the equipment and we will be able to see up close all the marvellous treasures the tomb has to offer. I believe I will have to return to Cairo to buy some more paper, but I am loathe to leave the dig at this exciting time, and I was asking Miss Darcy if she had any paper to spare. She has already given me some pages out of her sketchbook, but I fear there is no more paper to be had."

"Hmm. A grave problem," Darcy said. "One that I had not anticipated. I admit that even I thought you would only have to make a few sketches of palm trees and camels out here."

"This is indeed a problem," Edward interrupted, looking up from his own conversation with Saeed and Sir Matthew. "But maybe one that I can solve, at least temporarily. William, would you be so good as to go to my tent and find my documents case? I think I have some spare paper there."

William jumped up from the table, returning a few moments later with the battered leather satchel Edward used to file all his documents. He pulled out a wad of papers and began sorting through them.

"There you are, Paul. I knew I had some paper to spare."

So saying he handed Paul a thick notebook. It was very old and bound in battered red leather.

"You're most kind," Paul said, taking the book and skimming through the pages. "But are you sure about this? It seems to have some writing in it."

"It belonged to my father. He gave it to me years ago when I was a boy and he thought my interest in Egypt was just a passing fad. I think he hoped I would become bored by his notes, and indeed some of them make dry reading. My father was very interested in the agricultural innovations of the farmers here. You remember the problems we have always had draining the lower fields at our estate?"

Darcy nodded. "It never seemed to improve no matter what he did."

"Well, he wrote a great deal about the yearly Nile floods, and to be honest, I nearly did throw that notebook away. But further in he talks about the journey he and your father made, and some of the entries are fascinating reading. I thought they might be useful to us and so I brought it along, but I am happy to sacrifice the empty pages to Inkworthy's art."

Even his animosity to Paul had vanished, now that the tomb had been discovered.

"Thank you," said Paul. "If you will excuse me, I will make a start. I want to make some further sketches while the images are still fresh in my mind."

He made them a bow and then left them.

The conversation returned to the magnificent find. But just as Darcy was about to refill Elizabeth's glass, one of the Egyptian servants appeared next to her with a broom in her hand.

"Apologies. I see a rat in your workbasket."

Elizabeth jumped, horrified at the idea of a rat inside her embroidery silks. Seeing her distress, Saeed walked over to the workbasket himself and felt inside.

"There is no rodent in here, Mrs Darcy. The girl is just being overzealous."

"Thank you, Saeed, you're very kind," Elizabeth said, but she felt a strange uneasiness. She, too, had thought she had seen the workbasket move, but there had been nothing inside it. Then, dismissing it as a trick of the light, she turned her attention back to the dining table, for Sir Matthew had just risen.

"I will wish you all good night, ladies and gentlemen. It's been a long day and I'm not as young as I once was."

Elizabeth thought he looked pale in the candlelight and felt another unaccountable stirring of unease. She asked him if he felt all right but he smiled as he took her hand and said, "Perfectly healthy, my dear. Just the rigours of the day catching up with me. Please stay and enjoy the rest of the evening with your family. I'll see you all in the morning and then we will see what other wonders the tomb of Ammon and Husn has to offer us."

Elizabeth watched him leave, waiting until he was safely in his tent before seating herself back at the table. She joined in the lighthearted conversation, as there was still a great deal of laughter after the excitements of the day, and soon her feelings of disquiet were put aside.

Paul had his own moment of unease on his way back to his room. As he passed the girls' room, he heard murmuring coming from inside and stopped to listen, wondering if anything was wrong. He heard Margaret crying out, and although the words were indistinct he thought he caught the words, "No," and "…ware."

"Meg, be quiet," he heard Jane say.

He wondered where the girls' nursemaid was. She was meant to be sleeping with them, after Margaret's sleepwalking episodes, but his question was answered a minute later when the nurse-maid appeared, carrying a bowl of water.

"Miss Margaret was rather hot," she explained. "I just slipped out for a minute and went to get some water to bathe her forehead. Is anything wrong?"

"No, not really. I heard Miss Margaret calling out in her sleep and I was concerned, but she seems to be sleeping again."

And with that, he passed on and returned to his own quarters. He opened the book Edward had given him and for a time he was distracted by the account of Edward's father's excursion. The ink was somewhat faded now, but the words were still legible, and they told a fascinating tale.

"...today, George and I entered the tomb of the seven priests... the guides were against the visit from the start and refused to accompany us even after we offered twice the going rate... scorpions..." Here the writing became obscured by water damage, but he could make out enough of it to interest him. The tomb they had entered was unsafe but they were determined to explore it, as they were certain it was the tomb they sought. He managed to decipher the next bit: "...there was a landslide in the tomb, and as we had foolishly entered without guides we thought we were doomed. But luckily Wickham had remained behind as he was feeling a trifle unwell, and becoming alarmed at our absence he set out in search of us. Thank God he did! He worked tirelessly to free us, bloodying his hands raw and breaking a couple of bones tearing the stones away to leave an airway for us before going for help."

Paul frowned. Wickham. The name of the third man. But Edward had never mentioned that he knew the identity of the third man.

Now why would he keep it a secret? Paul wondered.

But the lure of the empty paper was too strong, and telling himself that it was impertinent of him to interest himself in Edward's honesty—or lack of it—he set about capturing the memories in his head and setting them down on paper.

Chapter 14

SIR MATTHEW DID NOT appear at breakfast the next morning. Edward was at first impatient and then annoyed, for he was longing to be off.

"Patience," said Darcy as he drank his coffee. "I am sure he will join us before long."

But when, sometime later, Sir Matthew had still not appeared, Elizabeth said, "He did not look well last night. I think perhaps someone had better go to his tent and make sure he is all right."

"Let me," said Edward, jumping to his feet and moving off toward Sir Matthew's tent with restless energy.

He returned a few minutes later looking annoyed and said, "You were right, Elizabeth; he is not very well. He seems to have a fever. He is tossing and turning in his bed and he feels very hot. The physician should be arriving later today, but…"

Elizabeth was on her feet at once.

"I will take a look at him," she said. "It might be some hours before the physician arrives."

She made her way to Sir Matthew's tent, calling her maid

as she did so. The two women went into his tent and discovered that he was delirious.

"Bring me my medicine box," said Elizabeth, as she silently thanked Lady Potheroe for advice on which medicines to bring.

The maid departed and returned quickly, whereupon Elizabeth prepared a tincture for Sir Matthew and managed to get him to take it. Then, leaving Sir Matthew in the capable hands of his manservant, with instructions for Sir Matthew's care, she left his tent and walked back across the camp.

The air was punctuated by frightened murmurs coming from the *fellahs*, and there was a good deal of wailing as well. She spoke little Egyptian, but the sight of charms being prepared left her in no doubt as to the cause of their fear: Sir Matthew had opened the tomb, and Sir Matthew had immediately been taken ill; therefore, the tomb had been cursed.

Shaking her head, she returned gladly to Darcy and to common sense.

"I am afraid Sir Matthew will not be coming with us today," she said as she reached the breakfast tent. "He is far from well. He will be in bed for a few days at least."

"This is the worst thing that could possibly happen," said Edward, looking glum.

"It is not so bad," she reassured him. "I am sure he will be up and about again before long, but not before the *fellahs* have decided his illness is a result of a curse."

He saw her face and said, "So, it has started. They have already decided. At best, it will cost me a pretty penny to persuade them to return to the tomb, and at worst they will refuse to go anywhere near it."

"I will speak with the men and find out what they are thinking," said Saeed.

He returned ten minutes later and said, "It is not good. The men are saying that the magician is angry and that he has struck Sir Matthew down for his meddling. They are saying that Sir Matthew will be dead before nightfall."

"But that is absurd," said Elizabeth. "It is a fever, nothing more. You must tell the men, Saeed."

"It will do no good. I have already tried to reason with them but they are convinced it is the work of a magician. And that is not all. They are now saying that a djinn was in the camp last night. One of the servants has been saying that she thought there was a rat in your workbasket last night, but that when the basket was opened there was nothing there. So they are now convinced that the rocking of the basket must have been the work of an evil spirit, one of the guardians of the tomb who is intent on revenge."

"We must put a stop to this at once. If not, the men will run away and we will be alone in the camp. Even worse, they could spread their panic among the sailors and persuade them to leave, taking the boats back to Cairo," said Darcy. "The best way to halt their flight is to show them that we are not afraid. If we cannot persuade them to come with us, then we must go ourselves to the tomb, just as if nothing had happened. When they see us setting out in good spirits and then, more importantly, see us return this evening, they will soon calm down—particularly when Sir Matthew shows signs of recovery. I suggest we start as soon as we are ready. Saeed, you had better stay here to make sure that Sir Matthew is given every care and to contain the panic."

Edward lost no time in ordering the donkeys to be made ready and laden with everything they would need, as well as giving instructions for the planks of wood they would need to cross the moat to be carried between the donkeys. Their intentions were soon plain, and a pitiable wailing went up in the camp.

"Do not go, I beg of you, *effendi*," said one of the *fellahs*, clutching at Edward most pitifully. "The magician will strike you down."

"Nonsense," said Edward, his eyes strangely bright. "There is no such thing as magic. If any man here is brave enough to come with me, I will give him double wages. If not, you must all stay here and wail like women."

But neither the gold nor the jibe could sway the men, and at last Edward mounted his donkey with only Elizabeth, Darcy, Sophie, and Paul for company and a selection of guards for safety.

Saeed made one last attempt to shame the *fellahs* into picking up their spades, saying, "See, Mrs Darcy and Miss Lucas are brave enough to visit the tomb. Will you allow yourselves to be shamed by women?" But it did no good, for although the *fellahs* shuffled their feet and looked at the ground, they would not move.

"I'll come!" said Laurence, who had been trying to persuade his parents to agree to his company all morning.

"See, even a child is not afraid!" said Saeed.

But although the men shuffled even more, they would not brave the tomb.

"Laurence, you can come with us another day, when we have made it safe," said Elizabeth, "but today you must stay here. Be a good boy and do what Saeed and Grandmama tell you."

"Never mind," said Edward, seeing Laurence's face. "We will soon make it safe and then you will have your fill of excavations, I promise. I would rather have one of you than ten of these milksops," he finished, looking at the *fellahs* in disgust.

Then, without further ado, they set out for the tomb.

George Wickham stood at the front of the boat with the wind rippling his hair. He was still a handsome man, and still very charming, still attractive to women. But underneath his superficial good humour, he was soured by his failure as a young man to marry an heiress. He had at last been forced into marriage with Lydia Bennet, having run away with her to London and compromised her beyond all hope of reclaim, and still bore a grudge against Darcy, who had forced the marriage.

It was Darcy who was to blame for every ill that had befallen him since then, for if he had not been forced to marry Lydia, he could have continued his quest to find an heiress and been living a life befitting his hopes and dreams, instead of one fitting his just deserts. And if Darcy's father had not behaved so shabbily to his own father, then he would have been wealthy from birth and a gentleman of equal standing with Darcy.

But now revenge was in his reach: not the revenge he had once planned, when he had attempted to elope with Darcy's sister, but still a desirable revenge and one which was capable of making his fortune.

"I do not see why we have to live on this boat," said Lydia. "I am sure there is no fun to be had here."

She had grown tired of flirting with the sailors, and she

joined her husband at the front of the flat-bottomed boat which had brought them from Cairo and which was now moored a mile upstream of Darcy's boats.

"Because, my sweet, this is where we will find the tomb. If my father had not destroyed his piece of the map, thinking it might lead me astray, we could go to the right spot and find the tomb ourselves, but as it is, we must wait for Sir Matthew to find it and then rob it of its treasures once it has been excavated."

"I thought he had already found it."

"He has found something, but whether it is the intact tomb we do not know. It could be nothing but another false doorway."

Lydia looked out across the green banks of the Nile to the endless sand dunes beyond and said, "I hope Sef is more use than the sailor you employed to steal the other parts of the map on the ship taking Elizabeth and Darcy to Egypt. He was not only caught but put ashore, and all without getting us the map. That was a waste of a pretty penny."

"The man was a fool, but Sef is more reliable, and what we give him is a small price to pay for the information he brings us," said Wickham. "Look, here he is now."

Wickham left his place at the front of the boat and jumped down onto the bank in his eagerness to hear his spy's news.

"*Effendi*," said Sef, as he hurried toward them. "It is the tomb you seek, *effendi*. He has found it! It is full of the most beautiful treasures, and your enemy goes there even now to claim them for his own."

"Why did you not bring me news of this earlier?"

"Because I waited to discover more for you, *effendi*. Your enemies' *fellahs* refuse to go with him. They are ignorant peasants, not educated men like me, and they are convinced the tomb is cursed. Sir Matthew Rosen, he was struck down with a plague when he opened the tomb, and there is an afrit loose in the camp, so they say."

"Well, well," said Wickham thoughtfully. "And so Darcy is going to the tomb alone."

"Not alone, *effendi*. He has his cousin with him and another man and two women. Then, too, there are some guards, though they will run away at the first sound of a magical wail, and if they do not, they can be bribed. Your enemies take many palm ropes and many planks of wood. They say there is a pit inside the tomb that none may cross, and beyond it lies the treasure, gleaming and tempting. But it is cursed, *effendi*. It will bring ruin to any man who touches so much as a single cup."

"I will touch more than a cup," said Wickham. "Ready me a camel and another for any of the sailors who will come with me. Let us see if they are made of sterner stuff than Darcy's men. Load the camels with sacks and let me know when you are done. Then we will see who will come away the richer man, Darcy or I."

Despite the setback to their plans, Edward, Paul, Elizabeth, Darcy, and Sophie were in good spirits as they returned to the tomb: Edward was feverishly excited, Sophie was intrigued, Paul was eager to sketch the wonderful treasures, Elizabeth was happy for Edward, and Darcy was quietly gratified that his father had not broken his health for nothing and that his young cousin had achieved his dream.

It seemed strange to see the site so deserted, for even those men left to guard it had fled, afraid that some terrible calamity would befall them if they stayed.

Elizabeth stopped for a moment and drank in the silence. It was something she never experienced at home. There was always the noise of the servants as they moved about the house or the voices of the children, and when they were occasionally quiet, there was the ticking of a clock or the shifting of coals in the fire. But here, everything was still. The sands stretched out in every direction, gleaming under the sun-drenched sky, and even the breeze did not stir.

Then Edward dismounted and said, "Let us begin."

Without another word, he disappeared inside the tomb, leaving Paul to help Sophie dismount.

"Tether the donkeys here," said Darcy. "We can carry the treasure across the bridges in sacks and leave the sacks stacked at the foot of the steps. Then, when we have retrieved as many treasures as the donkeys can carry, we can bring the sacks up to the surface and load them onto the donkeys before returning to camp."

"If I might make a suggestion," said Paul. "If I am allowed some time to quickly sketch the treasures in their locations before we move them, we will have a record of everything we take and where it came from. It might be of some interest to scholars, and I can then paint a mural on the wall of the Egyptian gallery at Pemberley, giving an accurate feel for the discovery."

"An excellent notion," said Darcy.

They agreed, and the men began to unload the ropes and planks of palm wood while Elizabeth lit a flambeau and descended the steps into the tomb, followed by Sophie and Paul. She went through the entranceway into the vast open space and stood looking about her in renewed wonder. The pictures on the walls were as fresh as if they had been painted the day before, with their bright colours and their odd, flat people together with symbols of daily life: wine, figs, bread, grapes, lotus flowers, and rolls of linen.

"Do you know, I think I would like an Egyptian style portrait of us," she said to Darcy as he came down the steps, carrying ropes over his shoulder.

Paul, following Darcy, immediately took up the idea.

"It has never been done before," he said with enthusiasm. "Those flat shapes, those strong blocks of colour, it would make a striking painting, or I could create a mural in the Egyptian style."

"Then let us have one, by all means," said Darcy. "And we must have some of these extraordinary symbols in the painting, too. Paul, you have been making a study of it. What do they mean?"

"The phoenix is the symbol of the sun god," he said, looking at the bird that stood, man-size, next to one of the human figures. "And see here, on this painting, there is a barge, the barge that carries the sun on its night's journey. The hieroglyphs in the background must mean something, and one day they will be deciphered. The pictures of food and drink are symbols of everyday life. I could paint you with bottles of wine instead of jugs and apples instead of grapes. I could paint some of the more attractive hieroglyphs behind you, too, although their meaning would be obscure."

"And you must be surrounded by all your treasures!" said Edward.

"And what of you, Edward?" asked Elizabeth, as they progressed through the vast space, their voices echoing as though they were in a cathedral and their flambeaux flickering fitfully, shedding dancing light on the painted walls. She fell back a little and put a hand on his arm to detain him so that the others should not hear. "You must take care how you treat Sophie, you know. She has been badly hurt in the past and the time is coming when you must make your intentions plain. Before, when there was no question of a marriage between you, it was different, but now you are in a position to take a wife and you must not lead her on if your feelings are not serious."

"I mean to marry her, or at least to ask her if she will have me," he said with a quick glance at Paul, who was some way behind them. "You know her, Elizabeth. Do you think she will say yes?"

Elizabeth hesitated, and Edward was quick to notice it.

"So she has not made up her mind," he said.

"She has never been asked to," Elizabeth reminded him. "You have been obsessed with other things."

"Yes." He passed his hand over his eyes. "Obsessed. That is how it feels. As if there are times when I can see nothing, hear nothing, think of nothing but the tomb. And yet I love Sophie—"

"You love her?" asked Elizabeth.

"Yes, I love her. More than anything else in the world, I want to make her my wife."

"Then you had better let her know your feelings. You are not the only young man on the expedition, and if she feels you are not serious, then you may lose her to another young man who is."

"You are right," said Edward, looking at Paul, who was talking to Sophie. "Curse him—oh, I had better not say that here. I do not mean it!" he said to the empty space. "I do not wish any harm to come to him, only that he will not steal my treasure away from me."

They passed the model of a boat they had seen the day before—"To transport the lovers in the afterlife," he said—and when they moved on, they found several casks which were locked and too heavy to move. On the casks were cartouches, and inside the cartouches were the names, in hieroglyphs, of Ammon and Husn.

"I knew it," muttered Edward. "I knew we would find it."

And suddenly his eyes gained a glazed look, and he spoke of Sophie no more.

He hurried on and Elizabeth had to remind him that at any moment the moat would open up beneath their feet.

"You are right," he said, moving more slowly and holding his flambeau so that the flames showed the floor until at last he stood at the side of the pit.

"I wonder how many men have fallen here," mused Darcy, raising his flambeaux to show the glittering treasures on the other side. "With their eyes fixed on the gold and jewels, they would not have noticed the moat until it was too late and fallen to their deaths."

It was a sobering thought.

"We must go forward carefully," said Darcy, addressing his flushed cousin. "There is no telling what other traps lie in store for us."

The men set about laying the palm planks across the moat to

create a bridge, and when it was done Edward set one foot warily on it. The plank creaked and sprang a little under his weight but otherwise seemed safe enough.

He edged his way across and at last reached the other side.

"It is even more magnificent than we realised!" he said. "There is another door at the far side of the room. I believe there is another chamber."

"I think you had better stay here," said Darcy to Elizabeth. "The plank is very narrow and—"

But she had already hitched up the corner of her skirt and was edging her way across the plank.

"It is as Edward says," she called back. "I believe we have only scratched the surface of the tomb. It is a wonderful find. Edward's name will be on everyone's lips when we return home."

Darcy quickly followed, with Paul helping Sophie, and they gazed in awe at the treasure trove in which they found themselves. Everywhere they looked there was the glint of gold. There were statues of people and animals—"Anubis!" exclaimed Paul, going over to a statue of the jackal-headed god and examining it in awe; golden hawks—"made of wood and covered in thick gold leaf," Edward said, upon examining them; a young Egyptian man with a spear—"hunting hippos, most likely;" and the figure of a young man being reborn from a blue lotus—"the symbol of rebirth." There were urns and vases, and over the walls were pictures of a lithe young man, engaged in his everyday activities as well as a young woman in a variety of poses.

"Ammon and Husn," said Elizabeth.

"Remarkable," said Darcy.

"And about to become more so," said Edward, as he approached the door at the opposite side of the chamber.

This door, too, had been sealed, and Edward could barely restrain himself long enough to open it with the proper care. When he had done it, they tested the air for foul gases with their flambeaux as Sir Matthew had shown them, and when all seemed safe, they went through into a smaller chamber. Their way was blocked by boxes. Edward opened the first one he came across, and its contents dazzled them. There were pendants of gold inlaid with lapis lazuli, scarabs inlaid with turquoise carnelian, arm bracelets of gold inlaid with jasper, amulets of Anubis and Horus—a dazzling array of jewels and trinkets all twinkling in the dancing light. He whirled round in the centre of the room in high spirits, gazing at the blues and reds and golds that dazzled from every corner and from the magnificent sarcophagus in the centre.

Elizabeth lifted her flambeau to see the walls and gasped.

"The paintings," she said. "They are the same as the paintings on the frieze of Aahotep I saw in the British Museum, where I first met Sir Matthew."

"Aahotep must make amends," muttered Edward, reading the hieroglyphs beneath the painting.

Paul was already busily sketching, his hands moving rapidly as he sought to make a record of everything he saw in its original place.

"And now the work begins," said Darcy.

"Yes." Edward shook his head as if shaking strange imaginings away. "We have to transport the treasures back to the camp. But where to begin?"

Their activities soon became more methodical. Returning to the first antechamber, they began to wrap the smaller items and place them in the sacks, and then the men carried the sacks across the plank bridge and deposited them there, ready to be carried to the donkeys later in the day. When they had removed all the portable pieces, they went through into the farthest antechamber and began to empty the chests, filling the sacks with jewels and pausing every now and then to rest and drink, for the air was stifling. But their spirits were high and they scarcely noticed the heat or the closeness of the air, working on willingly as the morning passed into afternoon.

"I think this must be the last one," said Elizabeth, as she put a final pendant into the sack beside her.

"We can stay another hour and still be back at the camp before dark," said Edward.

"I do not doubt it, but we have run out of sacks," said Elizabeth.

Edward was startled.

"Have we really collected so much?" he asked.

"We have. The rest will have to wait. It will all be here tomorrow, and the next day, too," said Darcy.

"But will it?" asked Edward. "I don't like leaving it unguarded. I think I will sleep here tonight."

He picked up his sack, Darcy carried a second one, and Paul, with every inch of paper in his book covered in drawings, picked up a last few items and put them in his pockets. Then they made their way into the outer antechamber and went toward the bridge.

"That's odd," said Paul, who had walked more quickly than the others. "I could have sworn the planks were here."

"Have you lost them?" said Darcy jovially. "I am not surprised. You have not been back and forth all day as we have." But when he joined Paul he said, "It is not possible." He called to Edward, and Edward came up beside him. "The bridge," he said. "It has gone."

"Impossible," said Edward.

"I know. But it has."

"What is that, over there?" asked Paul, peering over the moat to the darkness beyond. "I thought I saw movement."

"I knew it!" said Edward. "The *fellahs* have overcome their fear and have come to rob the tomb. They have thrown the planks into the moat, and we were too engrossed in what we were doing to hear them."

"Not *fellahs*," said Paul, whose light shone farthest across the void, remarking in surprise, "An Englishman."

"An Englishman?" asked Darcy.

"Yes, an Englishman," came a familiar voice, which echoed and reechoed round the cavernous space.

"I must be hearing things," said Darcy.

"If you are, then I am too," said Elizabeth.

"Good afternoon, dear sister," said Wickham, coming to the edge of the moat so that the light of their flambeaux fell upon him. "What a coincidence, meeting you here."

"Sister?" asked Paul, surprised. "I had no idea you were related to Mrs Darcy. Why did you not say so when I met you in Cairo?"

"Do you two know each other?" asked Edward.

"Yes. Or, at least, we have met," said Paul. "This is Sir Mark Bellingham, the gentleman who offered me employment when I finished my work for Mr Darcy. He understood that I would be travelling down the Nile to Sir Matthew's dig but he said he would be prepared to wait. He said…"

"That talent like yours does not come along very often? That you are a genius?" asked Wickham, amused.

Paul was bewildered at the contemptuous tone in his voice.

"Then you are not a patron of the arts?" he asked as he tried to make sense of it.

"He is nothing of the kind," said Darcy grimly. "He is a liar. His name is not Sir Mark Bellingham."

"Then what is it?" asked Paul.

"Wickham," ground out Darcy.

"Wickham!" said Paul in surprise. "The man whose father joined your fathers on their ill-fated expedition?"

"*What?*" exclaimed Darcy.

"The third man. See, here, it is written in Lord Fitzwilliam's diary." He found the page and read, "…there was a landslide in the tomb, and as we had foolishly entered without guides we thought we were doomed. But luckily Wickham had remained behind as he was feeling a trifle unwell, and becoming alarmed at our absence he set out in search of us. Thank God he did! He worked tirelessly to free us, bloodying his hands raw and breaking a couple of bones tearing the stones away to leave an airway for us before going for help."

"And what did my father get for his pains?" spat Wickham. "A position as a steward! What a fine reward for risking his life to rescue two wealthy men who could have made his fortune without noticing the loss to their own pockets. And nothing has changed. Your fathers robbed my father of his rightful reward, just as you have attempted to rob me of my share of the treasure.

The map was split into three, but you did not let that trouble you. You planned your trip to Egypt and said not a word to me."

"We did not know the identity of the third man," said Darcy. "Or, at least, I did not know."

He looked hard at Edward, and Edward had the grace to look ashamed.

"I knew how you felt about Wickham," he said. "If I mentioned that his father was the third man on the expedition, I felt you would not lend me your support. I was planning to share the treasure with him, if any was found."

"And so you tricked me into it?" said Darcy. "This was a bad day's work."

"Not for me," said Wickham. "For me it has been a very good day's work. Perhaps it is cynical of me to doubt that you ever intended to share these riches, but I prefer things as they are. It was kind of you to leave the sacks of treasure all neatly stacked on this side of the moat for me and equally kind of you to leave a collection of donkeys to transport it for me."

"You will not get far," said Darcy. "You have no camp nearby—"

"But I do have a boat," said Wickham, "and soon all these treasures will be travelling with me to Cairo, where I mean to sell them to collectors and set myself up for life—something you should have done years ago, Darcy, for taking that brat of a Bennet off your hands."

"That is no way to talk of your wife," said Darcy.

"No? Well, perhaps when I have a fine house and enough money to buy myself time away from her I will not speak of her that way. Perhaps, the next time we meet, I will say she is the most charming woman on earth. Until then, I will bid you adieu."

And with that he turned on his heel and walked away, out of the flickering red light and into the blackness beyond.

"You cannot leave us here!" called Paul after him. "We cannot stay here all night; we have women with us! Return the planks at least, so that we might cross the moat."

But there was no reply.

Chapter 15

THE SOUND OF WICKHAM'S footsteps faded down the tunnel, leaving the five adventurers in stunned silence. The light from their torches was growing gradually dimmer.

"How could you not have told me?" Darcy said with too-quiet calm to Edward, who was still staring at the tunnel mouth sullenly.

"I did not think…"

"No, cousin, you certainly did not. You should have told me immediately. Quite apart from the danger you have put us in, you have brought dishonour to our family."

"What is done is done," Elizabeth said. "Let us begin to think practically. We cannot expect any help from our guards, who have either been tricked or bribed into leaving us, but we will be rescued eventually when the others back at the camp realise we have not returned. It will take some time and so we should think about preserving the light. I do not relish the thought of languishing here in pitch darkness. And we must see how much water we all have."

Since they had not expected to be imprisoned in the

tomb, their torches—wooden sticks with rags soaked in oil—
were small and light. They were not meant to last for long.
Reluctantly they agreed to extinguish all but one, and although
no one said anything, they were all thinking the same thought.
What would happen when the last torch was used up? The
tomb, which had seemed like an exotic fairyland of sparkling
jewels and priceless treasures a short while ago, was now
revealed to be a sinister repository for the dead. Elizabeth felt
her spirits sink. Her thin muslin dress, so practical in the heat
of the desert, was no protection against the dampness of the
tomb. She could almost feel the Nile waters seeping into her
bones. Seated beside her, Darcy felt her trembling and removed
his jacket.

"Here," he said, placing it round her shoulders. "Help will
soon arrive, my love."

Elizabeth nodded. "What o'clock is it?" she asked, and he
consulted his pocket watch.

"Nearly twelve."

"We started early. How soon will it be before we are missed,
do you suppose?"

Darcy hesitated. The days were still long and he doubted
anyone would begin to concern themselves before early
evening. Taking another look at the pitifully small torch, he
took a deep breath.

"Very soon. Have no fear, Elizabeth. We will be outside in
no time."

Elizabeth sighed. "I am sure you are right. Only what are we
to do until then?"

"We should look for another way out," said Darcy. "Edward,

you have made a study of Egyptian tombs. Do you think there might be another entrance?"

"It is possible. Sometimes the workmen created another exit, one which could be used to secretly remove the treasures after the tomb was sealed."

"And if not, we might come across something we can use to make another bridge," said Paul.

"A good idea," said Darcy. "I do not relish the thought of just sitting here for hours."

"Neither do I," said Sophie, glancing apprehensively at the flickering shadows that danced in black corners, making the painted faces on the friezes leer and grin.

Darcy picked up the torch and led them through the main chamber, where the treasures of the tomb had been piled up but were now depleted. He moved slowly, aware that he was carrying the only light they had. He picked his way past caskets and chests toward the back of the chamber until they had reached the wall of the cave.

"One moment, if you please, Mr Darcy," said Paul, his eyes lighting on a new frieze that had been painted onto the wall. "This is unusual. I do not think I've seen this style before."

Darcy held the torch up and they looked at the drawing. Paul was right; the painting was not like the other richly coloured ceremonial pictures which described the progress of two high status Egyptians into heaven, but was altogether more businesslike. The pigments were brown and red and seemed to be concerned mainly with two characters. One figure was twice the height of the other, a man with a crook and a flail in his hands. The other figure, depicted several times, always kneeling and in thrall to the first, was a woman, her beauty still clear for all to see but now less terrible than the many other representations they had seen of her.

"Aahotep!" Elizabeth breathed.

The likeness to the first time they had come across her painting back at the British Museum was unmistakable. She even seemed similar to the little doll Margaret had carried everywhere. But now the expression on Aahotep's face was no longer proud and vengeful. The woman in these paintings looked frightened and humbled and even a little tired.

"It seems she has been made to pay for her sins," said Sophie.

"The artistry is fascinating," Paul added, handing his sketchbook to Sophie so that he could trace the painting with his fingers. "She seems genuinely terrified of this character."

They all looked at the stern features of the man leaning down over Aahotep.

"What was it Sir Matthew said?" Darcy continued. "Aahotep was doomed by the magician Ptah to walk the earth until she had learned the error of her ways and made amends. This must be Ptah."

Edward nodded. "It makes sense. See here, he's surrounded by the head of an ibis, representing Thoth, the god of wisdom; the feather of Ma'at, goddess of justice; and the crown of Isis, who represents magic."

"Wisdom, justice, and magic," Darcy repeated. "It seems that Ptah has used all three to sentence Aahotep."

"And these symbols here," said Paul, pointing to the crook and flail the magician held. "They are usually carried by Osiris, the god of the dead."

"Aahotep must find a way to make amends," said Edward, almost in a trance.

He bent down, but Sophie was there before him as something gold caught their eyes. She bent down to pick up something which proved to be a necklace.

"How odd," she said. "It is the same necklace as the one round Aahotep's neck in the picture. I have never seen anything quite like it."

Elizabeth shivered as an eerie feeling washed over her. Darcy put his arm round her instinctively, just as a terrifying crack rent the air and the ground seemed to open up beneath her. Darcy pulled her back from the brink, but Sophie was not so lucky.

"Sophie!" Elizabeth cried, as Sophie teetered on the edge, her face a mask of horror.

Sophie swayed for a moment as she tried to regain her balance, and it seemed she would do so, but then she fell, throwing up the sketchbook and necklace as she reached for the sides of the pit.

Paul and Edward both lunged forward.

Paul threw himself at his sketchbook while Edward threw himself at Sophie, falling at full length on the ground in his effort to catch her as he let the necklace fall into the pit.

"I have you," said Edward as he looked into her panic-stricken eyes with his own suddenly clear ones. "You are safe. I will not let you go."

"My fingers are slipping," she said.

"Give me your other hand," he urged, reaching out for it.

But even as he spoke, her fingers slipped through his grip, and he could only watch in anguish as she hurtled down into the pit and landed with a sickening thud at the bottom.

"Noooooo!" cried Edward.

"Sophie!" Elizabeth called in horror. "Sophie, are you all right?"

She knelt beside Edward as Darcy thrust the torch downward to illuminate the pit. The dancing light revealed Sophie's face, now an unhealthy white in the weak illumination of the torch. Her eyes were closed and she made no reply.

"Sophie!" Edward shouted.

"Please, speak to us!" cried Elizabeth.

Slowly Sophie's eyes flickered open. She groaned and began to struggle to sit up, but then cried out with pain and sank back down again.

"Lie still, Sophie. I will soon be with you," said Edward, before pulling back and sitting up then rising to his feet.

"That pit is at least twelve feet down," Darcy said quietly. "It is a miracle she is still alive. The sides are smooth and without any footholds. I don't see how we can get down there, let alone bring her up."

"I am going down," said Edward in a tone that brooked no dissent. "I brought this upon her and I am not going to leave the woman I love alone in that hellish pit."

"So, you love her," said Darcy.

"Yes, I do, and when we get out of this situation I mean to ask her to be my wife." Adding under his breath, "If she will have me, which after today's misadventure I very much doubt."

Quickly he retrieved three of the remaining torches from their original resting place near the entrance to the tomb and returned to the pit, lighting them from their one glowing torch and handing them to Paul and Elizabeth.

"I was wrong about there being no footholds," said Darcy,

taking advantage of the better light as he peered down into the pit. "If you look carefully, you can see there are some stones sticking out around the wall. I will hold onto you for as long as I can. When you are at the bottom, I will throw a torch down to you."

Edward nodded and began to inch his way tentatively downward. Elizabeth held the torch as near to him as she could in order to give him as much help as possible in seeing stones to balance on and crevices in which to slide his feet, while Darcy took a firm grip on his shirt.

"Be brave, Sophie," Elizabeth shouted as Edward cautiously descended. "You will soon have company." But this time there was no answering call, and she and Darcy exchanged worried glances.

There was a frightening moment when Edward slipped, but at the last minute he managed to regain a foothold. He jumped the last few feet and they heard the echoey thump of his boots on the packed earth before seeing him gather Sophie into his arms. He pulled her closer and as he kissed her, Elizabeth nudged Darcy's hand so that the torch no longer shone on the young couple.

"If you see Edward kissing her, you will have to speak to him sternly about it," she said. "They are not yet betrothed."

"But if I do not see it?"

"Then you will not have to object!"

Then Sophie's weak voice could be heard as it echoed round the walls, saying, "You ignored the necklace. You saved me!"

"And you saved me. When you fell, it cut through the strange obsession which has gripped me these past few months. I knew I did not care if I never saw another tomb again, but I could not live without you. Sophie, this is neither the time nor the place, but I cannot wait any longer. Will you marry me?"

And around the walls reverberated the echo, "Yes... yes... yes."

Elizabeth glanced at Paul, and for a moment he looked downcast, but then a look of calm dawned on his face and Elizabeth thought, *He loves her but he loves his art more, and now he realises it and he has accepted it.*

After giving the newly engaged couple a little more time, Darcy called down, "Are you ready for the torch, Edward?"

"Yes, cousin."

Darcy threw the torch down and they saw Edward hurry to pick it up before it was completely extinguished. In the flare of light from the pit they saw that Edward was now examining her.

"How badly is she hurt?" called Elizabeth.

"I cannot tell in this gloom. I think her arm may be broken," said Edward. "We must get her out of here as quickly as possible. I will look around down here and see if there is anything that will help, a piece of rope perhaps or something similar."

His torch began to move, and suddenly they heard him give an exclamation.

"Good lord!" he said. "There is something down here. Can you see this?" He moved the torch until it lit something large and made of gold. "It is a small sarcophagus. And lying on top of it... the necklace. Almost as if it led us here," he added musingly.

"Were the Egyptian dead not often buried with objects that would be useful to them in the afterlife?" asked Elizabeth. "Perhaps there will be something in the sarcophagus we can use."

"It is worth a try," said Edward as he knelt and examined the gold box. "There are no carvings of any kind on it and the lid is far heavier than I would have expected. I cannot remove it—hello, what's this?" He sat back on his heels. "Really, I can hardly—"

"What is it, Edward?" Elizabeth shouted impatiently.

"The sarcophagus," breathed Edward. "The markings on the lid are quite clear. This is the sarcophagus of Aahotep."

Back at the camp, Mrs Bennet sat beside Sir Matthew's bedside with a cloth in her hand.

"…and as soon as Mr Bingley moved into the neighbourhood, I knew he would end up marrying one of my girls, for as I said to Mr Bennet—"

"Grandmama," protested Beth, trying to halt Mrs Bennet's endless flow of words.

But Mrs Bennet was enjoying herself and ignored her.

"'Jane cannot be so beautiful for nothing.' And so it proved, for…"

Beth gave up and took the cloth out of her grandmama's hand so that she could bathe Sir Matthew's head, while outside, she heard William speaking in a dignified voice to Saeed. He, like Beth, had taken quiet charge when Mrs Bennet had proved to be unequal to the task. And while the younger children played, they helped Saeed restore some calm to the camp.

But as the day progressed, Beth was painfully aware how inadequate her actions were. Sir Matthew occasionally roused himself and apologised for inconveniencing her, but he was getting worse and there was little she could do. Mrs Bennet, tiring of the sickroom, retired to her tent with her nerves, so that Beth hoped her parents would be back soon.

As she sat and pondered, Saeed entered the tent. To her relief, Beth saw that he was accompanied by a new arrival, the camp physician.

"Here is Mr Knight," said Saeed as the physician took in the situation at a glance.

"Well, well, young lady, and so you are the nurse? And doing a very good job, I see. If I can just…" Mr Knight made a quick examination of Sir Matthew and then smiled reassuringly at Beth. "We'll have him up and about again in no time, you just leave him to me. Now you go off and play, my dear, or whatever it is young ladies like to do." He smiled kindly at her and Beth gladly gave up her place at Sir Matthew's side, going out of the tent and looking for William so that she could give him the news.

But when she found him, she found that her troubles, far from being over, were only just beginning.

"Have you seen Meg?" he asked.

"No. Why?" asked Beth.

"Because she seems to be missing."

"Are you sure?" asked Beth. "Is she not with her nurse?"

"No. She complained of a headache and her nurse took her to rest in her tent, but when Laurence and Jane wanted to play with her, having been set free by their tutors for an hour, they could not find her. They called John to help them but he could not find any trace of her either."

They exchanged worried glances as Saeed joined them. There was a small commotion by the girls' tent. Margaret's nursemaid, Jenny, was in tears.

"I swear I don't know what happened, miss. One minute she

was sleeping like an angel and I only popped out for a moment, and when I returned I couldn't find her anywhere."

As Beth tried to calm her down and make sense of what she was saying, Saeed glanced over at the *fellahs* congregating nearby, their murmurings unquiet.

"Please excuse me one moment, Miss Darcy," he said and walked over to them.

Beth nodded distractedly as William and John appeared with Laurence and Jane.

"It's no good; we can't find her anywhere," Laurence said.

"When do you last remember seeing her?" Beth asked, her mind whirling with this new problem on top of Sir Matthew and the *fellahs*.

"Not since breakfast," said John.

Beth noticed Jane's expression and said, "What is it?"

"I think Aahotep's been talking to her again," Jane said.

"What do you mean?" asked Beth.

"I know it's silly, but Meg thinks that horrid doll talks to her and whenever she does, Meg goes all red and hardly speaks to anyone. She's been all right for the past few days, but a few hours ago she started acting strange, and she was carrying her doll again. And just before I saw her last, she was arguing with the horrid thing and saying she didn't like the tomb because it smelled, but I think that's where she's gone."

From behind John's arm, Laurence seemed about to make some rude remark about girls and their dolls, before he was wrestled away by his older brother.

Beth was troubled but sent Jane and Laurence to find Mrs Bennet. "Tell Grandmama it is time for luncheon," she said.

"But what about Meg?"

"William and I will decide what to do, and Mr Massri will help us."

As she said this, Saeed came back to her. His expression was, if anything, even graver, and Beth felt her heart sink. But she was a Darcy, with the true Darcy spirit, and she was not about to give way to nerves like her grandmama. Instead, she was determined to make her parents proud.

"This is very bad, Miss Darcy. The *fellahs* say they saw the little girl wandering into the desert some time ago."

"Why did they not stop her?" she asked.

"Because they believe she is being influenced by great magic, and it would be bad luck to interfere with the vessel the spirits are working through."

"What nonsense!" said William, with an arrogance that made him sound just like his father. "She is probably looking for Mama and Papa. She never likes to be left behind and once followed them halfway down the street in London when they were going to walk in the park because she wanted to go too."

Beth was not sure whether he believed it, but she was glad of William's calm sense and commonplace explanation.

"William is right," she said. "We must find her and bring her back to the camp before we make any other decisions."

Saeed looked anxiously back at the *fellahs*. "They won't wait much longer."

"I can't help that, Mr Massri. Leaving Mama and Papa is one thing, but we cannot just allow Meg to wander the desert alone. You must do as you think fit, but William and I will look for her."

Saeed looked at her intently. She was so young and yet so much more sensible than Mrs Bennet, who had refused to speak to him after he had tried to get her to understand the gravity of the situation.

"Very well," he said reluctantly. "I will come with you and leave Josef in charge. He is reliable and will take care of those left in the camp, though I fear he will not be able to stop the *fellahs* leaving if they make their minds up to it."

"Then let us leave with all speed, Mr Massri," said Beth lifting her chin stubbornly, "and pray it does not come to that."

Elizabeth and Darcy sat in the damp silence of the tomb, listening to the soft murmurings of Sophie and Edward beneath them. Elizabeth dared not ask Darcy again what the time was. She had done so already three times, and it was still barely two in the afternoon. She leaned a little closer to him and he put an arm around her shoulder.

"Well, you have had your adventure now, my love," said Darcy, kissing her forehead gently. Elizabeth grimaced.

"This was not what I had in mind all those months ago at Pemberley," she admitted. "If ever I seem inclined to wander again from the safety of my home, remind me of this."

She glanced around at the ever encroaching darkness. The torch was gradually dimming, and she was sure she had heard the soft scurrying of rats—or something else she did not even want to think about.

Darcy laughed. "Even if I did, it would do no good. It will take more than this to dim your spirit. In a few months time it will be Christmas, and we will be shivering with the cold and you will be wishing yourself back in the desert," he replied.

"We will be celebrating with a great fat goose in front of a roaring fire," said Elizabeth, taking new heart from the cheerful thought. "And I may pine for the heat of the desert, but I can assure you I will never pine for this soft dampness oozing into my bones."

"I must agree with you on that—" Darcy began, but then they heard Edward's voice, attempting a loud whisper.

"What is it, Edward?" Darcy leaned forward and stared down.

He could just see Edward's white, strained face.

"It's Sophie," he said in concern. "I think she is delirious."

Elizabeth leaned over.

"It must be the heat. Do you need more water, Edward?" she asked.

They had thrown down one of the two canteens they had left after Wickham had gone. There was very little left in their own now, but if it would help Sophie, she would gladly give it.

"I think it might help."

Elizabeth threw down the canteen, and Darcy included Edward in their conversation to take the young man's mind off the fears of the present. But Darcy couldn't stop himself at last from looking at his pocket watch. It was only just after two in the afternoon and he very much feared the torches would not last much longer. And then all five of them would be sitting in the pitch black.

"I cannot see how she could have come so far," Saeed said for the fifth time in ten minutes.

Beth said nothing. Seated atop the camel, with William behind her, she looked back from where they had come. The camp was nowhere to be seen.

"She could be anywhere now," Saeed added. "I wonder if perhaps we should return to—"

"We should go to the tomb," said Beth.

"I doubt very much that Miss Margaret will be there, Miss Darcy," Saeed said politely. "It is a long way away and she has no idea—"

"No doubt you are right, Mr Massri, and at any other time I'm sure I would agree with you. But my sister Jane said that Margaret mentioned the tomb and that is where she will be going," Beth said clearly.

There was a silence. It seemed ludicrous that a little girl out on her own walking across a desert would have any idea how to reach the tomb. But eventually even Saeed nodded.

"It is as good a place as any to look," he said at last.

Chapter 16

THE TORCHES WERE VERY near the end of their life. Darcy could see there was hardly anything left to fuel them and even from twelve feet away he could hear Sophie moaning.

"It will not be much longer now, Edward," Darcy shouted down to him. "Very soon Sir Matthew will be coming through the tunnel entrance with a hundred *fellahs*."

"I pray you are right, Darcy," Edward replied. "Sophie's colour is ghastly and she will not drink even though she looks parched."

From above they saw him try to press the canteen to Sophie's lips, to no avail. The light from Edward's torch was almost gone, and things looked bleak.

"We have to do something," said Elizabeth. "If we look around, perhaps we can find something…"

"Yes," said Paul, even though they had looked around several times already and found nothing of use.

Elizabeth began searching again, but before long, the final flames flickered and died on the torch beside them. A few moments later they lost sight of Edward too, as his torch went out, and they were all plunged into darkness.

"Edward!" Darcy shouted.

"I am still here, cousin, but talk to me, please. I feel very alone down here. And as for Sophie… If anything happens to her, Darcy, I will never forgive myself."

"None of this is your fault," said Darcy.

"No?" said Edward. "I lied to you and deceived you, luring you into a trip that could very well end your life, and I have no idea why I did it. I was like a man possessed. I—"

"What was that?" Darcy cut across him.

"What?" Elizabeth strained her ears, immediately alert as she felt a change in him.

"Listen. Again. There, do you hear it?" Darcy asked.

"I hear it," said Paul, in a voice full of hope.

Elizabeth strained her ears. "I hear nothing—" she began, and then she stopped. At first it seemed as though there was the scratching of some tiny creature, and then the noises seemed to grow.

"It's someone calling your name, Darcy. A voice, calling for—"

"Papa! Papa! Where are you?" came the sudden pure voice of a little girl, cutting through the blackness around them.

"Meg? Is that you?" Darcy shouted in astonishment, and as he turned to the sound of his youngest daughter, there was the faintest flicker of light in the distance near the tunnel entrance, the warm welcome glow of an orange flame illuminating the darkness around them.

"Papa, where are you?"

Suddenly they heard other voices too, Beth and Saeed, and although they could barely believe it, William was there as well. Within minutes there were several torches bobbing and weaving their way down the tunnel into the tomb.

"Edward, we are saved!" Paul cried.

"Thank the Lord," came the heartfelt reply from below.

"Beware of the moat!" cried Elizabeth to the children.

Darcy and Elizabeth turned their backs on Edward's pit and went toward the bobbing lights, stepping carefully so that they did not stumble and keeping their eyes on their feet so that they did not fall down the moat themselves.

"What happened, Mama? Why are you and Papa standing here in the dark?" asked Beth.

"And where are the donkeys?" asked William.

"More to the point, what are you doing here?" asked Elizabeth, her fear turning to anger once she saw they were safe. "And why did you bring Margaret with you? She is far too young to be here." For Margaret was sitting on the edge of the moat.

"We had to come. Margaret wandered out of the camp and we followed her here," Beth said.

"Is that so?" asked Darcy. "Children, I am proud of you."

Elizabeth was about to protest when she caught the glow on William's face as he heard his father's words and her angry words died on her lips.

Darcy is right, she thought. *He is not a little boy anymore. And look at Beth, a young woman almost. And both of them sensible and intelligent.* And so she put her fears and admonition aside and said, "Your father is right. You are a credit to us."

"I'm glad we found you, Papa," sighed Meg. "Aahotep said I helped her find the tomb so that she could say she was sorry to Ammon and Husn, and so she was going to help me to find you and Mama before she went to her rest. She used to be very bad but she's not very bad anymore, she's just tired and sorry and she's glad you're safe."

Darcy took Elizabeth's hand and gave it a squeeze as William and Beth put a protective hand on each of Margaret's shoulders.

"What happened here?" asked Saeed. "Why are you in the dark? And where is the bridge? How did you get across the moat? And why did you not come back when your torches went out?"

"A long story," said Darcy, "and one which will be better told when we are out of the tomb."

Saeed nodded and set to work. The planks were lying on the other side of the moat and he and William pushed them across again so that Darcy and Elizabeth could embed them in the dirt.

"We need ropes and more planks," said Darcy. "Miss Lucas is hurt. She has fallen down a pit and we must get her out. I fear that she is in some danger if we do not get her back to the camp right away. Has the physician arrived yet?"

"He has, *effendi*," said Saeed.

"Good," said Darcy with relief.

They were all together now, the new arrivals having crossed the bridge. The men set to work by the light of the torches, lowering further planks to Edward so that he could make a makeshift bed for Sophie to be lifted out on, while Elizabeth hugged her children.

"Now, Beth, tell me what has been happening since this morning," she said to her daughter. "If I am not mistaken, you have a great deal to say."

Beth explained everything as the men worked, ending with "…Meg was almost here by the time we caught up with her. It is a miracle she got so far in so short a time. We had camels but she was walking. And Mr Massri is still unclear as to how she knew the way. But as we arrived she insisted we let her down and really she ran in before we could stop her, which is odd considering how frightened she was the other day when we visited the false tomb."

"Yes, it is," said Elizabeth, stroking her daughter's hair.

By now the men had managed to place Sophie on a makeshift stretcher and they were lifting her to safety. Elizabeth knelt down beside Sophie as soon as she was clear of the pit. Her face was a sickly white colour, but at least she was quiet at last.

"So the *fellahs* refused to come here," Darcy said to Saeed as he threw down a rope for Edward and Edward climbed out of the pit.

"I'm afraid so, Mr Darcy," Saeed admitted. "There was nothing I could do to get them to accompany me. They are simple people, easily frightened. They believe in magic and curses and all kinds of superstitions."

"Possibly," Darcy said quietly. "But I wonder if it really is all superstition."

Beside him Edward nodded. "There seems to be much that they understand better than we do," he agreed, looking down at the pit. Far below, the gold sarcophagus lay. It looked no different now than it had done half an hour before, but it felt very different. It felt as though the bones inside it were at peace.

"Time for us to go," Darcy said, lifting Meg in his arms.

As he shifted her into a more comfortable position on his shoulder, something dropped from her grasp. It was the little doll, now thoroughly drab and dirty from being held so long in tiny, grubby hands. Elizabeth picked it up.

"I do not think Meg wants this anymore," she said, looking at the face. "And I do not think the doll wants Meg. Aahotep has found her way home and made amends. It seems she was buried here, with her victims, though her spirit was far away. But now it will no longer have to wander the earth. It can rest in peace."

As she spoke, the doll seemed to shrink in her hands. She looked at it closely and saw that the painted-on eyes had been all but rubbed out, the mouth almost nonexistent. It was hard to believe they had ever found anything malevolent about it. It was just a worn-out toy.

"Put it where it belongs," Darcy suggested, and with a nod Elizabeth threw it down into the pit, where it landed on the sarcophagus.

As they moved off toward the entrance to the tunnel, Elizabeth could have sworn she heard the faintest hint of a laugh, and the paintings on the walls seemed to be smiling. But when she turned back, there was only the blackness swallowing up the tomb again.

She followed the others into the bright sunlight of the desert and felt Darcy's arm go round her shoulders. She put her arm around his waist and breathed in deeply, inhaling the sweet, fresh air with relief.

Back at the camp they found more good news waiting for them. Sir Matthew was no longer tossing and turning feverishly in his bed but was sleeping peacefully. It was Mrs Bennet who conveyed this piece of news, ascribing it to her own efforts, but

Elizabeth more wisely ascribed it to the efforts of Beth before she had left the camp and to Mr Knight, who had tended to Sir Matthew ever since.

His improvement had done much to allay the *fellahs'* concern, and they had been persuaded to stay on a little longer when the Darcys returned. The guards, too, had returned, coming into camp shamefacedly, as they were forced to admit they had run away at the sound of mysterious wailing in the desert and at the sight of a fleeing man who had told them to run because their excavations had angered the dead and an afrit was on its way.

The stories of fabulous treasure lying unclaimed in the tomb tempted the *fellahs* further, and they seemed at last to overcome their fear of the curse. If Sir Matthew was not going to die, then why should they, who were only humble servants, be struck down? And if they were not going to be struck down, why should they not benefit from the enormous amount of money they were being offered to bring the remaining treasures back to camp?

The camp physician set Sophie's broken arm and seemed confident that it would heal well. By the following day, she was well enough to sit in the shade, while Edward sat beside her and brought her drinks and fruits and anything else that would help restore her to vigor. Sir Matthew was still in bed, but he was so much better that he was able to sit up and take an interest in everything they had to tell him.

Saeed returned to the tomb with the *fellahs*, and Paul elected to go with them. Since leaping for his sketchbook at the expense of Sophie, he had been effacing himself and Elizabeth guessed he was glad of an excuse to leave the camp.

"It will take some time to empty the tomb," said Edward to Darcy as he sat contentedly by Sophie's side, while Sophie herself recovered from her ordeal by reclining against him. "Perhaps you will wish to remain in Egypt until everything has been cataloged and removed from the tomb, but I, for one, will be content to return home just as soon as I have rescued enough treasures to enable me to present myself to Sir William Lucas. My obsession with Egypt is over. As soon as we have Sir William's consent, Sophie and I intend to marry without delay."

"You must marry by special licence," said Mrs Bennet in delight. "And you must invite us all to the wedding."

"How could we not," asked Edward, "when you have been with us every step of the way?"

"I think we, too, are ready to go home," said Darcy.

He looked at Elizabeth, and she agreed.

"It has been a splendid adventure, but I confess I am ready to see Pemberley again."

"If we are really all agreed then I suggest we return to Cairo the day after tomorrow," said Darcy. "Sir Matthew should be up and about again then, and he has Saeed to help him until he has made a full recovery. There will be a lot of formalities to attend to in Cairo and a lot of people to notify of our find, and it will take some time to make arrangements for our return journey, but as soon as possible we will be on our way."

Saeed offered to go to the boats and tell the *reis* to make everything ready for their departure, and when he returned he was laughing.

"Ah, *effendi*, there is such talk on the river! Your enemy returned to his boat yesterday with donkeys loaded down with treasures. He put them all on his boat and said the *reis* must set sail. The *reis* said he would not—there were too many treasures; the boat would sink!—but your enemy had his way. Then the boat ran aground on a sandbank and the *fellahs* made off with the treasures. Not honest *fellahs* like the *fellahs* here—thieves, *effendi*! And when your enemy swam to the bank, it is said that the crocodiles chased him all the way."

"Well, I am glad your enemy was routed," said Mrs Bennet, adding, "Who is your enemy?"

Elizabeth, in the middle of her laughter, said it was no one. It did not seem the right time to enlighten Mrs Bennet; indeed, she thought the time would never come, and Mrs Bennet soon ceased to enquire. There were far more interesting things to do, such as eating dates and arguing with Laurence about the likelihood of him being allowed to keep a crocodile in the lake at Pemberley.

Epilogue

It was a year to the day since Edward had walked into the drawing room at Darcy House and announced his intention of visiting Sir Matthew at the British Museum. Elizabeth and Darcy had been back in England for months and were walking arm-in-arm through the gallery at Pemberley. Older paintings had been rehung or moved into the attic, so that one entire wall was now full of the paintings and sketches Paul had made both during and since the trip. In pride of place along the end wall was a mural in Egyptian style of their entire party discovering the tomb. The ochres, reds, and golds were bright next to the subtle colours of the Old Masters hanging on the other walls, and the large, flat shapes were an interesting contrast to the detailed sculptures that stood in the corners.

"It is hard to remember the terrible heat we endured in Egypt!" said Elizabeth as she looked at the pictures, drawing her shawl around her shoulders as she did so, for although the spring sunshine poured into the gallery, as yet it had no warmth.

"Paul has caught it very well," said Darcy, looking at the shimmer hanging over the pyramids in a large landscape.

"And just look at Laurence on this camel!" said Elizabeth, stopping by one particularly fine painting. "Is that not exactly his expression!"

"Laurence's? Or the camel's?" Darcy teased her.

"Both!"

Laurence was looking absolutely delighted, and the camel was looking disdainful as it walked past an oasis glowing with jewelled waters and inviting patches of shade.

The sound of carriage wheels crunching on the drive below distracted Elizabeth and Darcy from the paintings, and Elizabeth walked over to the window.

"I do believe the first of our guests have arrived," she said.

The carriage drew to a halt and Mr and Mrs Edward Fitzwilliam stepped out. They were both looking well and had an undeniable spring in their step. Edward jumped out of the carriage and then turned to help Sophie as she sprang nimbly down the steps. They were both elegantly dressed in the latest fashions, as befit their newfound wealth.

"We had better go and greet them," said Darcy. "It was an excellent idea of yours to have a house party for all the adventurers so that we could relive the trip and see Paul's work all together for the first time."

"And how lucky we were that Sir Matthew was back in England and that he could spare the time to join us," said Elizabeth as they went downstairs. "He will be here by midday."

"Paul, too. He is much sought after these days and has one of the most fashionable studios in London."

"It is ironic, is it not, that it is his portrait of Sophie which made his name?" said Elizabeth. "I am surprised he let Edward buy it."

"I think he felt he could not refuse. Besides, once he had exhibited it, he had no more use for it. I fear it reminded him of a moment he would rather forget."

"Yes, it was not well done of him to leave Sophie to plunge to her doom!"

"But it was very well done of Edward to catch her," said Darcy. "I never expected, this time last year, to have so much to worry about with my young cousin or to have so much to feel proud about when he found his true self."

"Sophie looks well," said Elizabeth as the butler opened the door.

"Yes, very well," said Darcy.

There were cries of greeting and Elizabeth ran down the steps to welcome her guests, kissing them both with delight and then standing back so that Darcy could shake Edward by the hand. Then she ushered her guests into the house. Once rid of their outdoor clothing, she led them through into the drawing room and asked about their journey.

"It was well enough, but I would have liked it more if we had come by ship!" said Sophie. "I find I miss the sea."

"I would rather have come by camel," said Edward.

"You came by camel?" enquired an excited voice as Laurence ran into the room.

"Alas, no," Edward admitted. "But I would have if it had been possible."

"Papa has promised me a camel to ride around Pemberley," said Laurence blithely.

"Papa has done no such thing," said Darcy. "You will have to make do with a horse like everyone else."

"Why, Beth, how grown-up you look!" exclaimed Sophie. "Your hair is most becoming. I like that style very well indeed, and your gown is delectable. Let me see!"

She admired the gown as Beth spun slowly so that she could see it from all sides.

William walked into the room with exactly his father's walk. John followed and greeted his guests with a bow. Jane entered behind them, and Margaret came afterward.

Sophie looked questioningly at Elizabeth, who smiled and nodded, and then she bent down to speak to Margaret.

"You look very well, Meg."

In response, Margaret put her arms round Sophie's neck and gave her a kiss.

"She has never mentioned the doll again?" asked Sophie as she and Elizabeth drew a little to one side, while Edward made a fuss of the children, drawing a bag of sweetmeats from his pocket.

"No, never," said Elizabeth. "Our little Margaret is herself again."

She looked fondly at Meg, who was just helping herself to a sweet and popping it into her mouth.

"And you?" asked Elizabeth. "How is your arm?"

"In full working order," Sophie replied with a smile, "although sometimes in the cold it aches. I fear I shall turn into a mad aunt who prophesies rain whenever a dark cloud appears."

"You shall be no such thing. And how is married life?"

"More than I could even have dreamed of! I feel like I am reborn. Marriage to Edward is wonderful."

"Good! Then you will not mind meeting Paul here?"

"On the contrary, I am looking forward to it. I am very pleased for him. He has made his mark in the world, and I am happy that in some small way I helped him to do that. And I am very grateful to him for the marvellous portrait he painted of me. It is too flattering, of course, but Edward insisted on hanging it over the mantelpiece, and so there it stays."

"And Edward is himself again?"

"Yes, entirely."

Elizabeth invited her to sit down, and the men followed suit, still talking to the children.

"And how do you like Edward's family?"

"Very well. They were a little intimidating to begin with, particularly his father, but they have all accustomed themselves to the idea of the marriage. Anne and her husband helped by saying what a good idea it was, how well matched we were, and how lucky it was that we had enough to settle on. They helped bring Edward's family round."

Refreshments were brought in, but hardly had the drinks been poured when another carriage pulled up in front of Pemberley and out of it stepped Mrs Bennet and Paul Inkworthy.

Elizabeth felt a momentary sadness that her father was not with them, but he was visiting Jane and intended to travel with his eldest daughter when she visited Pemberley the following week.

"Was this not fortunate?" said Mrs Bennet as she entered the drawing room a few minutes later. "Mr Inkworthy and I met at the coaching inn and he insisted on bringing me on in his carriage, for you know your father could not let me have our carriage and so I had to come in a hack."

Paul smiled and bowed and tried to look as though he had

been delighted to find himself with Mrs Bennet's company for the final stage of his journey.

He was looking much better than he had when he had joined their party as they set out for Egypt. Then he had been thin and pale; now he was looking healthy and prosperous.

There was an awkward moment as he saw Sophie, but then he made her a bow and she said how glad she was to see him, and the moment passed. He moved on into the room and began talking to Beth, praising one of her watercolours which hung beside the fireplace.

Their party was completed when Sir Matthew arrived, and they went in to luncheon.

The talk was convivial. They relived their adventures and caught up on all the news, and there was much merriment.

"I wanted Lydia and Wickham to accompany me," said Mrs Bennet. "Lydia was eager to come, but Wickham said they had a previous engagement. It is a pity, for I am sure they would have liked to have seen the pictures of Egypt. They have never been to Egypt, nor are they likely to ever go. Wickham has not had the luck he should have had with his profession. If *some people*," she said, looking straight at Darcy, "had given him the help he deserved, he would have been prime minister by now, and I daresay visited Egypt every year."

This remark was wisely ignored as the main course dishes were removed and various fruits and desserts were brought in. As well as apples and pears from the Pemberley orchards, there were figs and dates to remind the party of their sojourn in Egypt.

"And how are you now, Sir Matthew?" asked Darcy of his older guest. Sir Matthew smiled.

"Perfectly recovered, as you can see, my dear sir. The rigours of illness in Egypt can be frightening while they last, but all things pass."

"I am glad to hear it," Darcy replied. "However, I believe you must be of a hardy stock, sir. When my father became ill in Egypt many years ago, my mother feared the worst."

"My commiserations. Perhaps I should have said the rigours of a curse. My illness certainly concerned the *fellahs* at the dig. But since they thought it originated from a powerful magician intent on keeping an evil spirit at bay, I suppose one cannot completely blame them."

Darcy looked over quickly to his other guests, but they were engrossed in the story Edward was telling about the sun god Ra and no one took any notice of the two older men.

"I have often wondered about the curse, Sir Matthew," Darcy said. "Here in England it seems nothing more than a tale to amuse children on long winter nights. And yet sometimes I cannot help but wonder if perhaps there was some spirit at work on that day in the tomb. Almost everything that happened I can attribute to a simple explanation. And yet…"

"And yet still you wonder if there really was a tired restless soul longing for peace who took us to the site where so many others have failed?"

Darcy nodded. "Margaret has no memory of it now, but for the time we were travelling she took her doll everywhere— refused to be parted from it, in fact. Indeed, on at least one occasion, my wife removed it from her and hid it where it could not be found and still it made its way back to her. And without Meg…"

He trailed off. Without Meg wandering off by herself into

the desert, it seemed likely they might not have survived. Sophie almost certainly would have died, and all Edward's treasure would have availed him nothing.

"It is strange, is it not?" Sir Matthew agreed gently. He seemed to be about to say something else, but just then Elizabeth stood up and gaily declared the art gallery open and ready to be visited properly. Amid much laughter the entire company followed her.

For a good hour they walked up and down the gallery, admiring the paintings, much to Paul's embarrassment. Mrs Bennet insisted on taking his arm and making him explain every single nuance to her and then spoiling the effect by hardly listening to a word he said. The younger children became bored after a while and soon ran off to the kitchens, where they knew the cook would have pastries for them. But Beth and William remained and the atmosphere grew quieter as at last they all found themselves in front of the largest painting, a group picture of the family in front of the lost tomb.

Paul, it was agreed, had outdone himself with this picture. The sun was a fierce orange ball hanging low in the sky in the late afternoon, and although the sky was a bright blue and the green of the palm trees contrasted strikingly against it, there were shadows in the corners that added a somewhat sinister cast to the painting. Darcy and Elizabeth were seated in prominence in the middle of the picture, with Sophie and Edward admiring a large golden vase slightly to their left. The children were dotted around the painting in various poses, Laurence atop a camel, which had pleased him greatly. Margaret sat on her mother's lap, a doll in her hands, which could have been made of wood or just dressed in sombre browns. The little girl was pointing to the doorway of the tomb, which was shrouded in even more shadows. From within the tomb it was just possible to see flickering candlelight.

"A most striking depiction, young man," Sir Matthew said, taking a pince-nez from his waistcoat pocket and peering closely at the painting.

"It is marvellously executed," Edward said. "I have to confess I thought some of those sketches you took were a waste of time, but you've included details even I had forgotten about. But this is still my favourite," he added, pointing to a smaller painting on the other side of the gallery. It was a picture of Sophie smiling as she sat in the shade of a palm tree, her parasol half-open against the heat of the sun.

"It is most charming," Mrs Bennet said. "But look at this picture of the children and me at the oasis. I have insisted Lizzy let me take it home to Meryton so that her papa can see it. In fact, I think it would make an excellent addition to our parlour. It would take pride of place over the mantelpiece and Mr Bennet, I know, would be thrilled every time to…"

As she walked off with the young couple, Elizabeth and Darcy could not help but smile.

"This method of painting seems somewhat familiar to me, young Inkworthy," Sir Matthew said, looking intently at a dark area of the canvas near the corner. Paul nodded.

"It is called chiaroscuro—the use of contrasts between light and dark. It has been practised by the greats since the Renaissance, and although I know it might seem a strange style to use when painting such a bright landscape, I felt it helped capture the sense of mystery of the tomb."

"I believe your instincts were sound," Sir Matthew said.

Paul bowed. "You flatter me, Sir Matthew," he said as Sophie, laughing, called him over. With another bow he left them.

Sir Matthew continued to stare at the painting.

"You know," he said standing back at last and addressing himself to Elizabeth and Darcy, who were left standing with him, "the contrasts of light and dark are very dramatic, but at the edges there are certain greys which I believe can be just as striking and even enigmatic."

Elizabeth looked at him for a moment before exchanging a brief glance with Darcy.

"What is it that you see, Sir Matthew?" she asked evenly.

"Well, dear madam, I am not entirely sure, but here in this corner by the entrance to the tomb, just in the flickering play of the candlelight, I thought for a moment I caught the suggestion of a woman's face. It seems to have gone now, but…"

"I believe it will come back, Sir Matthew, when you are not looking for it," Elizabeth said with equanimity.

Sir Matthew looked at her.

"Ah, you have seen it too."

"Only in certain lights," Elizabeth confirmed.

"When the sun is upon it," Darcy added, "or when one holds a candle at a particular angle."

"Or one can hold it at the same angle and not see it again. And not everyone sees it," Elizabeth added. "And Paul swears he did not paint any face there, and I believe him."

"Does Miss Margaret see it?" Sir Matthew enquired with interest. He was staring intently at the painting, but there was nothing there to see and he knew he would find nothing. The face would find him if it wanted to be found.

"I believe not," Darcy said. "She much prefers the painting over there with all the monkeys at the market in Cairo. Although I have once or twice caught her suddenly looking back in this direction as though in response to someone calling her name. But she never says anything, and the gallery holds no fear for her as it might if a child feared ghosts."

Sir Matthew nodded. "No, I imagine it wouldn't." He said nothing for a moment or two.

"What face do you see, Sir Matthew?" Elizabeth enquired at last. The older man smiled at her.

"Why the same as you do, I would imagine, my dear Mrs Darcy: a woman who has finally found peace after many centuries of wandering. But of course, it is all nonsense. Fairy stories for children and simple nomads who know no better."

"Of course," Elizabeth agreed.

Darcy nodded. "Come, Sir Matthew," he said. "Would you care for a glass of canary?"

"That would be most kind," the older gentleman said as his hosts led him down the stairs and out of the gallery, the last of their party following them. Elizabeth waited until all her guests were out of the chamber before gently shutting the door. Just as she did so, she fancied she heard once more the faintest hint of a laugh, much as she had done that afternoon back at the tomb. She smiled.

"Good night, Aahotep," she said softly.

All too soon, it was the end of the holidays. The Darcys stood in the hall as the carriage was brought round. Beth was looking elegant and graceful, carrying herself with a new maturity. Her hair was dressed in adult style, coiled into a chignon instead of tumbling around her shoulders, and her dress no longer stopped at her calves; it reached the floor. Everything about her showed that she was a young lady and no longer a little girl.

William, standing beside her, was so much like his father that Elizabeth caught her breath. He had all the dignity and assurance of the Darcys, and he seemed to be growing every day. He was surely half a head taller than he had been at the start of the holidays, and he was closer to being a young gentleman than a boy.

John, who was striding around the hall, checking the trunks with military precision to make sure that nothing had been forgotten, was still reassuringly boyish in looks. But the Egyptian adventure had increased his confidence, and he was a more capable and experienced boy than he had been before they had all set out.

The butler announced that the carriage was ready and Elizabeth embraced her oldest son, feeling him stiffen slightly as he allowed her embrace rather than enthusiastically returning it. She sighed, sorry that he was too old now for such shows of affection, and turned her attention to John. He saluted and then held out his hand for her to shake, but she ignored it and hugged him close, pleased to find that he returned her pressure. She kissed him on the cheek and then turned her attention to Laurence.

Laurence was still refreshingly impish and looking forward to going to school for the first time. He had spent the morning asking constantly if it was time to go, running up and down the stairs, and generally getting in everyone's way—that is, when he was not whooping with delight and teasing Jane for being left behind.

Elizabeth gave him a hug, which he returned impatiently, and then stood back so that he could take his leave of his papa. He held out his hand in a grown-up fashion and Darcy shook it, but then Laurence launched himself at his papa and gave him a tight squeeze. Darcy picked him up and smiled into his eyes then set him on his feet again and gave him some last-minute fatherly advice.

And then it was time to go. They all went out to the carriage. The boys climbed in excitedly, Laurence riding on the box next to the coachman, while William and John climbed inside, and then they were off. Elizabeth and Darcy stood and waved until the carriage was lost to view.

Elizabeth stifled a sob as it turned the corner of the drive, and Darcy put his arm around her shoulders in silent sympathy. But the boys had been so happy that she could not be sorrowful for long. She put her arm around her husband's waist and they went back inside, with their daughters beside them.

Beth sailed indoors with the grace of a swan, but it was Jane who caught Elizabeth's eye. She was already more demure now that Laurence had gone. She was leading Meg by the hand, instead of running around and hollering as she would have been if Laurence had still been at home.

The girls were claimed by their governesses and Elizabeth and Darcy went into the drawing room.

As she looked around the familiar room, with its graceful furniture and its panoramic views of the glorious grounds, Elizabeth thought how lucky she was. She had a beautiful home, a wonderful family, many good neighbours, and a wide circle of friends. Her children were happy and growing up into fine men and women. And her husband… she looked at him with a lift of her heart. Her husband was the love of her life.

ABOUT THE AUTHORS

Bestselling author Amanda Grange was born in Yorkshire, England, and spent her teenage years reading Jane Austen and Georgette Heyer while also finding time to study music at Nottingham University. She has had over twenty novels published, including six Jane Austen retellings which look at events from the heroes' points of view. Her short stories have appeared in a number of anthologies including *The Mammoth Book of Regency Romance*.

Woman magazine said of *Mr. Darcy's Diary*: "Lots of fun, this is the tale behind the alpha male," while *The Washington Post* called *Mr. Knightley's Diary* "affectionate." The *Historical Novels Review* made *Captain Wentworth's Diary* an Editors' Choice, remarking, "Amanda Grange has taken on the challenge of reworking a much loved romance and succeeds brilliantly." *Austenblog* declared that *Colonel Brandon's Diary* was "the best book yet in her series of heroes' diaries" while *Austenprose* made *Henry Tilney's Diary* a top ten pick for 2011. Her paranormal sequel to *Pride and Prejudice*, *Mr. Darcy, Vampyre*, was nominated for the Jane Austen Awards.

Amanda Grange now lives in Cheshire, England. Please visit her website at www.amandagrange.com or follow her on Facebook.

Jacqueline Webb has published two acclaimed historical romances, *The Scarlet Queen*, set in Egypt and London, and *Dragonsheart*, set in London and Northern Africa. She is a French/English teacher. She lives in Merseyside, England, with her husband and two sons.

Wickham's Diary

by **Amanda Grange**

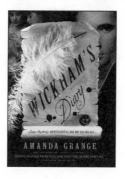

Enter the clandestine world of the cold-hearted Wickham...

...in the pages of his private diary. Always aware of the inferiority of his social status compared to his friend Fitzwilliam Darcy, Wickham chases wealth and women in an attempt to attain the power he lusts for. But as Wickham gambles and cavorts his way through his funds, Darcy still comes out on top.

But now Wickham has found his chance to seduce the young Georgiana Darcy, which will finally secure the fortune—and the revenge—he's always dreamed of...

"Grange, an obvious Jane Austen fan, has given an amusing and totally believable account of a wastrel's life. *Wickham's Diary* takes its place among her previous diaries of Jane Austen heroes."—*Historical Novels Review*

"A short, fast read that is just plain enjoyable, double if you are an Austen fan to begin with!"—*Fresh Fiction*

For more Amanda Grange, visit:

www.sourcebooks.com

For a celebration of all things Jane Austen, visit:

www.austenfans.com

Mr. Darcy, Vampyre

by Amanda Grange

A test of love that will take them to hell and back…

My dearest Jane,

My hand is trembling as I write this letter. My nerves are in tatters and I am so altered that I believe you would not recognise me. The past two months have been a nightmarish whirl of strange and disturbing circumstances, and the future…

Jane, I am afraid.

It was all so different a few short months ago. When I awoke on my wedding morning, I thought myself the happiest woman alive…

"The romance and mystery in this story melded together perfectly… a real page-turner."—*Night Owl Romance* Reviewer Top Pick

"Amanda Grange has crafted a clever homage to the Gothic novels that Jane Austen so enjoyed."—*AustenBlog*

For more Amanda Grange, visit:

www.sourcebooks.com

For a celebration of all things Jane Austen, visit:

www.austenfans.com

Mr. Darcy's Diary

by Amanda Grange

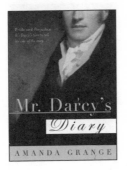

The only place Darcy could share his innermost feelings…

…was in the private pages of his diary. Torn between his sense of duty to his family name and his growing passion for Elizabeth Bennet, all he can do is struggle not to fall in love. A skillful and graceful imagining of the hero's point of view in one of the most beloved and enduring love stories of all time.

"A gift to a new generation of Darcy fans and a treat for existing fans as well."—*Austenblog*

What readers are saying:

"Brilliant, you could almost hear Darcy's voice… I was so sad when it came to an end. I loved the visions she gave us of their married life."

"Amanda Grange has perfectly captured all of Jane Austen's clever wit and social observations to make *Mr. Darcy's Diary* a must read for any fan."

For more Amanda Grange, visit:

www.sourcebooks.com

For a celebration of all things Jane Austen, visit:

www.austenfans.com

Mr. Darcy's Undoing

by Abigail Reynolds

What could possibly make a proper gentleman come completely undone?

What if Elizabeth Bennet accepted the proposal of another before she met Mr. Darcy again? In Abigail Reynolds's bold and playful retelling of the Austen classic, a devastated Mr. Darcy must decide how far he is willing to go to win the woman he loves. Consumed by jealousy, he knows that winning her will throw them both into scandal and disgrace, but losing her is unbearable. Mr. Darcy is going to have to fight for his love, and his life…

"Abigail Reynolds offers a fanciful story, replete with anguish and raw emotion, exploring another possible road not taken by Jane Austen herself… an inventive, fiery, Regency romance."—*Austen Prose*

"Abigail Reynolds, one of my favorite Austenesque authors, is a skilled storyteller, an ardent admirer of Jane Austen, and quite proficient at infusing a lot of emotion, tension, and passion into her stories!"—*Austenesque Reviews*

For more Abigail Reynolds, visit:

www.sourcebooks.com

For a celebration of all things Jane Austen, visit:

www.austenfans.com

Miss Darcy Falls in Love

by Sharon Lathan

The choice of a lifetime…

One young lady following her passion for music.

Two strong men locked in a bitter rivalry for her heart.

A journey of self-discovery, and a trap of her own making.

Georgiana Darcy is going to have to carve out her own destiny, however ill-equipped she may feel…

"The love, passion, and excellence of style, as well as the writer's superior talent with words is sure to win her new fans or satisfy old fans with this one."—*Long and Short Reviews*

"Lathan proves she is indeed a master at writing both Regency romance and Austen continuations. *Miss Darcy Falls in Love* positively oozes with yearning and sweet romance."—*Read All Over Reviews*

For more Sharon Lathan, visit:

www.sourcebooks.com

For a celebration of all things Jane Austen, visit:

www.austenfans.com

The Plight of the Darcy Brothers

by Marsha Altman

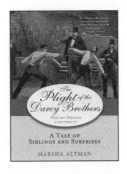

Once again, it falls to Mr. Darcy to prevent a dreadful scandal...

Darcy and Elizabeth set off posthaste for the Continent to clear one of the Bennet sisters' reputations (this time it's Mary). But their madcap journey leads them to discover that the Darcy family has even deeper, darker secrets to hide. Meanwhile, back at Pemberley, the hapless Bingleys try to manage two unruly toddlers, and the ever-dastardly George Wickham arrives, determined to seize the Darcy fortune once and for all. Full of surprises, this lively *Pride and Prejudice* sequel plunges the Darcys and the Bingleys into a most delightful adventure.

"A charming tale of family and intrigue, along with a deft bit of comedy."—*Publishers Weekly*

"I've read various Austen sequels, but this is the best so far."—*Historical Novel Review*

For more Marsha Altman, visit:

www.sourcebooks.com

For a celebration of all things Jane Austen, visit:

www.austenfans.com